I AM ALESSIA

Persia West

For my father, Archie Brooks,

who taught me to read

Cover design: Doug Davidson

Layout: Andie Davidson

Published by PersiaWestWords

ISBN 978-0-9572775-2-6

Pero yo ya no soy yo,
ni mi casa es ya mi casa

But now I am not myself,
nor is my house now my house

from *Romance Sonambulo* by
Federico García Lorca

Acknowledging his inspiration for my story from his play,
Bodas de Sangre, Blood Wedding.

Chapter 1

It seems to me now that all the catastrophes and blessings that suddenly erupted into my life during those few astonishing days of November last year must have been destined, that somewhere in the macrocosm of moving stars or forgotten deeds from my invisible past—actions in another life, some seed acts of childhood, who knows—was the source of this great gift of freedom and myself. As is true for the source of almost all things in my life, in the final analysis, I really don't know. What I do know is that I am in fact humbled, not proud, when I look back on that single weekend that made me into what I am today by teaching me about love, about tenderness, about the power of being true to oneself and the vast range of possibilities that lie for the taking in this sweet world of ours. In truth, I don't care so much about understanding these things anymore. It's enough for me to fully live every golden moment, watch my lovely life unfold with such intricate perfection, and, just sometimes, look back with wonder at the mask I used to wear for a life made for me by someone else.

Come what may, come November the Fifth just last year there I was getting married, taking the plunge into happily ever after then coming out into a renaissance of my once lost soul through blood and the ashes of my sweetheart's dreams, his broken heart pulsing enough to see me alive, truly living, my own heart beating with the hot blood of passion for the first time this fast-fleeting life.

I was thirty three years old—no child anymore and had that sinking feeling that comes with being all alone as time ticks on and you wonder if bitterness is the taste of the future years. Dreams of something fine and true seemed to be nothing more than traces of movies I once saw where a good life full of beauty, light and love was a mirage with no substance on this earth for me. I gave up holding out and sold out instead, faced reality and the flimsiness of the vague, glittering dreams which ruled my life like a phantom lover and whose fruits were the denial of ordinary goodness. Without a sigh I moved in with Charlie the boyfriend and pretended to take compromise to heart. Was this the way of the world? Is the only way to live on our blue planet to give up hope and live in common greyness? Is it better to accept who and what you are, meaning total surrender to the mundane, grow up and stop being a fantasy princess and start living the life that was before you?

That's the way I came to feel, and believe me, it was the death of a part of my soul, the part which always sparkled with just maybes which never, yet, came to be, but you never know, right? If this sounds hard on Charlie, well it isn't. Charlie was who he was and was just fine about it. He was smart enough to know me and who I was too, so he needs no sympathy for that stage of the game; not in the end either, actually, even after all that happened.

He was a good guy, really, worked as a lawyer, made money and quietly helped those without, professional and tough with a heart of gold. And he was good for me, brought me into his home and treated me like a treasure, thought I was beautiful and told me so, bought me flowers, held me when I cried, made love to me with sweetness and power, told me I was the best girl in the world and he loved me to death and wanted to marry me and live happily ever after in a future of babies and long-lived happiness. Couldn't be faulted, right?

All this happened when I lost my job, made redundant, axed from a so-called career I had come to detest being mummy to some little emperor businessman, what was called executive P.A., but which had moved gradually into making coffee, paying his credit card bills, buying presents for both his wife and his girlfriend, and even listening while he told me his troubles, mostly to do with his wife and his girlfriend. I was almost glad when the creep's career collapsed, despite the fact that I found myself without income, lost and uncertain and needing something to cling to—surely not, I think these days, not just another man to give me a sense of direction and existence—so I moved in with good ole Charlie, to cling to him just for a while, right? He'd look after me. Why do we girls still imagine even after everything we've seen that the answer to completing our incompletions lies in the hands of some incomplete man? And, of course, the same goes the other way round. What mad delusion of Charlie's led him to believe that I would, or even could, fit into his own dreams and hopes and fill in the feminine void where he imagined a girl like me would make his dreams come true?

To do my bit at the end of his erratic days there I started to be, no longer the working girl so no reason why not, waiting with the big meat-and-two-veg dinners he liked best. Discomforting shades of the world I had just left; different man, different place, same sense of being some addendum to what really mattered, the male, the sun at the centre of the world.

Good girl, he said, patting me on the bottom like a good dog, sitting down to wolf down food like his mother made, or like his prep school made, and I sat there and watched with folded arms, chewing away at my upper lip, wondering; I could feel myself being drawn into being a ghastly mix of his mother and mine.

But it was like being in quicksand; all you do is walk into it and stand still and gravity alone sucks you down and down, and struggling just makes it all go faster. What was being sucked away was me, Michelle, something shining and special, a Devi, a star, vanishing down into the quicksand of everyday suburban life, and I could see no other way to go. For how many years had I waited for the Golden Path while I suffered the indignities of being a serf to men in offices? Freedom, romance, glitz, passion, power and certainty all seemed to be for other people who lived in other distant worlds. Within me was a disquiet, a rumbling, an itch that was never scratched, but it was so indistinct, formless and ungraspable that I had learned to live with it as some sort of minor and chronic affliction, not knowing that I was on the brink of this faint whisper rising to the fore, bursting into flame, passion and ecstasy, and engulfing my life.

But that was still weeks away. In the meantime there we were, me, Charlie and the cat. Where once there was just me and the cat. And before the cat just me, but those days of being myself in my own world were fading fast, blurring in my mind as I lost the remains of myself in the everyday round and round world of the suburbs of Chester. I had little money of my own, due to an open hand and the unending needs of my restlessness, and Charlie had his own house, a cottage of some charm, as comfy as an old slipper and it soon became home. I had food on the table, clothes in the closet, no hurry, no reason to find another job, an Indian summer lay over the land, Chester was cute and rich and all was well with the world, so I relaxed, let go of my ancient doubts and lived the pleasant life that was given to me.

I seemed to be the last one of all my pals to settle down, get married and have kids and live the life, but now I had time on hand I could meet the girlfriends I knew and chat, when their kids were asleep or at school. So, with an ease that slipped up on me, like twilight in summer, the life that seemed my inevitable destiny enveloped me step by creeping step, and although I knew what was happening I stopped listening to the whispers of warning from inside, and took firm steps into my destiny. Which was written, inevitable, imminent, and not at all what might have been predicted from what could be seen.

Tracy used to work in the same office that I just got laid off from, got married to this guy Colin who was doing really well, as they say, with some computer company of his own and was providing her with all a girl would ever need. Detached house, purple car, two kids, five and three, holidays on the far side of the world, meals in swish restaurants. The Life.

'Michelle, sweetheart, great to see you, come in.' Peck on cheek, take my coat, and there we are with two other friends of hers I didn't know, Kerrie and Sam. Smiles and hi's as we're introduced. The house, one of a bunch of new ones in a dead-end road all of its own was as immaculate inside as out. Green lawns as trim as billiard baize with washed cars parked just so made way for grey carpets trim up to every wall with coffee tables and shiny magazines parked just so and hardly a sign of child to disrupt perfection. They all have kids of the same sort of age in the same nursery school and get together to natter over coffee and cakes in Tracy's conservatory while their kids are off their backs. I took my place at the green plastic table while they carried on talking. They were all dressed more or less the same, jeans and big jumpers and make-up, and I felt out of it and over-formal, old-fashioned, in a suit which was one from a rack of the same, as if I was going to work. But, as there is nothing worse for a woman than being the odd one out in clothes for the place and the time, at least I knew what to wear for my future. See the quicksand? See the fear of being different dragging me into being the same? And how being the same meant the end of the difference that was me?

'... and then he said that he didn't care, right? So I thought, well, up yours, make your own dinner if that's how you feel.'

'Good for you, girl,' said Tracy. 'You've let him run over you enough. Have one of these cakes, Michelle, go on, be naughty.'

Well, why not? What to lose? Chocolate éclairs, just the thing for comfort on a wet Tuesday. But my goodness you could see the change in Tracy, was she ever podging out, take a look at those thighs. Maybe it was having children, I thought, as I bit into the cream and chocolate.

'Me too,' said Kerrie, all blonde curls and pink lips. How did she manage two little kids with nails as long as that? 'I just don't have the interest in sex like I used to, you know how it is, but for Richard it's bloody frantic. Honest. Getting worse if anything. Maybe it's a kind of stress release or something. You know what I mean? Get all wound up at the office and let it all go by throwing me on the bed and being macho man.'

The other women sneered and giggled, sipped their coffee and licked cream from their sticky fingers, and so did I. Men.

'So how's life with Charlie, then?' asked Tracy, and the others looked eagerly on. New grist in the soap, what was the same ole story with me and my man, what were we doing in minutely fractioned difference from all the other boys and girls in town?

'All right,' I answered vaguely.

'Is that all? Just all right?' She turned to her friends and flashed her wickedest smile. 'Tell the truth, I always quite fancied Charlie.'

More giggles.

'You going to get married then?' asked Kerrie.

'Married?'

'You know,' she said, 'rings and things, you've heard of it.'

'Don't know,' I said. 'Don't know. Charlie wants to.'

'You're not going to find anyone better, believe me,' said Tracy. 'Nice guy, good job, thinks the earth of you. You'd be mad to let him go. And how old are you now? You've got to think of having children, can't leave it too late.'

The other two were nodding their fluffy heads. Leave it too late and you might lose the chance to be like us. Fate worse than death, or a death worse than any fate, depends how you look at it.

'Look,' I said, lifting my hands in an attitude of surrender. 'I just don't know. Is it what I want? I ask myself.'

'What else do you want, Michelle? Honest to God, if you don't make up your mind soon you'll lose everything.' She leaned forward. 'What's the alternative? Ageing spinster in some little bed-sit listening to other women's kids laughing and regretting not having some warm man to give you comfort on cold nights.'

In the echoey conservatory silence that followed the creed, the three girls who were on The Right Track looked at me with a mixture of pity and compassion. I could feel something in their eyes pushing and urging me to take the only sane way forward. All they seemed to do was to bitch about their men and be fatigued about their children, but bottom line it was the only and good way of all women, the single way to fulfilment this single life, right? So why did I doubt, hesitate, hold back? What on earth was I waiting for? I was soon to know, and when they knew too I would no longer be invited over for éclairs.

The silence was broken as the girls looked at their watches and made little cries of concern for the toddlers in nursery school and must be off. Pecks on cheeks and promises to get together again soon and I was off by myself walking alone down the damp streets, the first fallen leaves of autumn scudding along the pavement in the gusting wind, feeling barren and discontent, dissatisfied with everything, mostly myself. I made my way in time down to the centre of the city, threading through the ancient buildings, the shops on their two levels, the brown sandstone cathedral, the Roman city walls and down to the river to walk along the banks frowning to myself. Everything in my universe was drawing me inexorably towards my fate. It was as if there was the river of life like the River Dee by my side, and everyone was flowing down it in the way that rivers flow and people live, and I was standing alone against the current, holding out against the inevitable. A rowing boat passed by with little children leaning out trailing their fingers in the water; the boat, the children, the parents and the yellowing autumn leaves behind them all reflected perfectly in the smooth water, looking so sweet my heart panged. There was no doubt that the desire for my own children pulsed in my female depths, but it felt remote from me even as it existed, like someone else's spent passion. I sat on a damp bench and watched the silent flowing river, feeling the pull of the world matching with the desires of my heart—babies, security, a man to keep me safe and warm, no need to face the battles of the world alone, companionship, love, an eternal friend, all the solid goodness of the life my mother bore me to live.

So what was this hesitation? What held me back from the brink? Nothing but the unformed dreams of something fine and free that I had never known, some race of the heart, some exultation, some passion, some abandoned wildness that had never been mine. And the river flowed quietly on, liquid beauty in depth and restraint, a fineness I knew and could see. Why cry for the moon and end up with nothing? Better to grow up and take the world as it is, take what I have and be the envy of many a woman. After all, I wasn't getting any younger. My flush of pretty youth was maturing into womanhood, and although my form still drew the eyes of men, it was fewer than before and the numbers would dwindle and fade with the passing of time, no doubt. My options were narrowing. If I could have seen the shadow, even the hint of something else, anything to give substance to some ache of heart that had reached out so long to nothing and nobody that I was beginning to believe it was all a sweet fantasy that would lead me to nothing other than a souring with the passing of time.

All of a sudden the inner clouds cleared and vacillation vanished. Hell, Charlie, I think I'm yours. Michelle Brown I would be. Oh, yes, that was his name, Charlie Brown, just like in the comic strip. Charles Brown, but who could resist it? Charlie he was and Charlie he liked. I felt a wave of warmth pass over me, a wave that swept away doubt, cleaned my vision of haze.

I was filled with the overwhelming sense of certainty that Charlie was such a good guy; strong, tall, very sweet, had his expectations, had his moments, but who didn't? He had a temperament as even as the river. What Tracy said seemed to me to be true; I could never find anyone better, what was I waiting for? The more I thought about it, the more I smiled to myself. Good ole Charlie. Good ole me. Good ole us.

And at some profound level, as I entered into the happiness of that particular delusion, at some place within my ancient soul far beyond my vision or understanding, the doors to my cataclysmic destiny opened, silently, invisibly, until the coming of their time.

That night Charlie Brown, lawyer, came home to find his cottage in candle-light and his girl in a little dress I knew would quicken his blood, as tired and worn as he was after yet one more long long day treading the treadmill.

'Angel,' he said to me, proving once and for all as he always did that he knew nothing of what boiled away in my devil depths. Is it the poor fate of men to be entranced so easily by the transient form that we girls cannot resist creating, for their hopes and doomed dreams to be shipwrecked upon?

'Charlie,' I responded, smiling the siren smile that always came so effortlessly to me, firing up his eye-produced fever by playing with images that I knew would entrance him, bewitch him, please him, arouse him, make him malleable, at least for a while .

'To what do I owe this honour?' he asked, and kissed me with passion before I could answer. To hell with reasons. Some inner change, a surrender in me translated into the melting response of my body into his and he responded with fervour. Tiredness fled. He unzipped me from my dress and fell upon the nakedness I concealed underneath with hunger, made frantic love to me right there on the carpet, still in half his clothes, the smells of the day—cars, tobacco, mint—highlighting the urgency that rose with animal fangs, almost frightening me, certainly thrilling me with its feral power, from the hidden depths of a Charlie I had previously not known.

Then we lay there while he took breath, his weight beginning to weigh, a draught from the door chilling me.

'Come on, love,' I said to him. 'I'm freezing to death.'

'What?' he mumbled. 'You're cold?'

'There's a draught coming under the door.'

'Oh, sorry, gosh, I didn't realise.' Charlie; passion and apology.

He rolled off me and I picked up my dress, gave him a kiss on the cheek and went off to the bathroom to clean up. Oh, it was good; predictable, powerful, exciting—and short. It was my body, my image, my smell, my skin which flipped a switch which ran a machine and where was I? Once more this life I wondered if that sense of something missing was nothing more than the emptiness that followed in the wake of unattainable dreams. I patched up my face in the mirror, looking past the big brown eyes and waves of hair into the soul of me. Was it true that I loved to interest men with my image, but then found that once they had bitten at the bait I wanted them to toss it aside and touch upon the real me, the heart of me beyond the entrancement and they never did or would, and that was the odd Catch 22 that led to yet one more sell-out and compromise? As I brushed my hair, still looking at myself in the eye, I realised that the hope for love beyond the seen was as dangerous a fantasy as the overwhelming feminine illusion that Charlie would sell his soul for, and a normal reality without flash or expectation that would never be met was maybe not a sell-out at all, but a simpler reality that may lead to a simpler happiness.

Was it compromise or was it love? I made a great slavering steak dinner for my man, the blood red on his lips, while I picked at a little pasta and salad. I had not eaten meat for years and could hardly abide even touching the great hanks of flesh that I was learning to cook. In contrast to me, he was a man at peace with himself over the table, feeding his male body that filled me with a strange mix of desire and misgiving with red blood and red wine. Was this what men were made of? We had hardly spoken since he came home, and I sat there in my little dress, holding back the desire to change into something that covered my skin more and wondering why the certainty I felt earlier about my future with Charlie, that which had produced the display he had come home to, had now withered and was replaced by gnawing uncertainty.

'Great meal,' he said, looking at me fondly, tiny reflections of candles reflecting in his pale grey eyes.

I smiled and shifted my gaze. 'Dessert?' I asked brightly, and made to stand. He reached over the table and held my forearm down with his large hand, as big as two of mine.

'Let's wait a while,' he said, voice rumbling, and leaned back in his chair. He certainly was a good-looking man in the soft light of candles and their purple shadows. My ebbed feelings for him flowed once more; I was a tidal creature, my heart subject to the pull of moons unseen.

'It's good to have you here,' he said. 'Brings the house alive.'

I sat and looked, lifted a finger to my mouth to chew a nail, noticed what I was doing and let it fall. 'Good.' I said.

One of my candles began to flicker; we both looked over at it at the same moment, and then, catching the synchronicity, at each other.

'So this is what I can expect every night, is it?'

'What do you mean?'

'What do I mean. Candles and fine food, sexy dresses. You trying to tell me something?' The lawyer missed nothing; he was sharp and fast in the ways of men, and women.

I fidgeted and shrugged. In some odd way I felt like a fourteen year old with a first boyfriend a lot older than me. 'I s'pose so. In a way.'

'Well, whatever it is I like it.' He paused. The mood in the air thickened, deepened. 'I do love you, Michelle.'

I swallowed. He was such a sweet guy, and he did love me, I knew it. In that moment I could have turned away and let the whole thing go, but there was some movement of star-written force beyond my choosing, and the manic fluctuating tide in me flowed towards him with the heat of all that was to come.

'Charlie, love,' I said, 'it's time.'

'Time?' he asked, 'time for what?'

'How many times did you ask me to marry you?'

He shrugged, kept my eyes in his, waited. We fell into silence, him looking at me without moving, still waiting.

'I think it's time.'

His face lit up with a happy smile. A great part of his charm was the genuine simplicity that held together the complexity of his lawyer life. He leaned over the table, took my face between his hands and kissed me on the forehead. A small tear squoze out of one eye and rolled down my cheek, and I had time to feel its coolness on the warmth of my skin. I sniffed. At that moment the world seemed like an opening rose. In a flash I could see that it was commitment that made dreams come true, that it was the hesitations of the past that had brought vacillation, misgiving and discontent, and my folly had been holding onto those mad fantasies that never came to anything, which served only to deny me what was truly mine. Such is the nature of what we believe to be true at times of confusion and emotional power.

'Come here,' said Charlie, holding out his arms for me, and I went to what I thought was my future willingly, relishing the familiar frisson of being overpowered, a woman surrendering to the power of man.

Chapter 2

By the next day, the very next day, I had a ring on my finger. Charlie met me after his work for a drink and presented me with this chunk of sparkle in one of those little plush boxes that swing open like a treasure chest. Who could resist it? The little thing slipped on my finger like it was coming home and I sat there in the bar of the Grosvenor Hotel moving my hand in the light to flash and twinkle my very own diamond best friends, besotted, thrilled, delighted. Everything seemed so right. Flash went my diamonds. All sense, adulthood, intelligence, and discrimination were lost as the magpie in me gazed at the bauble which reduced my mind to rubble. If it isn't falling in love which creates the madness which turns future years of drudgery into magic dreams, it's one of the other devices which suck you into signing on the dotted line. I was cheap; for me a mixture of desperation and diamonds was plenty enough.

'Gosh, Charlie, look at all the colours. Nothing like a diamond, eh?'

He reached across to me and took my hand. 'I'm glad you like it, love,' he said, and I was pleased to see his great paw of a male hand on my smaller, bejewelled, female one. It helped set off the diamonds, me, and him. I look back on this display of feminine narcissism with embarrassment; what I loved was myself, my own beauty as the gem in the centre of my adornments; a man, two hands, a diamond, a swish hotel. Wasn't I just something? And what was I thinking?

Why had I held out so long? This gluttony of romance was so sweet it seemed mad to have had doubts. What funny creatures we are. It's the contrast of sharp glitters against the duller soft skin that makes it so perfect, I thought, lost in my own mad world.

'Michelle, love,' said my man, a second player in this drama, second to his diamonds. 'Look at me a second.'

I tore my eyes away from my ring and onto its giver. For no more than a moment he looked heavy, ponderous, angry even, as I left my world of pretty light and wonder to listen to what he had to say. A tiny flash of petulance passed through me. I hoped that there was good reason for him to drag me away from my little world of magic.

'I'm here,' I said, working hard to look him in the eye, telling no more than a half-truth. 'I just love the ring.'

'I know,' he replied, with a touch of patience. 'And I'm glad. It makes me feel like you're really mine, at last.'

I was startled. What? Is that what rings did? Gave some sort of possession? A feeling rose from my depths which wanted to take off that ring that moment and hand it back with apologies and a last kiss to the stubbly cheek, as there was no price at all for ownership of me. But the alarm rose and fell and passed over me easily enough and was gone, with the ring still there looking just great. I was dying to show it off to my friends. I wondered if Tracy was having her pals round for coffee again next week.

I looked at Charlie, remembering he was there, and he was back again, the kind and rugged-looking guy, slightly tired and worn enough to make me feel like looking after him, looking at me with a touch of impatience. He wanted my attention. I snapped to, focused, looked him deep in the eye and smiled sweetly, shifted my body slightly and put my free hand on his. Men are easy to charm; to a point, and when that point is reached and our lure no longer functions and power fades, danger begins.

'I'm ever so happy, Charlie,' I said, diamonds forgotten.

'Me too,' he replied, then took a breath and scratched his ear. A change in mood, I knew his signs; there was some news for me, and maybe not the news I wanted to hear. 'I talked to my mother today. Told her about us.'

Oh, God, I thought, his bloody mother, the spectre at the feast, and a tremor passed through my new-found certainties. 'And what did she have to say?'

'She was delighted, thought it was wonderful.' He scratched his ear once more, oh, no, what now? 'And she insisted we call round for a little supper. A celebration.'

'When? You don't mean now? Not this evening, please.'

Charlie looked like a guilty schoolboy. 'This evening. She wouldn't take no for an answer. You know my mother.'

Oh, shit, yes, I certainly do. Well, I guess diamonds don't come cheap. Nor Charlie's. But how about me? Such awkward questions could be answered with time, no doubt, I hoped, I thought, and another shudder of doubt passed through me. How odd this all was to live, moving through such contradictory forces so consciously, as if it was not my choice at all, as if I was playing my role in some cosmic drama written by someone else. Which was almost true, except for the fact that in the end I found that I wrote it all; it's just that the me that wrote it was not the me I was when I got to understand my complicity was in fact my authorship.

'Oh, good,' I said brightly. 'Seems like the right thing to do.'

He sighed with relief. 'I know you two'll get along so much better now,' he said. 'I think she was just worried about me.'

'Worried?'

'Well, not being married at thirty seven. No sign of grand-children, you know how they are about these things.'

Ah, they—so his father was allowed to creep into the picture then, poor old bugger. He was usually included in with his mother, no need for plurals when you had the royal She. Well, I had to face the old cow sometime, and better sooner than later. Give her a couple of grandchildren and she'd be a different kettle of fish, I suppose. GIVE? There seemed to be deep water at every turn. I twinkled my ring in the bar light. Gosh it looked good. Maybe I would grow my nails just a bit longer. Dig out that old topaz ring I got from my grandmother for the other hand, start to use my hands more when I talked. But this time the thoughts were forced, they were a way of distracting myself from my inner discomfort.

'Another drink, darling?' asked Charlie. It was the first time he called me darling, and for some creepy reason I couldn't put my finger on it made me feel panicky, like I was losing control in a vortex of someone else's fate, and for the second time that evening I felt like tearing off the ring and fleeing into the night. But I had nowhere to go, and it felt as if my path was set.

'Definitely,' I said. 'Make it a large one.'

Charlie's folks lived in Parkgate, a posh district on the Wirral where Admiral Lord Horatio Nelson used to come to visit his mistress, the gorgeous and desirable Lady Hamilton. She must have been quite a girl, I thought, as we passed by her very house, indifferent to the tongues of lesser beings as she flaunted her forbidden love for the hero who had England at his feet. I wondered if I had what she had, the feminine power to rule the Navy, looked down at my hand and in the darkness my little ring didn't flash at all.

We turned into the rhododendron drive of the Brown's sandstone pile, which, in the daytime, gave a view right out over the silted estuary of the River Dee, a great sad plain of reeds and tides that reached far over to the hills of Wales. With a shock I suddenly realised that one day this could all be mine, that in time I could be sitting at the window, ageing and wrinkling, painting the shifting light and shade and cloud in water-colours, just like my mother-in-law to be. Was I no more than a rider on a destiny forewritten? Was I simply the container for the continuity of what was demanded by the house, the family money, the lifestyle, which would turn me into its own creation? The thought gave me the creeps, evidence of at least a partial truth.

As Charlie's car, his fast and eager Jaguar, his one great indulgence of love for machine, crunched to a halt on the gravel outside the front door and the engine and lights died at a touch, he turned to me in the darkness and said, 'I know my mother can be hard for you. But she only wants the best for me, that's all.'

'I know,' I said, touching him on the arm and wondering to myself if I was that best and knowing that in my heart of hearts that no-one could ever be. Especially a girl from the wrong part of Liverpool, with maybe traces of that accent still lurking behind the years of education and trying hard, and her own unmentioned parents in their council flat in the Dingle.

A long way from the oak and glass door that swung open to show the rich light of the hallway of the Brown palace. My heart sank; Mrs Brown came steaming out, a slight figure in smile, tartan kilt fastened with a large pin, cashmere sweater and pearls, white hair in tight curls.

'Charles,' she said, receiving her homage on offered cheeks. I found myself averting my eyes; he always seemed to turn into a little boy at these times, and I guess another mummy I didn't want to be, as time moved on and my youth faded into a reflection of Margaret's years. I stood to one side, fidgeting with my ring, while she ignored me for the few moments that reminded me of my place in the order of things. Then, to my utter relief, Geoffrey, her husband and Charlie's father, appeared from the lit hallway, his eyes going straight to me.

'Hello, gorgeous,' he said, and gave me a kiss on the cheek and a hug that felt like coming home. He was twinkle-eyed, white moustached, wearing a cardigan that sagged at the pockets and he smelled of pipe-tobacco, whisky and retriever. The old boy squeezed me again and asked, 'How've you been keeping without me? These young men treat you right?'

'Not for a minute,' I said, 'but I suppose the only way is to find 'em young and train 'em well.'

'Ah,' he replied, with one of his innocent asides that told me just how much he was acutely conscious of his world. 'Margaret's theory entirely.'

At the sound of her name, she turned from her little boy to me. She stood back, no embrace, no kisses, phoney smile under hard eyes. 'Michelle, darling,' she said—what was it about that word that chilled me to the core? 'You don't know how thrilled I am.'

I didn't believe her for a moment, disliked being told what I didn't know, but smiled back, equally phoney, twisting my ring round and round my finger and said, 'I'm so glad.' Which I wasn't.

We stopped there for few seconds in a strange little void filled with strange little undercurrents, all of them dark, none of them sweet, till Geoffrey said in his rich, plummy voice, 'Come on now, come inside, what on earth are we doing keeping you freezing to death out in the cold?' And he ushered me, hand on waist, into his warm home, followed by his wife with hand on arm of her big boy.

It was already late so we were led straight to the dining table, all candles, polished wood and polished silver. I would have preferred a Chinese take-away in the car to this stage-set. Geoffrey sat us down and filled our rainbow-flashing crystal glasses with no-doubt fine wine while Margaret busied off to the kitchen.

'Cheers,' he cried. 'To you!' And closed his eyes while he nuzzled into his greatest love of all, his oldest and trustiest friend, his blood red Claret. Charlie turned to me and smiled, leaned forward and kissed me quickly. 'To us,' he said, raising his glass and looking at me with great happiness. He was in a different world to me; none of the troublesome currents of doubt which troubled my heart troubled his.

'To us, Charlie,' I replied, smiling to his simple goodness, and drank deeply. Mmmm, what wine. I looked down at my ring and my diamonds looked back at me, at home there with the twinkling silver, crystal, and eyes of Charlie and his father, both looking at me in a way that made me feel happy to be a woman.

In came mother, carrying a hot serving dish with a towel. 'Make a space! Geoffrey darling, move the cruet, come on now!'

He dived into action and she banged her meal onto the table with a flourish. 'Beef Stroganoff,' she announced with pleasure, looking at Charlie. 'Your favourite.'

He almost flushed. 'Gosh, thanks, mummy.' he said. I wished to hell he wouldn't call her that. Beef Stroganoff. Jesus. I mean she just knew I didn't eat meat. Oh, hell. Not for the first time in that house I felt tied in awkward knots; the outsider.

The serving began. My plate first.

'Oh, er, no beef for me, thanks. I don't actually eat meat.'

Margaret stopped dead, serving spoon in hand. 'Still?' she asked, as if that peculiarity belonged to a past that was not relevant to my new Brown life, giving me a chance to relent, renounce my childishness, become more like her, begin my surrender on the spot and begin to be her kind of real.

'Don't worry,' I said with my best bright good girl smile. 'I'm really not so hungry. I'd be happy with just vegetables.'

'Well, suit yourself.' She served me with a small pile of potatoes and peas that embarrassed the hell out of Charlie and his father, not to mention me, and the rest of the meal was served in a troubled silence she alone seemed brightly unaware of. Such was the nature of Margaret Brown's house.

'So when's the happy day, Charlie?' Geoffrey mumbled through a mouthful of dinner, pointing at him with his fork. 'Or are we ahead of things?'

'Well, not really, Pops. We thought next month. Why wait?'

'Why indeed.' Geoffrey smoothly sank another glass of claret heaven. What did he care?

Margaret put down her knife and fork neatly against her plate, dabbed her palely lipsticked mouth with her linen napkin, and said, 'Oh, Charles, not November! What a time for a wedding. And we'll have no time to prepare, it's impossible. Change your mind this instant and move your ideas to spring, I implore you.'

I sat there picking at my peas and feeling hungry, watching. Would Charlie capitulate? Would he give in to his damned mummy and betray me, and in that way set the tone for the whole of the future? The whole idea that I had and he agreed with was to get the actual marriage bit all over and done with simply. No fuss, no phoney priests and divine blessings, just the essentials which did the job. We worked it all out in the car on the way over. Took just a few minutes, it was so simple. Just a few friends, family if we must, register office, no fuss, small sweet reception, champagne and a few dirty jokes, off to the airport on our honeymoon in the Caribbean and Bob's your uncle. What would Charlie do? Was it me or her?

'No, mummy, we've decided. I know you'd love it, the big thing, but we're going to deny you that one, I'm afraid.' He shrugged and licked his lips, waited for her response. I tried not to smile in victory and focused on spearing up a few of my miserable peas so she wouldn't see my eyes.

Margaret laughed her odd, choked, mirthless laugh, and threw her hands in the air, every action, to me, contrived, artificial. 'No, no, darling. November you want, November you shall have. But can I help? You'll need it.'

'Of course. We'd love that, wouldn't we, Michelle?'

I nodded enthusiastically. 'Oh, please,' I said. My lines were few in this particular scene of the drama. My time was yet to come, and even then it was action rather than words that fitted my part.

'Oh, good,' she said. 'You'll be amazed at what can be achieved in a month.'

Her husband reached for another bottle of wine, raising his eyebrows theatrically. 'Here we go,' he pronounced, with equal drama. 'Mountains will be moved.'

I glanced nervously at Charlie, but he was busy brushing crumbs from the table with his hand, and didn't notice. A murmur of fear without known cause moved in the centre of me. There was so much hidden agenda in this family that I never knew what the hell was really going on. Gave me the creeps. So different from my roots, where nothing was hidden, all doors were open, so much so that I had to flee to find any sign of who I really was, what was so deep within me it was unseen in the desert of arid openness.

To my relief the main meal finished and dessert arrived, a great cream and fruit gateau made without compromise. After a few miserable peas and potatoes it looked like heaven. And tasted like it too. The fickle tide in me turned once more, and I forgot the tricky bits of the Brown life as I looked around at the solid opulence, took another bite of gateau, relaxed.

Now this was living, I thought. In my family it would have been something frozen from the supermarket. How nice it will be to have the money to make such things for people. Holidays in the villa in Tuscany. With the clothes to match ...

'... don't you think, Michelle?' My name woke me from my reverie.

'What? Sorry, I was off in my own world.'

Charlie laughed out loud. One of his favourite themes was that I was a dreamer. 'She's a bit of a dreamer,' he told them, predictably.

'Well, that's all right,' said Geoffrey, indignantly. 'Many great men were. How we got to have an Empire.'

'More like how we lost an Empire,' said Margaret, tartly. One more point for her. Eight hundred million points to Margaret Brown, zero to everyone else. Minus four million for Geoffrey, who compensated by downing one more glass of wine.

'I was wondering,' she said, 'if you would like the Cathedral for the wedding.'

'What? The Cathedral?' I said, almost shouted. 'I thought we were going to do quiet and small at the registry office.' I looked around for support. Charlie!

'Well, I don't see why not,' he said meekly, looking up through his eyelashes just like the Labrador, now curled up asleep under the table, its rank smell apparently only detectable by me. 'It can still be small. It doesn't have to be big. You only get married once, for God's sake. You see, Pops knows the Bishop. Went to school with him, reckons he can fix it.'

'Easily done, beautiful,' said Geoffrey thickly. He must have drunk almost two bottles of Claret with the smooth ease of the much practised, which slowed him down to a snail's pace but had never—yet—stopped him completely.

Well, surprise, surprise, control was being eased from my grasp. In fact, the job had been done. And done by a master. I sighed. And smiled as I gave in. 'The Cathedral's very beautiful.'

Margaret, who was fussing round with coffee, looked over and smiled in return. Our eyes met. Charlie was right, we were beginning to get along. Hell, why fight a battle you could never win? I may as well enjoy the Life. I suppose she only wanted the best for us. And everything had its price, right? Compromise wasn't a dirty word, it was the way of intelligence, the way of the world.

'You know, Michelle, dear,' she said, slipping a small cup of the blackest coffee onto the table in front of me, 'I bet we could fix a really beautiful wedding gown through Annabella Wise. D'you know her? Fashion Editor of Harpers for years. Knows everybody in the rag trade. You me want to have a go?'

I shrugged, and smiled. 'We could try.'

'Try we will,' said Margaret. 'What the bride wants is what the bride gets.'

I had an odd feeling that I'd lost the thread completely. Is that what I wanted? Well, I suppose it was, really. Why not make it as Princess for the day? Maybe we could get Charlie into his old Major's dress uniform too—in for a penny, in for a pound, eh? He'd left the Regiment years back, one of those following in the footsteps of fathers routines and had worn the splendid costume for me once when I found it in the back of the wardrobe, and I just loved it; certainly brought out the surrender in me.

The coffee drunk, Geoffrey sank back into his favoured haze of food and booze, a contented man. He burped without embarrassment. Charlie was chatting to his mother about some friends in common and the legal problems they were having with fishing rights. I was sitting in front of the rest of the gateau, wondering if it would be OK to ask for more. The evening was coming to a close. Suddenly Geoffrey sat up and we all looked his way; he had an idea.

'Sweetheart,' he said to his wife. I wonder if he ever referred to women by name, it always seemed to be darling or gorgeous or sweetheart, arm's lengthening us in some way that kept life safe, in some way that made me feel sad. She looked over.

'Final thing.' He stood up, animated. 'Blessing for the happy couple and all that. Dig out that bottle of extra-special Amaretto, remember?'

'You mean that ancient bottle we picked up in Lucca, how many years ago?' Margaret wrinkled her nose.

'The very one. Marvellous stuff. Show you a trick.' He pulled himself to his feet without staggering, showing all the control of the practised lush, and walked slowly off to his study across the hall, wavering only slightly from his line. The three of us sat there in silence, tolerating one of Geoffrey's little foibles. After all, he did pay the bills.

Back he came, odd-looking bottle in one hand, four tiny stemmed glasses upside down through his fingers in the other. With difficulty he extricated the glasses and placed one at each of our places with sozzled concentration. It was clearly a ceremony. We watched as he then poured precise measures of his prized Amaretto right to the top of our glasses, meniscus showing. This was a breathless achievement, not a drop spilled even as his hand wavered. We all three watched this performance with absolute concentration, hardly able to breathe.

Right, done. He looked up in triumph. We all breathed again. I felt like applauding.

'Nest,' he said, 'the lights.'

Click and click and the lights went off in the room and floodlights silently filled the garden, manicured lawns and shrubberies framed brilliant in the darkness of the night by the huge window.

'The glasses,' said Geoffrey, swaying slightly, 'fit the drink. Antique Italian. Hand made hundreds of years ago. Bought them in Florence on our honeymoon, bloody expensive even then.'

We sat in disciplined audience silence. So far, so good.

'Now watch,' said our host, and went round the table once more, this time with a cigarette lighter, and put the flame to each of our glasses. Obediently, vague little blue and yellow flames licked up in the half-light. It looked very beautiful, the four little flames in our darkness, the bright garden beyond luminous in its own. We sat there in appreciating silence while years of money shone beautifully for us; the garden, the glasses, the Amaretto, the silver, my diamonds.

Then, one after another, there were four fast and tiny noises—ching! ching! ching! ching!—as our four antique Italian glasses split from top to bottom with the heat of the flames, which burned on regardless as the remaining Amaretto spilt onto the beeswax-polished antique table top. For many moments we sat there in silence, a mixture of awe and horror freezing us into stillness.

'Oh, fuck,' said Geoffrey.

Such was the nature of the Browns that there was a fast clearing up of obvious disaster, without discussion or even mention of the incident, and Charlie and I departed soon afterwards. It left me feeling scared, looking out of the window of the Jag as we sped back to the city, watching the lights of cars and houses flee by. It felt to me like an omen, a warning finger of fire from the power that was the hand in the puppet that was our world, but a portent of what I had no idea.

Chapter 3

Then the madness that ended in the phoenix rising from the funeral pyre of my life truly began. The surrender to Charlie was an act which unleashed forces in and around me that I had never before witnessed, forces of a power and unpredictability that left me feeling like a wild-eyed bystander at the volcanic eruption of my own self. But still it seemed to me that I was on a track of certainty to a life which entranced me with the glitter of wealth, the warmth of security, the dubious simplicity of a future assured. This folly taught me never to trust the images of life as they seemed, and in the end to ride the point of uncertainty that lies around the corner of each moment like a surfer on a wave. But at that time I was a long way from such inner balance, at that time I was still lost in the drama of the time, still believing that the soap opera of my life was real.

Which brings me back to Margaret Brown. At that time it seemed that all tracks led back to her, the centre of all things in that world that now has gone. The last thing she said to me as we left that fateful evening was that she was looking forward to meeting my parents. It was all terribly polite, the niceties of her middle-class way of being, all shine on the outside and something far darker concealed and yet visible beneath the surface. Maybe they would like to work together on the wedding arrangements? Maybe. And there again, maybe not. The whole issue of my unfortunate family was one that was not so hard to avoid when Charlie and I were just being girlfriend and boyfriend, no commitment so no certain future, so avoided it was, but impossible now the Great Event was looming. The time for the revelation of eluded realities had come.

Charlie, not surprisingly, had become more and more curious. And the more elusive I became, the more intrigued he became, of course. It's recommended that if you're going to buy a puppy, see its mother first, check out the bitch, see the bloodline in action before you commit to what may be years of avoidable misfortune. In my experience the same goes for the girl you're thinking of marrying, guys. Even more so if she is pretty and desirable; as a skilled operator of feminine charms myself, a caster of delusion, a projector of image to match your longings, I can tell you to take care. What you see is certainly what you don't get.

And if, as in my case, there's some avoidance going on, know there's something going on your sweetie doesn't want you to know, for very good reasons that don't match up with the delights you see, so you are then investing in future uncertainties. To say the least. Charlie was still innocent of such things in those days, still charmed by me enough to ignore signs that would have normally sent signals of alert through his acute lawyer's mind. But sense flies out of the window at times of romance, death, and intense desire, so he noticed nothing. It seemed.

'Were your parents pleased?' he asked one night, sitting by an open fire while he honed the blades of his knives, a legacy of his army past. What creature lurked, rarely seen, in Charlie Brown, lawyer, that showed in the flickering firelight and the flash of sharpening blade? He looked to me for some moments like a man from a primal past, a primitive, a hunter making ready for the kill, and my feminine heart was caught in-between the thrill that male power brought and my fear of it.

'Of course,' I replied, struggling with the ironing of one of his damned shirts. A fresh one every day. Ironed just so. He'd done it himself since he left the army, and a great job he did too. I still couldn't figure out how I'd begun to take over this task that I hated. Irons in my hands burned holes, snapped off buttons, welded in wrinkles. It was one of the many items of business that I'd deal with later, after we were married, when we'd have time to talk about such matters. To me it was the sort of thing that you get the cleaning woman we didn't have to do—I should know, it's work my mother did for years when I was a kid. Before she discovered a talent for removing almost anything from shops under the eyes of just about anyone, that is. It was as if she was blessed with some special magic, which, as a good Catholic, she believed was God-given and made a fruitful career from her special aptitudes, which she confessed regularly and so had no burden of guilt to sour her joy. When I called to tell her about my new life she just started talking about herself, what a great week she'd had in the shops and how she'd got hold of this amazing new television by a means that made me bite my lower lip when I heard. Got it fixed up for satellite by our Jimmy so she didn't have to pay a thing, and on and on. Did she listen to me even once in my life? Did anyone, including myself? Certainly not the other half of the genes that made me, my dad, the ole man, Big Al himself, the other great non-listener.

'Dad,' I told him on the phone, 'I'm getting married.'

'Great,' he said. 'You'll never guess who showed up the other day.'

'I bet I won't.'

He caught the sarcasm in my tone, of course, it was a game we'd played for years, father-daughter cat and mouse, me begging him for attention, love, him denying me, in one unsubtle way or another, on and on. It was a dance that I had danced throughout my life to that point, but, oddly enough, with the roles reversed with all others and me in the lead.

'Well, if you don't bloody well want to know,' he said, and of course I did. I always wanted to know what was denied me, I always wanted the things I couldn't have. I could hear the glugging of beer from a can, the faint sound of TV down the phone, the background noises of the culture from which I sprang.

'Come on, dad, of course I want to know.' Funny the way the Liverpool accent rose so deftly in me, took over my speech from behind, reminding me of who, or what, I was.

He burped with the baritone resonance which came with a lifetime of practice. 'Your long-lost cousin. Ada's girl, remember?'

How could I forget? 'Alexandra,' I said, pulse quickening. 'She's back?'

'That's what I said, innit?'

'I'd like to see her.' Truth is I'd love to see her. She was my girlhood heroine, five years older than me and light-years faster. By the time she was eighteen she was long-gone, and the last we heard from her came in the form of occasional, fewer and fewer post-cards from exotic locations around the world—Kyoto, San Francisco, Manila, Guatamala, New Delhi, like messages from another planet. Throughout my teenage years these cards appeared erratically, and I would steal them from where they were thrown on the kitchen table and treasure them in my room, staring into the colourful pictures as if I could will myself to enter them and reappear in another world, anywhere but where I was. Before she vanished she once gave me a present from one of her practice runs across Europe, one of those times when she would hitch-hike alone, indifferent to apparent danger, disappearing without trace for weeks on end and then returning with small gifts for everyone. What she brought me was a bracelet from Venice, a cheap metal chain with tiny pictures of scenes of the city—Saint Mark's, the Bridge of Sighs and so on—stamped on tags that hung from the chain and jangled when they moved. It was a treasure of mine, a sort of talisman, and I had it to that day, twenty years later, dulled with time, at the bottom of my jewellery case, oddly predicting my oncoming future. When I heard she was back in town, I had the odd desire to take out that bracelet and wear it, in case we met again and she needed reminding of a point at which we had once touched.

'Who're yer gettin' married to, then?'

'His name's Charlie. Charlie Brown. He's a lawyer.'

'A bloody lawyer,' sneered Dad. The enemy class, the hoity-toities, the overpaid and under-worked, he knew all about Charlie.

'Oh, dad, he's very nice, not at all like you'd think.'

'They're all very bloody nice, Michelle, till you get them cutting you to pieces in the dock, fuckin' yer life over so that they can send their bloody children to fancy schools.'

'But I do know him, dad,' I pleaded, begged, whined. 'You should get to know him too.'

'Bring him over, girl, go on. We've got to meet yer meal ticket some time. How 'bout Sat'day. We'll go out for a bevvy, see what the bleeder's made of. Come over to our place.'

'All right.' I hesitated, licked my lips. 'Dad, how can I get to see Alexandra?'

'I dunno,' he said. 'Give Ada a call. She can come slummin' with you and yer lawyer on Saturday if you like.'

So when Charlie asked about my parents, I had a time and a place for once. Saturday in Liverpool. Things were firming fast.

'All right,' he said, looking up from his knives, the light from the fire flashing for a moment in his eyes as he looked my way. 'Jolly good.'

It took me three calls to Ada to get through and find out that her wandering daughter was off in London doing something or other that Ada disapproved of without knowing what it was, but yes, she said, she'd be back, I'll tell her you called. How strange it made me feel, almost trembly inside, to think of seeing her again after how long? Gosh, it must be twenty years. All I could remember was dark eyes and dark hair shining to the waist, an aura of speed and impatience and remoteness from me. Remember that when she was eighteen I was thirteen, and she had no time of day for the hesitant, fat-faced kid I was then, while for me she was all I wanted to be. If I had had the nerve, which I never did.

Saturday arrived, as Saturday always does, and I was more nervous than ever in my life. I got Charlie dressed in jeans and checked shirt to hopefully fit in to the Dingle world better and still he looked like an officer in the Household Cavalry. His jeans were ironed to a fine crease, for God's sake—not by me, I must tell you—it's the nature of Charlie Brown, he did it without thinking. And he looked fantastic to me, a genuinely handsome man, quite a hunk in his own way. No problem to get the girls on my side, I thought, as we drove through the Mersey Tunnel. It was the Old Man himself. And more than that, how Charlie took to them. It all seemed quite hopeless, one long tunnel of my life without light at the end.

God, but the Liverpool we emerged into depressed me. It looked seedy, run-down and future-less, the world from which I came. I was born in the Maternity Hospital, grown up in the Dingle, and normally doomed for teenage motherhood, whining about my fate as I fattened up on chips and pizza, smoking myself to an early death in a council flat. Then I was rescued by that single teacher that can make the difference to a life, a young priest called Father O'Brien who taught us English and found my intelligence and natural ambition, fanned the spark into a fire and showed me how to buy my own ticket out of the life I seemed doomed to through the magic power of education. I wonder about that man to this day. With the wisdom of hindsight and years of living life I can see that there was more to his generosity than professional dedication, and I hope all worked out well for my priest.

'This is where you grew up?' Charlie gestured towards the grey streets.

I nodded. 'Yep. But it was better when I was a little kid. More life going on. Different world from yours, Charlie.'

'True enough,' he said, nodding, face expressionless, showing nothing. As I watched him driving in the glow of the passing street lights, lighting and fading, lighting and fading like my own certainty for the correctness of my commitments, I felt a real love for the man, a respect for his goodness, an attraction to his solid frame, his bearing, his certainties. He would make a good father, of this there was no doubt. The only doubts were in me, not great, not enough to make my engagement to him a lie, but enough to make me sit there next to him in his lawyer's car in the Toxteth streets and feel a niggle of unformed wondering that would dim the brightness of my own love. Until it passed me by and the light returned, and I knew that doubt was nothing but a passing weakness of a mind practised in doubting.

'Here we are, pull over. Park anywhere, best under a light.'

I felt in my bag for a lipstick and ran it over my lips in the half light, catching sight of my own eyes looking wide and wild in the sun-visor mirror. 'Oh, hell, Charlie, I feel scared to death of you meeting my family.'

He laughed, reached over and gently massaged the back of my neck under my hair, a habit of his I found deeply sensual, and which soothed tensions from me at a touch. I wanted to make love to him there and then in the car under the street light, using passion to erase my uncertainties by overwhelming them; just one more way of avoiding the legacy of my past. 'Come on,' I said, reaching back to him and running my fingers through his short hair, my nails tinily scratching his scalp, almost sparking with electricity, such was the power of the unexpressed desire that longed between us. 'Time to meet the crew.'

'Don't be concerned, Michelle,' he said. 'I know who you are.'

Thanks, Charlie Brown, I thought, smiling back at him, thanks for your faith, even though in my heart of hearts I know you don't know who I am any more than I do myself.

We lived in one of those blocks of maisonettes that were built on land that was cleared when the old terraced streets, the blood vessels of the old heart of the city, were razed to the Saxon earth. An abomination—cheap modern style, bright brick now covered in graffiti, soulless places, young kids smoking in the doorway, glancing up at us as we passed in and up the stairs.

Ding dong on the doorbell and I waited there in a buzz of anticipation. Any mood you care to name might open the door—what was it to be tonight? I touched Charlie on the hand and smiled up at him, but he was as calm and at ease as almost always, it was me that was seeking reassurance.

The door opened and there stood my dad, squat and wide, unshaved, tattoos showing on his hefty arms, can of beer in hand.

'You're Charlie,' he said, giving a broad friendly smile, reaching out with his hand. 'Come in, lad, make yourself at home.' He winked at me. I was relieved, he'd been drinking long enough to have reached love for the whole wide world. I just hoped he wouldn't keep drinking to the next predictable phase.

'Nice to meet you, Mr Rafferty,' said Charlie.

'Cut the crap,' dad replied. 'The name's Al.'

We went into the lounge, took a seat on the black plastic sofa, the TV chattering away to itself as always, the plastic flowers on top needing dusting as always, the table littered with empty beer cans as always. Home Sweet Home, as it said on the sampler I sewed in St. Agnes' Primary School too many years ago, still hanging on the wall next to the picture of Jesus with his red heart exposed, rays of metallic love pouring out to give us the blessings we all no doubt desperately needed.

'Drink?' asked Dad, benignly.

'What are you drinking yourself, Al?' asked my lawyer, sounding too well educated by half to my over sensitive ears.

'Tetley's bitter,' Dad answered, watching for reaction.

'Great,' said Charlie. 'Love a glass of Tetley's. That'll do me fine.'

'In a glass?' A further test.

'Not for me, thanks, Al.' All men together, cans in hand.

Hmm. Dad was pleased. Good ole Charlie. We'd agreed that he would drink and I would drive back, which suited me and suited him. Tell the truth, he was a bit of a chip off the old block, so to speak. Meaning that he drank with the disconcerting ease of his father, and sat there with Big Al, sliding warm Tetley's down his wide throat in immediate companionship. Who would have guessed?

The football results came on the giant television, state of the art, fabulously expensive, and from a source I would never reveal to Charlie. Immediately the sound was turned up to booming. As dad loved to recite like his own private litany, from the lips of the saint of Liverpool FC, Bill Shankly himself; football wasn't a matter of life and death, it was more important than that. I fell into the silence expected of women at that holy time.

At that moment there was the sound of the front door opening, and in came Tee, my mother. I don't think I ever called her mum in my life. Even as a little kid she was Tee. It was short for Teresa, but no-one ever called her that either.

I stood and grinned, tiptoed over to her and hugged the rogue. She looked exactly the same, ageless at some undetermined middle-age, skinny and bright-eyed, hair dyed a lurid orange, clashing lipstick smeared on her wide lips.

'Michelle, darlin', great to see you,' she whispered, dropping her bags on the floor and hugging me tight. She was more like a naughty sister than a mother, lousy for childhood warmth and stories in bed, great for telling lies to boyfriends and borrowing skirts from when I was a teenager, never a reprimand even when I wanted one.

Dagger looks of warning from Al on the sofa. The holy service was still being intoned, don't you bloody women disturb me.

'Come on, kid, let's go in the kitchen. Tell us about yer feller.' Tee looked at him and made a face. 'Cor,' she said, 'looks like a bit of all right to me.'

There we were, back in role, talking about men. I think she was just one of those women born without maternal feelings. The problem wasn't hers, it was ours, although I think that my brother Billy missed what he never had more than me. Maybe boys need their mummies more than girls. So what Billy did was to marry one—fair deals, eh?

It was just great, ten minutes after arriving back home there we all were, perfectly in role, men on the sofa, beer cans in hand watching the footy results and women nattering in the kitchen about the men. What surprised me was just how easily Charlie fitted in. To tell the truth it worried me more than a little. If a Dingle male lurked inside my boy, what else lived in there that I'd missed? Something shifted uneasily inside me; in a way I couldn't put my finger on I sensed that life in the Brown palace and life in the Rafferty madhouse had something in common but upside down, so it looked as different as chalk and cheese until you stood on your head and looked at it right.

Tee and I chatted on about this and that. She was either innocent or half-mad, a creature unto herself, not looking for approval from anyone, beholden to no-one, coming and going like a wraith. And somehow she matched her man, who was as solid and present as a block of flats. My parents; the butterfly and the bull.

Ironically, dinner was the Chinese take-away I would have preferred at Charlie's parents and hated the thought of with mine, the four of us sitting round on the black plastic furniture while we all watched Bruce Forsyth on the TV that never slept. Charlie paid for the dinner, of course. I just knew that swine of a father of mine would find his pockets empty at the critical moment, and in that moment betray all his principles of equality and pride, a lifetime of fighting for the rights of his so-called class. Oh, the men of my family. When Charlie offered to take the empty containers into the kitchen, Dad waved his helpfulness aside. 'Leave 'em on the table, he said. 'They're not goin' nowhere, bet you anything they'll be there when we get back. It's only after a coupla weeks they start crawlin' round the floor.'

Then he started roaring at his own joke, the way he did, bent double, tears at the corners of his eyes, clutching at the old sofa for support, while Charlie and I smiled and Tee ignored him totally.

'Come on,' she said, 'if we're goin' let's go. Where are we goin',

Al? Down the Waterloo?'

He stopped laughing and stared at her. 'I don't never go to the Waterloo,' he said testily. 'Not since Billy Sanders choked to death in there. He was eating an egg and it went down the wrong way or somethin'.'

'Billy Sanders?' said Tee. 'I didn't know he was dead. Could've sworn I saw him the other day.'

'That's why I don't drink in the Waterloo,' Dad explained patiently. 'The place was never the same.'

'I didn't know you don't go there no more.'

'It's been four years and then some. Don't you listen to nothin'?'

It all made me feel right at home as this conversation carried on down the stairs and into the street. What a family. It took the wedding of their one and only daughter to get them speaking enough to catch up on deaths of friends and actually drink together in the same pub. The thought passed through my mind that if men marry their mothers then this meant I was something of a Margaret Brown, and if women marry their fathers then Charlie was something of my Dad. The thought made me nervous, because I knew of the furies inside my father, and nothing much of what lay in the deepest part of the depths of the heart of Charlie Brown. Then for amusement I thought of Margaret and Al in the same bed, and to my surprise I could imagine them getting along just fine in a bizarre way. But the idea was comical enough to make me giggle, and Dad was sensitive about other people's humour. Who knows what, or who, they were laughing at.

'What you laughin' at then?' he demanded.

'I was just thinkin' of them take-away containers crawlin' round the floor,' I said, reverting back into Liverpool-speak with an ease which scared me. 'Couldn't help laughin'.

He started wheezing away to himself again as we turned the corner and started climbing the hill. There was the smell of the sea in the air and something in that salt-sea smell reminded me of childhood, walking up that same street in icy fog on the way to school, listening to the foghorns of the big ships booming on the river. I wondered what was it in that time of the ending of a life within a life that touched the ancient loneliness in me that I carried up the hills to school, and then from there throughout my entire life.

I noticed with surprise that Dad's wheezing was not just the end of laughter; climbing the slope was beginning to be work for him, and I had my first intimations of the mortality of what always seemed eternal. Change was crowding in from all around; old certainties were crumbling and the new had not yet formed. What I didn't know at that time was just how far and how wide and how swift would be the ending to come, how soon, how unexpected, and how sweet would be the emerging of my butterfly self from the chrysalis of my lingering past.

Chapter 4

The pub which was chosen for the occasion was an old Dingle hangout called The Camel, one of the few remaining from the old days when men were men, women were men, dogs were men, and a place that I remember shyly creeping into as a little girl to get me dad and bring him home for his tea, which was baking dry in the oven. Funny he should be back in The Camel. Things seemed to be moving in circles, or maybe spirals, the same points and the same people touched on once more with the passing of time, the only difference being all that really changes and all that really counts in the end is our attitude and perspective to what we live.

It was one of those stained with the tobacco of years, thick with the tobacco of now, red mahogany bar and yellow brass foot-rail type of pubs. My brother Billy was there keeping seats for us, with his wife Sally frowning next to him. He was one of those people who always come on time and fret if you're five minutes late, balding at twenty six and mercilessly mocked for it by Dad, who gloated over the thick black hair which stayed unchanged on his bull head.

'All right, Billy,' I said. 'How's tricks?'

Not too bad, Michelle,' Billy answered. 'Makin' a decent woman of you at last then, are they?'

'Trying their best. This is Charlie. Charlie, my little brother Billy. And Sally.

They looked up at him with pale, strung-out, weasely faces. No wonder I never got to see them anymore. In comparison Charlie looked lush, tall, well-fed and watered, a thoroughbred in a paddock of pit ponies. My past and my future passing through now with me torn in two odd ways between the two. 'Good to meet you,' he said, well brought up, polite as always. 'Can I get you a drink?'

What sort of family were mine? Within five minutes of arriving Charlie had bought drinks all round, him the guest, the stranger in their territory. I couldn't believe it, despaired of my beginnings, the meanness of spirit, the cavilling, the pettiness. This is why I never wanted Charlie to meet them, I suppose, in case he saw the shadow of them in me, in case there was the shadow of them in me.

We all crowded round a tiny table, the six of us, three couples, and drank to Michelle and Charlie, then the women crowded round my flashing ring and made the right noises while the men talked of war. They knew that Charlie had been a soldier, had seen action in Northern Ireland, and violence and death were a language they could speak, a flavour that had given spice and meaning to many a mean Dingle life.

The Camel was not only a pub from my past, it was full of people from my past, who came and went, bought us drinks, checked out Charlie, looked at me like a creature from another planet.

'No, I don't believe it. You're not little Michelle. Well, well. Seems like just yesterday.' And so on. My old world, the one I fled from many years ago, bowing to me where I made my first stage appearance in the drama of my life as it left forever.

At the bar, three women, ageing now, faces familiar from my past, glancing over their shoulders, clearly talking about me. What were they saying? Why did I feel so ill at ease? I caught Sally's eye and she glanced at them, then back at me.

'They're just jealous,' she said, touching me on the arm. 'Take no notice of them, silly bitches.'

'Jealous?' I asked, puzzled. 'Jealous of what?'

'Because you're so beautiful,' said Sally.

I felt like running. 'Beautiful?' I said, feeling a tremor of contained panic running through me instead. 'Me?'

Sally smiled. How come I'd never seen the depth of goodness in her before? Perhaps it was because she looked worn out before her time, anxieties from her core heart of hearts lining her face, sagging her eyes, denying us the vision of the sweetness of who she was, the image of what I would have become without the good fortune of my singular destiny. How I hated the smallness of where I was made, how I hated what it did to people, what it had done to me. 'It's how you look to us, love,' she said. 'Isn't that right, Tee?'

'It's why your dad always gets so mad at you,' said my strange mother, casually tossing a shaft of insight my way, and in a flash lighting up a huge piece of what I never quite understood about my young life and why I had to run from home and why I found men so hard to trust.

'Oh,' I said. 'I see.' And I almost blushed. How come I was so naive? How come so many women find their own beauty so hard to believe and then to bear? I looked at my Charlie. It's what he always said about me, but to me it was just the sort of thing men always said, and how many times in my life had I had the eyes of men staring at me and not me at all, so I could never quite believe in what they were seeing and even less in what they said, what they promised, what they believed. For a moment I felt dizzy, lost, uncertain, till Charlie at last caught my eye and gave a smile which told me that all was well with him, then turned back to his conversation with his new friend, Big Al. Right there in the noise and the heat of the pub I felt that old cold sense of aloneness from the damp cold and alien non-belonging I part-lived in so long ago. I felt isolated, not belonging to any of the worlds around me, and something inside me wanted to go out into the street and walk through the fog once more with the sound of ships I never saw moaning on the invisible river.

'Good news,' said Charlie, turning back to me. 'Your parents think it's fine to have the reception at my folks house.'

'Practical, innit?' said Dad. 'If they got the space. You'll never find anywhere half-decent round here anyway, late as this.'

And it won't cost you a penny, I thought. Miserable bastard. But it was my choice too. Better the Brown luxury and style of my future than some scrappy working men's club in Toxteth that was the fading taste of my fading past.

'Righty-ho,' Dad pronounced. 'What yerall havin'?' Oh, good, he was buying drinks. What a relief. He took orders and pushed his bulk sideways through the press of Saturday night people at the bar. He wouldn't take long to get served; nobody was before Big Al at a Dingle bar.

Charlie leaned over the table to speak, and I leaned over to hear. 'I like your family,' he said. 'At least they're real.'

I smiled back into his eyes, inches from mine, in our own little world for two in the middle of bedlam. 'I'm glad,' I said, thinking that if my lot were real, what were his? What was he? But to look into those bright eyes of his melted all these traitorous thoughts, and the shifting sands of my emerged feelings swayed over to the simple longing for love in my own heart. 'Oh, Charlie,' I whispered.

Our little reverie was broken by the sound of breaking glass and a bull-bellow I knew so well, the sound of man rage that always made me cringe inside with stark fear, the sound of the feeling that I had spent my life avoiding. My Dad, oh no, oh hell, what was he up to now, in front of my lover, my fiancé, my future?

As if to answer my question the mass of people at the bar parted like the waves of the Red Sea, and there he was, eyes red with rage, jaw pushed out, fists like hams, and in front of him three younger guys in attitudes of aggression, one with a bottle broken at the neck in his hand, and on the floor in front of them broken glass in a swill of beer. I was gripped in fear, my hands up by my mouth, my eyes wide. Oh, no, not this, please, not the living nightmare that haunted the recesses of my soul, everything I feared most manifesting before my frightened eyes.

'This is it, yerole fucker,' shouted the one with the bottle. 'We've had enough of ya. Enough!'

Dad was swaying slightly. God knows how much he'd drunk, God knows what he'd done or said, standing there in brute arrogance, looking with contempt from one to the other of his latest foes in a lifetime of unending war. I knew him, I knew the bastard, he'd never back down, horror may be moments away. 'Come on, then,' he rumbled, sneering into the jaws of his doom. 'Yer just kids full of wind.'

It was like watching one of those wildlife programmes on TV when the young lion fights the older lion on the dusty plains of the sunlit Serengeti when his day at last was come to become top cat himself; the power of the time leaving behind who was once the king. Big Al, my Dad, had fought his way through years of this jungle and survived, but now you could feel his prime had passed, and with it there came fear for him in the place of fear of him, and with it a certain sadness, despite his outrages. It was a snapshot moment in a life, played out on his favourite stage.

For a measure of time there was stillness, the calm before the storm, the only sound the Beach Boys cheerily singing of waves and girls in California on the jukebox, all the people in the pub frozen still, almost not breathing, all eyes on one place.

Then, to my amazement, Charlie stood up and walked swiftly over to the bar to stand between Dad and the boys, facing them.

'Enough's enough,' he said calmly and with the expectations of command. 'Put the bottle down. None of us want any more trouble, do we?'

For a few slow, tickless seconds, not a move, not a word, everything hanging in the balance. Nobody breathed. The record finished. Then the chief lad sagged slightly.

'Yeh,' he said. 'He's not fuckin' worth it.' and threw the bottle in the corner with a crash, turned on his heel and pushed through the gaping crowd, followed by his mates. 'What d'you do that for?' Dad glared at Charlie.

'Didn't want you to dirty your hands, Al,' said my man, giving him the way out, and not without grace.

'Bloody right,' mumbled Dad. 'Whose round is it anyway?'

Conversation started from where it halted. It was like throwing a stone in a pond—first the splash, then the ripples, then all action vanished, nothing had happened at all. Except that the rite of passage was not from Dad to those lads, the younger generation of local yobs, the mantle had passed to Charlie, and it didn't please me one bit.

'Some feller ya got there, Michelle,' said Tee, picking at a pile of peanuts one by one, like a bird, but slow, as usual off in her own world.

Sally and Billy raised their glasses to me, and drank. Homage to the woman of that man. All well and good, but not enough. Somehow I'd been sidelined again. Pretty Michelle how nice you look, what a fine man you have, and something inside me wanted to stand on the table and shriek at them all. In some way I couldn't grasp at the time I felt that I wasn't escaping from anything, and the past I was flying from was changing form to become my future, like a demon in a myth. But I sat there and waited while Charlie and Al, pals—the surprise of the night—made their way back to the table with drinks for everyone.

Soon after the evening folded and we made our way back down the hill to home, said our goodbyes in the street and I drove the smooth quiet Jaguar, slowly and carefully, through the Mersey Tunnel once more, then I gathered speed as the road opened up on the other side of the river. Charlie was fast asleep by that time, arms tightly folded, head back and mouth open, and the car was mine. Rain speckled the windscreen and I touched the wipers into life. There was nothing on the road, and despite the lights all around I felt as if I was alone in the world, as if there was only me, driving to nowhere from nowhere. It was a taste of a wilder future soon to come, but I knew nothing of it yet.

There it was again, the bass note warning of the imminence of something as yet unknown, looming just beyond my sight. I felt a mixture of fear and strength, driving at speed into the darkness, not knowing what was coming my way but in the same way I had faith in my driving and the correctness of the road, I had faith too that I would handle whatever it was in my unrevealed future whenever and however it came.

In the daytime I followed Margaret Brown around, feebly helping as she bulldozed what would normally take a year into a single month. Wedding dress? No problem. What could take six months took an afternoon in London, doors opening for us, gorgeous dresses appearing from I never knew where, and falling in love with myself in this dazzling creation of cream silk and lace, grimly approved of by Margaret, and there we were on the train back to Chester with all a girl would ever need to be an immortal princess in a silver frame on the piano for the rest of eternity.

'I've been planning Charles's wedding in my mind for years,' Margaret confided to me. 'I'm not going to let anything get in the way of my dreams.'

Time passed, the days accelerating through the million and one and more exhausting details of food and wine and tablecloths, cars and honeymoons, churches and priests. The Rafferty's, my family, were as religious as Las Vegas, but the bog Irish blood in them still feared the consequences of dallying with religions that were not the Pope and the One True Church, and even to make a visit to the Church of England made them nervous of the consequences of mortal sin. We solved the problem by making two ceremonies, the main one in the Cathedral in Chester, where connections had made the impossible possible, and a second one small and for forms sake alone, in a Catholic church in the Dingle, with the whole business made all right by the local Irish Father. It seemed cock-eyed to me, but it made some sort of sense to everyone else. Our priest, the Church of England one, was a fat little guy who talked to us with inspiration of the sanctity of marriage and God making man and woman and so on, while he seemed openly gay to me. It was the way he talked and moved and looked at me. Maybe it gave him a better perspective on such things. Whatever, I liked him a lot, more than any priest yet in my life except for the man who taught me from the heart when I was just a child.

Margaret and I spent hours deciding on hymns, aeons on the kind of script for the invitations, longer deciding who to invite, and even longer who to ignore. It was exactly the circus I had hoped to avoid, but when it came to it I was sucked in like any other sucker, dying to dazzle up the theatre of My Day.

Flowers for the church, flowers for the house, bouquets for the girls, buttonholes for the boys. Heated marquee on the lawn, dance band, even a magician for the kids, no detail ignored, no price not paid. And because we had ended up by chance being married on November the Fifth, the day when the whole country was ablaze with bonfires and candelabra-ed with fireworks, an enormous bonfire and the greatest of fireworks was to be the finale of the Great Day. It astonished me. From nothing at all to all this in no time at all, and the more I became involved with this production the more I became drawn in, the more it became mine.

That quicksand again, finding weaknesses in my resolution not to be drawn in to that life, then expanding them until they became myself, and who I really was became lost in the complexity of holding the steps together in the dance which filled my days. And, without my own good fortune, would have filled my future too. Is this what happens? Is this all we are in the end, a character in a stock drama, a dancer to someone else's steps? And beneath it all, in the swirl that rivers us on from day to day, year to year, lies first a vague perplexity, then deeper than that a lostness, an aloneness which serves to drive us deeper into the dance.

Geoffrey Brown, long surrendered, stayed at home and planned the wine through an elaborate and dubious system of tasting everything his wine merchant could supply and writing the results of his selfless research in a tiny script in a tiny notebook. But he was happy, as much as I felt he could be, being helpful and part of things, and you could be sure the wine, from champagne to port, was going to be just great. My goodness, they spent money.

It was the first time I had ever been an insider with money power in that way, and I soon developed a taste for its delights, in the form of the best and most refined, silks and fine leathers and fawning waiters, the nectar and the flower. Why not the best? Everyone sells out for something, why not make the price high? Looking back from where I am now, a different creature in a different world, I can see myself being flattered into feeling I belonged, easing myself into a rich and flavoured top-cat life and pretending it was a mere nothing to me, that I could take it or leave it. Thank the Lord I escaped that particular form of doom, enticed into a one-way honey trap to feast my way to nowhere, perhaps ending up as rich, thin and lost to herself as Margaret Brown.

Alexandra, the cousin, had vanished into thin air, which was her way for as long as I had lived and known about her, but this time I felt some disquiet, a restless impatience. She just had to come to the wedding. Alexandra, where are you? I phoned my auntie Ada's number more times than I should looking for that cousin, but at least I knew she would get the message, and who knows, even she might materialise for a short time in our dimension, appear in the flesh for long enough to be witness to my marriage. Something in me ached for this, the seeds of my destiny having long been sown.

Those short weeks between the engagement and the wedding were the best with Charlie, as sweet as pie. The image of that time which rolls out of my memory with deep warmth and fondness is of Charlie and I walking and walking through the dark autumn streets of Chester, wrapped up in far too many clothes, me clinging to his arm, hardly talking, completely happy. In such a form betrayers come, it seems, death of the great and good arising from the tenderest of their kisses.

God, it was cold that year. By the end of October, just days before the Great Day, there was ice on ponds and a white frost on the world in the early mornings that remained in sheltered places throughout the whole of each bitter day.

'What a time for a wedding!' cried Margaret, fretting over the power of the heaters for the marquee, the incompetence of the bakers, the cost of hiring plates. It seemed madness to imagine we could get everything ready in time. I was overwhelmed with detail, tired of it all, just waiting for the whole business to be over and me and my man to be off on our honeymoon in the distant warmth of St Lucia. And through my tiredness came fresh doubts as I saw that my life was no longer my own and I was powerless to fight against the current that was now carrying me with overwhelming speed to its own choice of destiny. I still had simplistic ideas of the workings of that fate, you see, but my mind was soon to be expanded and widened way past any expectations I suffered within. Very soon. It was a lesson in appreciation of the now, because as I was to find, the best was in those long walks which led us back to the cottage and the blaze of log fire waiting for us, the cat basking in the heat, and making love right there and then in front of the fire and the indifferent cat.

After our fevered love-making he always became a dead weight, crushing me, making it hard to breathe as he started to inevitably fall asleep, so I pushed him without ceremony onto the floor from the great sofa which was our favoured place for passion. He was a heavy guy even now, muscled from those army days, but what would happen to it all with the passing of time? Hell, what would happen to me? Would my slender waist survive babies and middle age? What was to become of us? It was as if even then I knew in my heart of hearts that we were living the best, that the peak had been reached early and from there, there was nowhere to climb to.

'Charlie,' I said, looking down on him, lying there where he landed, naked and glistening, staring into the flames. 'Did you shoot at people when you were in the army?'

'Of course,' he shrugged. 'That's what soldiers do.'

'Where? Northern Ireland?'

'Mm.'

'I didn't know you were there.'

He shrugged again. 'I was there. Falklands too'

I rolled over to the edge of the sofa to see him better. 'But did you actually kill anyone?'

'Michelle, I don't want to talk about it. It's finished, gone, I'm a lawyer now and all that stuff's behind me.'

I sat up. 'Charlie, I need to know. I'm not going to spend a lifetime with someone who has secrets.'

'Right,' he said, sitting up on the floor before the fire, naked and beautiful in the flickering orange light. ' You don't know what you're capable of, Michelle.'

'You mean I could kill someone?' I leaned up on one elbow, my own nakedness stretched out along the sofa.

'I think we all could. I've seen it, done it. Any one of us could do just about anything.'

The fire behind him lit up the hair round his head like a halo, and his body glowed, shone, and in the warmth of after love and the heat of the fire I thought he looked like a God, but not a benign divinity; this was a thrilling and frightening God of War.

'Shooting at people is nothing. After the first time it's just another thing to do, and it's all remote, far away on the other side of the valley, and the bodies you see later are just bodies.' He turned his head and grinned like a schoolboy. 'I think it's a natural thing for a man, actually. Sounds like a terrible thing to say, but it's true, it's something we've always done, right?'

I lay there watching and listening to this alien creature, this male of the species, talk of the world from his mind and through his eyes. He lived on a different planet to me—as he talked on we seemed as distinct as giraffes and grasshoppers—and I was fascinated by this insight into his particular universe. Something in his awful violence both attracted and repelled me at the same time. So this is how they think. My goodness.

'I know I killed people, men. How many I have no idea, not a clue. Like I said, it's what soldiers do.'

Amazing. This still one with waters running deep began to intrigue me in a whole new way. What else had he done in all those secret years before I knew him? What other beings lurked in him unseen?

'But Charlie, love, did you ever see someone die, someone you killed?' I insisted.

'Now, now, Michelle. Calm down. We should change the subject.'

'I'm fine, Charlie, believe me. I just want to know. And I'm not bloodthirsty, if that's what you're thinking. It's just the most interesting thing I've ever talked about. Tell me, go on.'

He smiled and cocked his head. 'All right,' he said, and turned to lie out, stark naked male on the rug in front of the fire. 'Once,' he began, 'we attacked with drawn bayonets. You know what a bayonet is?'

'Of course I do. The knife affair you stick on the end of your gun.'

'Near enough. It's something we'd done in practice for years, yelling and shrieking and sticking the bayonet into a sack full of animal innards. Gives you the right feeling.'

'How bloody horrible you men are.'

He grinned again; the schoolboy caught putting a spider in his mother's bed. And was it the right feeling? When you really did it.'

'Pretty close to. Except for the bony bits.'

'How repulsive.'

'It's you who wanted to hear all about it. You're worse than me.'

'Crap. Charlie Brown, you're nothing but a homicidal maniac.'

'No, I'm not,' he said, yawning and stretching, unashamed, still glistening from making love to me. 'I'm a heroic patriot.'

Chapter 5

That freezing year, November the fifth fell on a Friday, the only day we could get for the Cathedral at short notice, even with influence and a name that counted for something in the Conservative Party and the Church of England. After the night when my warrior hero told me his almost all, or at least more of his all, I felt differently about him. A part of those hidden depths had surfaced, and with it an enhanced curiosity from me, who wondered how much more there might be down there, and what that more may be. I had seen enough to know that within that external placidity and good-naturedness, clothed in those gentle qualities, was a ferocity, a passion, a power that could take life with violence. Whatever lay in my own depths, swimming at its own pace to my surface as I lived those yet unexploded days, it was not that, and those alien male qualities fascinated me. I kept watching at him out of the corner of my eye, looking for signs of other men's blood written in even the faintest of guilt in his light-filled grey eyes, and I never found a trace. He truly lived easy with his past; there was no burden for him in duty done.

But you know what? I was also on guard for other hidden pasts that might emerge. Find one hidden depth and secrets of savage deaths hidden there and who knows what else may be tucked away round hidden turns. A man of some mystery, and it intrigued me, pulled me in, gave me something past and beyond the easily visible, a void to cast my fantasies upon.

'Charlie is a deep one,' I mentioned to Margaret one afternoon as we drove back from haranguing the unfortunate caterer in Chester.

She glanced sharply at me. In an odd way we had surrendered to each other, we had what we had and might as well make the most of it, and from that openness had come a certain understanding and warmth I would never have expected this lifetime. Perhaps our outer differences disguised some thread in common that we had at first fled from and now accepted. A thread that was more than just the increasingly enigmatic male son and lover; rather it was that shared need, or desire, or fantasy, that had created the same presence in our now shared lives. Come what may, there were times these days when we were at ease with each other, and at those times we could talk, actually be open and relatively free.

'Even as a boy there was always a great part of him I never knew, something he never showed me,' she said, threading through heavy traffic, the focus of her eyes on the road ahead as to not reveal more of herself than need be. 'Perhaps it's the source of his charm, we are always reaching for something, always trying to grasp something in him and never making it.'

Well, well, uncertainties, depth, acuteness, in Margaret Brown? The Bentley leaped forward as the traffic cleared and she glanced over to me.' I'm glad you know him well enough to know you don't know him totally.'

'Does anyone?'

'What? Know him totally? Oh, I don't think so. It's something you're going to have to live with, Michelle. We all do, in one way or another.'

'Could be worse.'

'Indeed. And look at what you can see. I hope that one day you too can have such a son. You don't know what he means to me.'

Ah, the vulnerable Margaret. How sweet to share the uncertainties and fears of another, the disappointments with her own man, a constant curse of womanhood, running unspoken beneath her hopes for her one and only child.

A small chill ran through me as I realised that hopes and dreams and expectations existed only to be unmet, and their bitter fruit was inevitable disappointment. What unspoken fruit did she expect from me? What did I expect from Charlie? What did he expect from me? Once more a cold hand fell on my heart as with some form of prescience I felt the oncoming storm rising in my vaguest inner distances as my fate spun out its unstoppable web.

'So you're happy with the menu?' Margaret asked, and my attention snapped out of its distant inner gaze to the car, the woman, the menu, the drama which was unfolding before me. What was going on? Some unformed inner world kept pulling me away from the most concrete of real realities, there was something going on which troubled me, excited me, and which I didn't understand at all, which competed with the more tangible realities I was living, in that car, at that moment.

'What? Oh, yes, fine.' The wedding. Five days to go and I had cold feet as my feelings swayed without reason from what seemed like one reality to what seemed like another. What was I doing? How had this happened so fast? I was being swept along in this swift river now, and for a moment of clarity I could see how I was losing myself in the theatre of it all, and in time may be gone without trace. Michelle, where are you? The chill was in the thought of the greater complexities of my future role—would I survive them intact and never really belong, or would I lose myself in them completely? The answer to that lay in the panic I felt, but I was in the river up to my neck and the current was strong and fast and there was no way out that I could see. And remember that a great part of me was happy with what was coming my way, the hesitations were just sometimes, in moments of stillness when I stood apart and could see all that was boiling on around me.

Then my focus would return to dresses and bridesmaids and cake and those impossible caterers and soon I would be lost once more. Is this life? Do we become no more than a reflection of all the baubles and troubles that surround us?

Talking of troubles brings me naturally to my dear family. Notice that the Browns had taken over the function of the bride's family, paying for and arranging everything. No-one had ever discussed this, it had just happened, and everyone knew why. While in Liverpool the raging bull of my bloody father, who had to have his presence known in everything that happened in life, started making objections to this and that, in fact to just about everything he heard of that was going on. Typical. Tee was off on her usual planet with no opinion at all but generally pleased with everything. I don't know which of them irritated me more.

All Dad's objections came over the phone—he never came to Chester and we never went to Liverpool. The old bugger called himself a perfectionist, that wonderful excuse done to death by fault-finders the world over. The tone of things went like this:

'Yeh, that's right, dad, a band. You know, guitars and saxes and drums and stuff, you've seen them.'

'Don't be sarky with me, young lady, I know what a bloody band is. The question is, why not a Liverpool group? They're the best, right? Remember the Beatles?'

'Yes, dad, I remember the Beatles.' Wearily. 'But those lads you have down at the Labour Club aren't hardly the Beatles.'

'What's wrong with them? Eh? You're gettin' too big for your boots, girl. And what's wrong with the Labour Club anyway? I think you need a bitta bringin' down to Earth. Who do you think you are anyway?'

There it was, the question of questions. Who do you think you are. Every time you try to escape, make something of yourself, fly off into the big wide world, it's who do you think you are. Reminds me of a story I once heard about this village that made their money catching and selling live crabs. Such was the nature of these crabs that the villagers just piled them in boxes without lids, right to the top, and sent them off on the train to the big city. When people asked why they didn't just dash off out of the boxes and escape, the villagers told them that if one of the crabs on top tried to do just that, then the crabs in the box under them grabbed them with their pincers and dragged them back in again. No need for lids when you got friends and family. Looking back at that time I can see that the sense I had of being repressed, held back, held down, was accentuating as my need for freedom was rising. I was becoming conscious of the tightness of my bonds, evidence that their time was running out, if I had only known it.

Those bonds took the shape of my Liverpool world; my old dad and his cronies, his sister Ada—my cousin Alexandra's mother—my podgy friends from school who all seemed to chew gum and smoke at the same time; I could feel their invisible pincers dragging me back into the box from which I came. The whole of my past life seemed claustrophobic. Had I never breathed free? Then there was the chilling thought that flashed through my mind without me wanting it to—was I just moving from one box to another? From one type of crab to another? Everything in its time, Michelle, take it easy. Right now we have the chief crab on the line, asking me that question. Who do I think I am? Well, one hell of a lot more than you'd ever let me be, you sod, I thought, but didn't have the nerve to say.

'I'm just getting married, dad,' I whined in frustration, pulling myself back into my self-made box. 'Let me be, will you?'

'Just getting married,' he sneered and mocked, and glugged a throatful of his only love. I could hear Ada, his poisonous sister, tittering in the background. It was the story of my bloody life, those two sucking any vestiges of power and self-decency away from me, tying me up in knots and leaving me weeping with frustration. Would I never be free of their ancestral curses of smallness?

'Just getting married' echoed through my head. What do you mean, just? Just this, just that, just my life, just little Michelle, diminished, wrapped up and tossed in the corner, and all of a sudden I'd had enough.

'Dad, you goin' out anywhere?'

'Out? No? Why?'

'Don't worry about the why's. Wait there. I'm comin' to see you.' Funny the way I fell back into the old Liverpool-speak when I talked to him. It was as if all pretence was stripped away, all the veneer and polish I had crafted so carefully for myself over the years was tossed aside as I made ready for action.

'Now?'

'Right now.'

So I did; I drove, right now, left the room as I was, walked out to the car and drove to Liverpool, with single-minded thought-free clarity, utterly determined. The time had come, the first of many.

The force was with me that night; the car seemed to cut through traffic, fly through the air, flow with power, and in what seemed like no time at all there I was parking under the same light Charlie parked under not long before, gathering my bag, no touch of lipstick this time, and straight into that miserable block of flats.

Dad opened the door, beer-can in hand. 'Well,' he said, grinning. 'Look what the cat brought in.'

'Dad,' I said, 'sit down.'

'What d'ya mean, sit down?'

'I mean put your great arse on the sofa.'

'You can't talk to me like that.'

'Dad, sit down.'

He sat heavily next to Ada, a bony creature with a permanently pursed mouth and sharp eyes eternally searching the world for something else to disapprove of, and, as ye seek so shall ye find, so she found her acid joy at every turn.

'Please turn off the telly, Ada.'

'I will not.'

'I've come to tell you something. Both of you. You need to listen. Dad, tell her.'

Something in my voice was different from anything he had heard from me before. Never had I been who I was that night with him in all my years. For reasons unknown, fear had fled. I meant business. He was stopped in his tracks, uncertain and wary, the game was being played with new rules. 'Turn it off, Ade,' he said, and she fumbled with the control. It was as if no-one had ever turned it off before. I waited patiently, in no hurry at all while she poked at buttons and waved the control at the TV. Channels changed, sound volume rose and fell, then suddenly there was a flash and silence. Two faces looking up at me, the faces that had terrified me as a child, monsters from my personal deep, blinking in the odd silence that followed the death of the TV.

'Right,' I said. 'First, don't speak till I'm done.'

'I'll speak when I want,' said Ada. 'I won't have you telling me what to do.'

'In that case, you can leave now. I have things to say to your brother, my dear old irreplaceable dad, which won't wait and won't be interrupted. What's your choice?'

'I'll do as I wish,' she said primly. 'I'll stay.' The baggage couldn't resist being there for the drama, even at the price of her own humiliation. So much for the demons of childhood, creatures that feasted and grew strong on a diet of my own fear.

'Right,' I began, 'what I've come to tell you is that I'm having no more controlling, sticking your oar in, making objections, bitching in corners, criticising me, making snide remarks about Charlie and his family. All of that stuff has to stop, right this minute, and stay stopped forever, understand?'

Dad took a casual swig of Tetley's. 'Or what?' he asked. 'We're only trying to help out, aren't we, Ade?'

She nodded, her lips tight. 'You need to know your place, young lady,' she said.

'I do,' I said, 'at last I do.' The old accent of my childhood had vanished. How easy it was now that the time had come. It seems that every tide has its turn, its time its own. I was utterly relaxed, calm, patient, unhurried. 'It's like this. Dad, you stop your interfering, bullying—' he made to object, who me?—'you know what I mean, don't give me that.'—and sank back into his plastic sofa all shifty-eyed; he knew all right. 'And if you don't stop it right now, once and for all, I'll walk out of here and you'll never see me again. No wedding, no me, no grandchildren, no nothing.' I paused, looking down at that face. 'What's your choice?'

He blinked, scratched an ear. 'Well, er, I dunno.'

'Not enough. Will you stop bullying me once and for all, right now? You'll never see me again, finish, finito. I'll walk out of here this minute and never come back. Well?'

How different when the words aren't empty. How sweet it was to be so sure. Every clear syllable was played for keeps. He took a deep breath. 'All right,' he said. 'Don't go, love.'

Ah, the sweetness of victory. Under it all the old bastard didn't want to be left alone, to be any more alone than he was and always had been. I was touched; he might have been a bully whose time had finished, but he was human after all, he was my father, and I meant something to him.

'Same goes for you, Ada.'

'Auntie Ada to you.'

'The days are gone when you call the shots, Ada, what is it?'

'I don't care if you come or go. In fact, I've got one like you already and to tell the truth I'd be better off without her.' She looked at me sharply. 'Have you been speaking with Alexandra?'

'Not yet. Why do you ask?'

'You're beginning to sound like her. Trouble. No respect.'

'Well, I can't wait to meet her, Ada.' I glanced at my watch. 'So tell me, are you going to join me ole dad and keep your charming thoughts to yourself in future?'

'Just for Al's sake. But don't think for a minute that I approve of this behaviour.'

'Who gives a shit?' I said cheerfully, and her eyes rounded in horror. What language! 'Oh, and Dad.'

He looked up obediently.

'You got a good suit for the wedding, like you said?'

'You want to see it?'

'No, I trust you. And another thing—don't get drunk at the reception. Got it?'

'I get the gist,' he said, popping open a new can, jaw stiffening, drawing a line. It was the signal for me to leave.

Twenty minutes later there I was accelerating out of the Mersey Tunnel once more, a different me once more, and it struck me with amusement that this me had moved a shade nearer to Margaret Brown. I had learned something at the knee of the master, who never took no for an answer and made the impossible come true. Maybe not a bad thing, I thought to myself with humour, at least she gets things done and is beholden to no man. Except, oddly enough, her one and only son Charlie.

If only it wasn't so cold. I spent those days shivering, always trying to get warm and never seeming to make it. Every day was icy before its time—we seemed to have January in autumn—with winds that cut through clothes and made straight to the bone, now and again made savage with a thin rain. What a time to choose to get married. I began to have severe doubts in yet another form. Why couldn't we have waited till spring? And when I thought about the sweetness of June, well, I began to feel I was mad. Surely spring, or early summer was the season for new beginnings and hopes and new love? I couldn't bear thinking about what a dark and grim, Arctic November wedding might bring, not knowing that it was the perfect, pre-ordained time for the pre-birth death of who I used to be.

But at least the Cathedral was beautiful, ancient, serene, remote from the passing pettinesses of life. I began to be awed at the prospect of being married in that sacred space, and said as much to our podgy priest as we strolled round the worn sandstone cloisters.

'That's the whole idea,' he said. 'Make great cathedrals to awe us with the power of God.'

'You sound a trace cynical.'

He looked at me with surprise. 'Not at all, I mean it. I think all of us get so lost in the thousand and one things of the world that we need a reminder of the power to awe, that something greater going on that holds our world together. I am not at all embarrassed by my amazement at the power of God.'

We carried on walking in silence. At that time of year the tourists had almost all gone home and the great pile of brown sandstone echoed to the sound of our feet alone; his solid, heavy, and mine the sharp sound of tapered heels. To me the Cathedral in Chester is very fine; not massive and towering but intimate and friendly somehow, a particular balance of passed time and window light and heavy stone.

'To tell the truth I've rarely even thought of it,' I said, after a few minutes of thinking of nothing else.

'Thought of what?'

'The something greater going on.'

'So you don't believe in God?'

'I don't know. The nuns of my childhood scared it out of me. I don't know what God means. All that remains is this sense of awe sometimes. It's as if I turn a corner now and again, almost by mistake, and draw back quickly before I see what's there. Does that make sense to you?'

A small group of Japanese girls tittered their way before the altar. They were dressed in angora and mini-skirts, leather and denim, with green streaks in their hair, children of another God, late tourists from the other side of the world. In the background the organ began playing softly, running up and down scales, flexing itself, filling the space of light with sound.

'Oh, yes,' said my priest. 'It makes sense to me. I think you're a deeply spiritual person.'

What? I looked at him open mouthed. Me, a deeply spiritual person? 'I think you've got the wrong girl,' I said. 'Apart from weddings and funerals I've hardly been in a church for years.'

He smiled. 'You know what I mean, Michelle.

'I don't know if I do. I do know you're making me feel very unsettled.'

'Then I'm doing my job.'

'I thought your job was to get me and Charlie married.'

'Oh, that's certainly part of things.'

'Only part?'

'Listen a moment,' he said, holding one finger up in the air, and we stopped dead where we were and let the music of the great organ sweep over us. From his first gentle explorations the organist was now playing with fire, music rising and falling in dizzying spirals, thundering and fluting, touching something in me that felt fear, as well as great joy, leading me into places in myself where I never went. I felt tears pricking at my eyes as this divine music resonated with what lay behind opening doors in the centre of my heart. What was going on? Every day brought another step towards the oncoming moment of the turning of my destiny, another preparation for what was to come. I face my father and the demons of my girlhood one day, and so taste freedom; another day I am filled with trepidation and an odd yearning; yet another and I am touched by a sense of the divine, if only I knew. Never in my life had I listened to music like that, in that way, me and my sweet priest standing stock still, both lost in the power of what once inspired that beauty.

In time it came to an end. 'My God,' I said. 'What was that?'

'You said it.' He smiled. 'Bach, in fact. Johann Sebastian Bach. He said he never wrote a note, that God did it all for him.'

'How come I've never noticed it before?'

'Not noticed what?'

'Not noticed the music. No, not that. Not noticed what's going on behind it all.' And in truth never before experienced feelings that I was feeling right at that very moment, a strange criss-crossing of waves of emotions, wonderful and uncomfortable at the same time, overwhelming my body. This priest of mine paused in the Cathedral stillness, as if he could sense what was going on in me before he replied.

'Maybe,' he said, initiating a phrase which would echo through all those days. 'Maybe your time has come.'

Chapter 6

I hardly slept a wink that night that led to the day of the Fifth of November, which had suddenly arrived as peace after the maddest maelstrom month of my life. So far, that is. All that night I tossed and turned in my bed at the Brown's where it had been decreed by someone other than me that I spend my final virgin night alone, with space to hang gowns, have my attendants fuss, and be away from my man in a way that actually suited me well. I lay there, tacky and hot, my hair in rollers, my great silken wedding dress glowing faintly in the traces of half-light like a ghost, and my mind racing with images of my past life, doubts, and downright fear.

I felt like a sacrifice at some pagan religious ceremony—such was my sense of being the victim of forces outside my control—and in the wild-mindedness of the early and darkest hours it would have been no surprise to me to be taken to the top of some previously unknown pyramid, and there have my pumping heart dragged from my bosom. In fact, by the time dawn began to show, late at that time of year, I would have preferred it to the fate which seemed to be assuredly mine. But the first light over the frosted fields brought some warmth and hope, and the dark thoughts of the night that seemed to be my single and only reality faded into the nothingness from which they came. Instead, my dress, which through the blackest hours of my own night seemed palely evil, possessed of a strange malevolence, began to look beautiful, which it was. My own dawn had come, and a charge of excitement ran through me. Gosh, my wedding day.

With that first light I got dressed in jeans and boots and sweater and walked down by the banks of the Dee estuary, all alone in a world without movement. There was not a breath of wind, not a cloud in the brilliant sky, with the brighter stars and a sliver of moon still showing before the sun tipped silently over the horizon. There seemed to be no life at all, as far as I could see over the still and frosted reeds, a whole world in shades of white and grey.

Well, well, well, I thought, so today you get married. This is it, girl, no backing out now, things have gone far too far. Not that I wanted to, actually. After the horrible night and the assault of the grimmest demons my frailties could summon I felt ready, happy, excited. This was my day. Over to my left the sun swelled over the low hills, white and bright, and lit up the first stage-set of my frosted and radiant wedding day. I felt very happy, all by myself, clumping along in boots and sweaters and scarves, watching the cold beginning of the day of days that began with ice and certainty and would end in fire and the dissolution of my world. Of this I had not a trace of foreknowledge; I was innocent of what was arising in me, believe me. All that happened was created by a force that was beyond anything I had ever known on that fine morning as I walked as free as a child under the dark blue sky.

By the time I got back to the house the action had begun, the drama of the day was in motion and my quiet aloneness by the river vanished as completely as the fevered night that preceded it. The next reel in the movie of my life began.

'Oh my goodness,' said Margaret. 'There you are. We were worried sick, weren't we Geoffrey?'

'Hardly sick, sweetness. We did wonder if you'd done a runner though.' Geoffrey twinkled his eyes at me. I hoped Charlie would bring more of this tenderness and humour out of those hidden depths of his with the passing of the years. Like father like son? Is this what I wanted? Well, not all of good old Geoffrey. There was a quality of defeat in him which I would wish on no man. And no wife of a man.

'Geoffrey! What a terrible thing to say. Honestly. Don't listen to him, Michelle, we thought nothing of the sort.' Humour was not one of Margaret's greatest qualities. Let's hope it wasn't like mother like son. Well, only time would tell. And once more my simple happiness was tainted by doubt. For just a moment my mind thought of the secret depths of my Charlie being the worst secret of all; that he was a mix of the worst of his mother and father.

We sat at the kitchen table and the lady of the house, the wedding-master like the ring-master at the circus, went through her check-lists. If things had been different she would have been the boss of some giant corporation or a minister like the other Margaret. From where I am now I wonder if she suffered like so many under the burden of not being herself, and we around were nothing other than the victims of her understandable frustration. As it was we sat there and she ran our lives. It was as natural to her as breathing, and there was one side of me which relaxed and let her take it, and another side which wanted things done a little differently. Was I letting myself in for a life of biting my lip and holding back just one more time, until my time came and I became what she was but in my own way? I had made the decision to let her run the whole wedding business after just a token of resistance at the dinner table, and since that time I got out of the way entirely. It would have been fighting all the way against an irresistible force, and as I was not an immovable object I surrendered.

As had Geoffrey a long time ago. We sat together and drank coffee, watching the sun come up over the lawn, melting the frost into drops of dew.

'The gods are smiling on us today, gorgeous,' said Geoffrey. 'It's a good omen. And look, that awful wind has dropped.'

'The marquee. Heating, flooring, tables, flowers, sound system, band, decorations, make sure they change those hideous drapes, name cards for all the guests ...' Margaret was in her own world of focus on lists, details, things to be done.

I sipped at my fine coffee, made from beans freshly ground which came from the best earth on the best mountain in Kenya, and who was I to know any different? 'Do you think it might be warmer today, Geoffrey?'

'It already is, sweetheart. I tell you, the Gods are smiling on you.'

'... the bonfire should be finished this morning, in fact the men said they'd be here by this time, where are they, for God's sake? Can these people never come on time? The fireworks are fixed, the cars are ready, must give the Bentley a final polish ....'

'More coffee, sunshine?'

'Thanks, Geoffrey. And talking of sunshine, it should make the Cathedral gorgeous.'

'All you deserve, honey. And wait till you taste the Bordeaux at lunch.'

'... the photographer—don't forget the confetti for the guests who don't have their own—I hope we have enough toilets. Margaret paused. 'Geoffrey ....'

He looked her way with weary expectation. 'Yes, sweetness.'

'Will we have enough toilets? Perhaps we should ....'

'Forget it,' he interrupted. 'We can manage. There's always the shrubbery.'

Margaret glared at him. 'Don't be disgusting.'

He looked at her evenly. 'No more toilets,' he said. And in that moment I saw that the power at the bottom of the pile was his after all, which made me instantly more optimistic about Charlie. Who I had hardly thought of all day. 'I'm sure the ladies who are desperate will adore the shrubbery, eh, Michelle?'

I giggled, despite the ice in the air from the Lady. 'Just the thing in a Lucretzia Ferrari wedding gown,' I said, and caught Geoffrey's eye. Maybe he had the same image come to mind, not just me in my billowing cream silk, but a host of poshly dressed ladies squatting under the rhododendrons in clouds of steam, and we burst out laughing till tears were running down our faces. The wound up pre-wedding springs running free, releasing us for the rest of that day. Margaret pursed her pursed lips tighter and stalked out into the garden, where workmen had just appeared—late of course—with even more wood for the already massive bonfire.

Geoffrey and I laughed and laughed, and I swear during that next hour when we couldn't look at each other without giggling all over again I was as close to him as I ever was to any man. In fact, the mood was set for the rest of the morning. The rising sun brought us a little warmth, like gold after all that bitter cold, really as if some benign force was smiling on us. The house rapidly filled with caterers and cleaners and flower arrangers. Sound systems were tested while the hairdresser started his work on me, the queen of the day, pampered and oiled, perfumed and massaged, remote somehow from the drama that was boiling away in the rest of the house.

I was in a dreamy state, no longer wound up and full of conflict, a girl painting my perfect nails while Annabella Wise herself fussed with my fabulous gown, adjusting pearls and silken bows, laying out the headband of dried flowers and rhinestones, necklaces and earrings in pinkish pearl, cream stockings with lacy tops, matching underwear in even more silk and lace, while outside in the garden the sun shone on men busying round the blue and white striped marquee and the bonfire reached dizzying heights.

The ceremony was at two, the morning was short and full of a million things to do, but it floated by me slowly in a sweet and timeless haze. I drank coffee, brought up by the ever-thoughtful Geoffrey, whose priorities were always clear, and we sat at the window committing the sin of lounging round nattering while there was so much to do and so little time to do it in.

'I've lived long enough to know it'll all get done, even without me,' said Geoffrey. 'Lovely day.'

I was sitting there in final rollers, part made-up, in woolly slippers and a tartan robe, the star in the dressing-room before the show, very relaxed, not a trace of stage fright, yet. 'Look,' I said, watching a familiar figure in an unfamiliar suit come rolling round the side of the house. 'My father. He must have just arrived.'

'Ah, yes,' said Geoffrey, watching him stop and light a cigarette, the blue smoke rising clear in shafts of sharp sunlight, then stand and size up the garden, the marquee, the busying staff. The socialist, I thought to myself, seeing the world he had been invited to in terms of money. Margaret appeared from one side and we watched them meet. Handshakes and smiles, a few words, a gesture, and the unlikely couple wandered off-screen together.

'Shall I go and bring him up?' asked Geoffrey

'No, for God's sake. We'll see plenty enough of him later. I've seen more than enough of him this life already. Who's that?'

'My brother in law, Henry. And that's my sister Georgina joining him. Can't stand her, never could. Look at that bloody hat, for God's sake. Who does she think she is?'

'Michelle,' the voice of the hairdresser behind me. 'Time's hurrying on, princess. Perhaps we should finish making that gorgeous face this side of Christmas.'

Geoffrey rose, feigning guilt. 'See you later, doll. Must go and check on my fireworks. Make sure the bonfire's ready. Count the wine bottles. All the important stuff.'

In front of the mirror, there am I. Richard my hairdresser easing my perfect waves into perfect place for little moons and stars to sit and twinkle. Caroline with brushes and tubes dabbing colour onto the skin of my face, ah, the touch of the professional, so subtle, so clever, why can't I do that?

Time seemed to have slowed right down; I was in my own little princess world, miles from the busying, besoming, frantic Margaret world in the house below, light years from anywhere Charlie—who seemed hardly more than a distant memory—might be, remote from Cathedrals and guests and pasts and futures in a limbo between all things.

'No lipstick till you've eaten your sandwich,' said Caroline.

'Oh, a sandwich. Great.' I just sat there and the world came to me. Being a princess was more than just looking the part. I could get into this. Well, as I was into it, what I meant is that I could stay in it. 'Do me a favour, Richard.'

He glanced over. 'What is it, darling?'

'Find Mr Brown. Tell him we need a bottle of wine. Glasses for us all.'

Without a word, just a check on himself in the mirror over my head, and a touch of his own perfect high-lit hair he slid off into the house.

'Where's Charlie?' asked Caroline, beginning to pack away her brushes and paints.

'In Chester. Did the stag party routine, last night of freedom, stayed at home. Didn't know you knew Charlie.'

'Not well.' She stopped and joined me at the window. 'I used to see him at parties and things. Half the girls in Chester were after him at one time. We all wondered who he'd end up with.'

I glanced at her with curiosity. She continued looking out of the window at the garden, where the action still eddied about, not catching my eye.

'So now you know.' I said.

'What?' She turned and looked at me.

'You know who Charlie Brown ended up with.'

'Yeh.' She smiled quickly and turned her eyes away. Why hadn't I noticed how pretty she was before?

'Did you ever go out with him?'

She started to fidget with her rings. 'Once or twice. But it was never anything. Ages ago. Years.' She glanced at her watch.

'I bet he went out with lots of girls.' I didn't mind; it was curiosity, more snippets to collect of the Charlie puzzle from the unknown years before I arrived, not that long ago.

'Oh, yes,' she said. 'Of course.' Just straight talking. Then she realised the deep water she'd entered, talking the past secrets of the groom with the blushing bride. 'Well, not lots, exactly. Some. It was when he was in the army'

I burst out laughing, and so did she. Girls together.

'Never fancied him for yourself, then?'

'Not really,' she said thoughtfully, and then backtracked quickly. 'I mean he's an attractive man and everything, don't get me wrong. There's just something about him I could never get hold of.'

Another something that I couldn't get hold of shifted uneasily inside me. I was just about to ask what she thought it might be, but it was too late now for old truths that might change things. At that moment she and I—and Charlie—were spared by Richard, one of the few who could freely enter the bridal inner sanctum, pushing open the door with a bottle of wine, cork half out, in one hand, and a clutch of glasses upside down through his fingers in the other. He reminded me instantly of Geoffrey on the night when I got engaged, bringing in fire in the Amaretto, the night that revealed the first signs of coming unknown things. The uncertain mood that talking to Caroline about Charlie's past had brought up in me mingled with the mood of the memory of Geoffrey's flaming Amaretto, and the intangible foreboding of some gathering darkness that portent had offered. Once again simple certainties were fertile ground for unsettling feelings.

It was almost time for my final dressing. The three of us held up glasses of golden nectar, somehow a trio of conspiracy, a triangle of understanding, them drinking to me and then me drinking to them, the final private ceremony of farewell to a life and a me that was ending before my costumed arrival on the stage of the world.

'And we all loved happily ever after,' said Richard. 'Have you finished your sandwich?'

I had indeed. The lipstick then, and no more food for me. Then it was into the great gown, bejewelled, be-pearled, shining with silk cut to give me a waist like a wasp then cascading out into a froth sewn with twinkling moons and stars to match those in my hair. Flowers, all pale, cream roses with no thorns, freesias, my favourite, scenting November with spring, and my attendants stood back in awe at my beauty, while I gazed at myself with wonder.

'Well,' I said, in the thickest Liverpool accent I could muster. 'Not at all fuckin' bad.'

'I think Charlie Brown's a lucky guy,' said Caroline, who knew him, and for a flash of a moment, even at that time, I wondered why.

'How about me?'

'Luck's got nothing to do with it,' said Richard, and for a few moments there we were in my last private silence that day. It was an odd minute or two where the three of us looked at me in a detached, dreamy, way, objectively sizing up this dazzling illusion of super princess mirage that was no more me than it was the mirror I was looking in. Nevertheless it overwhelmed and bewitched us all, men and women equally, into suspending reality to believe that this sacrificial offering had any relevance at all for the rest of life unavoidably spent firmly on planet Earth.

A rap on the door.

'Come in.'

In came Margaret, who was creating her own dream fantasy to satisfy some ancient longing and hunger in herself, for which how I looked was vital. She came in and clasped her hands in delight. I had made it.

'Oh, Michelle,' she said, just another sucker turned to jelly, bedazzled by the vision of the bridal me. 'You do look lovely.'

Lovely was the word of the day. It was all to do with loveliness, being exquisite, gorgeous, romantically charming, something from a dream—this was girls dressing for themselves and other girls, it was all about romance, fantasy and beauty. None of that flash of leg for the hungry fellers here. At that moment was I cynical, cool and detached? Forget it—I was sucked in as deep as any, dazzled by myself, and it was great. I took on a new way of being, like a Goddess or a Diva, eyelashes drooped in false humility as I basked in the adoration of the mortals who had gathered to worship. It all came very naturally. I loved every minute of it, lost in this Wonderland, gone, no hope left, at least for a time.

Then it was out of my private sanctum and into the big world, adoration everywhere, my father, the ole man himself with wet rims to his eyes—he'd reached that stage of alcohol in the brain, no doubt ably assisted by Geoffrey, who understood these things. Very good, as long as he stopped now. What a delicate business. Got to know how to handle the booze for the relatives, get them oiled enough to feel relaxed and involved and not a drop more before the Cathedral, afterwards they could look after themselves.

Into my carriage, an ancient, beautiful and draughty Roller that took me and these three second-cousin of Charlie's bridesmaids, red-faced, fat-faced, fat-assed all, from almost home from home to the Cathedral, no less, not bad style for a girl from the Dingle. It was the first time in my life that I truly felt beautiful, and I loved every moment of it. All I needed was an audience. The girls were useless. They ignored me and just talked horses, withers, gymkhanas and such, as we rolled in state, the princess me in my Rolls Royce from the jazz age followed by a line of cars, creeping unnoticed at 1925 speeds past sunlit giant factories where men were working with booming and crashing machines, while I drifted by, a dream of fantasy just yards away and seen by none of them.

Then, in time, we progressed to the suburbs of Chester where at last I was noticed. People stopped and pointed, and I found myself waving one tiny hand and smiling like the Queen as I passed my subjects by. It was great, and strange as I sat there, half-involved and half remote, watching myself and the world running out yet another of its eternal dramas.

The journey seemed slow to the point of unending, a perfect dream, me floating exquisitely towards a passage in my destiny, thought-free, the past gone, and Geoffrey was right, the Gods were smiling on me. What a day. The bitter wind faded now and golden sunshine made brilliant the colours of our autumn world. Was this all for me? I wondered, not for the last time that weekend, if some benign force was shaping even the weather around me, opening up a box of magic that would change my life forever.

Perhaps it was the springtime bride in autumn that turned the heads of people, an out of season exotic fruit in the back of an ancient grey and cream Rolls Royce, the chauffeur in his dove grey cap and coat stealing the occasional glance at me, my bridesmaids quietening now and in some magical way losing their redness and heaviness, changing before my eyes into angels as we drew up outside the Cathedral. My timing was perfect. It was precisely two o'clock.

Chapter 7

Cars and people and fuss, a sorting out, then me on the arm of my one and only dear old dad, who was so sobered and overwhelmed by the greatness and gravity of the whole drama that he briefly became a man of such poise and dignity he could have been an ambassador. We passed through the doorway into the Cathedral, a narrowing and darkening, and then there I was in the light and space of my own passing paradise. We stood at the back of the Cathedral, my father and I, close and still for the first and last time this life, waiting for the organ to finish playing that Bach I had been so moved by not so long before, and was duly being moved by once again. I was full with excitement, electrically alive with expectancy, looking down the length of that settled, medieval building.

Before me golden November sunshine poured in through the windows, shafts of light angling down onto those assembled, who turned and looked back as the Bach ended and the wedding march began to catch their first glimpse of the Beauty of the Bride. Not for the last time that fated month I felt like the Diva in some grand opera, my stage the ancient church, my audience the congregation, the music grand, my passions rising but as yet unsung.

We walked slowly down the aisle, me smiling, not at all

nervous, in a strange world all of my very own. Every step moved me: I became more acutely aware of every molecule of air as it passed through my bridal veil, every minute change in temperature, every cough and shifting of foot, every colour in every resounding note of organ. I was serene and balanced, ready for Charlie standing up there looking every inch the Prince for me, glancing over his shoulder and breaking into a wide grin when he caught my eye. For a moment there we felt like little kids playing a naughty game as I grinned back down a shaft of our own private understanding. Then he turned back to face the altar and my priest, as I glanced left and right into the people gathered there together, catching and relishing the eyes of friends, who winked and smiled, all of us falling secretly out of role for fleeting moments then returning to join the cast in the unfolding drama. It was wonderful to be the star, walking slow in that impossibly beautiful dress, unashamed in my own beauty, presented for all to see. I was adorned in all the beauty woman could muster, on the arm of the male whose thrust created my body, stepping up the aisle to the altar of sacrifice. At that moment I could understand the madness that seized so many women and drove them into futures they regretted, just to taste that ephemeral fruit of being the magically empowered, bedazzling Goddess object of worship and veneration in a living play before the eyes of their own adoring captive world.

I reached the row of pews before the front, and there, on my side of the church my relatives, far fewer than Charlie's, and my eye skipped briefly along the faces, knowing them all well, hopping from eye to eye, smiling. And then there was a face I knew and didn't know, between Ada and Sally, a face out of a distant dream I once had of far-away futures. My eyes locked on hers for a moment; they were brown and unsmiling, but calm and even, sweet and strong. In a flash I knew who it was; my cousin Alexandra transformed and transmuted and returned after most of my lifetime, and time stood still for an eternal moment that went beyond all the life I had yet known. The recognition and depth of that meeting of eye and soul sent a shock-wave through the air, through my heart and to the core of my soul, and I stumbled, a few paces away from the altar, yet another portent of doom for what was apparently visible to all and yet actually never to be. I was caught immediately in the iron grip of my father and with that grasp my attention was brought to the living moment of the tangible: my wedding, my man, the priest, the organ, and there I stood, eyes closed and almost trembling. The music stopped, followed by a void of silence that hummed with all the resonance of the occasion, within which there was a sharper note within me that shrilled with the thrill of the wild unexpected. The service began.

'Dearly beloved,' began the calm, practised voice of our fine priest, 'We are gathered together in the sight of God and Man ....'

And I lost him. My mind was on other things. Could I dare peek back and see that creature once more? Was I mistaken? Was this some delusion? Had anything actually happened at all? As is so often true in our lives, my mind doubted the voice of my heart. The words droned and I took a chance and turned my head, peeping through the veil and yes, there she was, looking directly at me. Once again there was a bolt, a shock, an intrusion of some power that was unknown to me. I swallowed, turned back and went through the movements expected of me, but the magical dream bride state had gone, and now

I felt oddly agitated and impatient to move swiftly through what now seemed to be a thin drama, be done and out of there and away.

Charlie and I stood, we sat, we knelt, we sang hymns of a church unknown to me, and then there we were at the crux of the whole matter where there was just me and Charlie and our priest and we were pronouncing our marriage vows. First we had Charles Brown's clear voice resounding through the Cathedral, taking me to be his wife. And by this time my attention had wandered into an odd confusion that had taken me right out of the feelings expected of that time. Then it was my turn—Do you, Michelle Teresa Rafferty take this man ... and of course I did, the time had come, all of my precious fate had led me to that moment, and then we were pronounced man and wife. Charlie lifted my veil and kissed me above and beyond the call of duty, and we turned to our world as the bells began to ring and the organ played trumpeting music of celebration.

Every face was smiling, joy was in the air, and I dared to peek at her once more as we began our walk as one couple back down that aisle. My God, I thought, how she'd changed from the long haired round faced girl I remembered, and now she was smiling too, looking at me with such sweetness that I felt free to be sweet myself and once more part of the wonder of the day. I hugged Charlie's arm tight and he glanced down at me with shining eyes, seeing what he wanted to see in the shimmer of the different magic that had entered my heart, which was fluxing in mood with every turn in that day which was marked in the heavens.

In Chester Cathedral there is a garden surrounded by cloisters, a square of seasoned and sacred buildings made of worn sandstone and glass. In the centre of that square is a sunken square pond, and in that ancient pond is a very modern sculpture, two figures curved into an elegant circle, one dripping water into the held out bowl of the other. It was here in this place of quiet and other-worldly beauty that we came to have our wedding photographs taken. Even with my exposed shoulders it was almost warm in the gift of sunshine that the God of that place had brought us, and for that short time it seemed as if we had somehow cheated the force behind the seasons and had created our very own spring wedding right there in November.

It was a lovely place to be, and once more I relished being princess for the day, the centre of all attention, the receiver of congratulations and kisses, admiration of my loveliness, hugs and smiles. One group of this lot of relatives, one of that, one of friends, one of everyone, all bossed round by this fat little woman photographer with a mass of auburn hair frizzing to her waist that lit up in the sunshine like a great halo. She kept pushing her hair out of the way as if it was some kind of enemy, while she shrilled orders in an abrasive voice that echoed off the stone and cut through the chatter of the crowd and the noise of dripping water from the statues over the pond, and we obeyed her like children in a playground.

It was a time of great mirth, bawdy jokes and good humour, especially when Charlie and his cronies from the army had their own picture set up, and they horse-played round like teenagers. For once I was standing alone, all the attention not on me, so I wandered to one side and looked down at the water in the old fish-pond and the statue which rose from it. There was a quotation from the Bible engraved around the stone base on which the statue stood, and I started to mouth it aloud, like a child, and to walk around the pond as I read, the only way to read the whole quotation.

'Jesus said,' I read to aloud to myself, 'The water ....'

And a voice behind me said, 'The water that I shall give will be an inner spring, always welling up for eternal life.'

I turned in surprise, and right there was my cousin, the long-lost one, Alexandra herself. For the first time I could see her properly, standing there in the bright sunshine. She was tall, as tall as me, her dark hair cut short and swept back at the sides, her eyes rimmed with black Kohl but no other make-up, her skin pale, her face sculpted over prominent cheek-bones. She was wearing a trouser suit with a black jacket like an old-fashioned military uniform, buttoned up to the neck with high collars, severe and sharp.

'You know the quote?' I asked, feeling oddly shy, addressing her for the first time for many years.

'I came here before the ceremony. This is a wonderful place.' Her voice was clear, unhurried and strong, and she stood there tall and erect but very relaxed, poised, at ease with herself, extraordinary in her black amongst all the bright dresses and lunatic hats of the other women, like a visitor from another world.

'I'm so glad you could come,' I said, feeling oddly uncertain of myself, not knowing what to say and falling back into social niceties that were, for once, very true.

'Me too. I knew I had to be here, and now I see you I know why.'

I felt bashful, reached out to touch the water dripping from the inner spring, a picture from an ancient myth in my dress from a dream in that place from a thousand years ago, with her next to me in sharp black contrast, and brought my wet fingers back to my mouth, where I tasted the promise of eternal life.

'Tastes like any other water,' I said, and had to restrain myself from touching her lips with that water so she too could taste what I had tasted.

'Your husband is a fortunate man,' she said, but not in the social way people say these things; she seemed to look calmly into my depths and see treasures there not even I ever suspected, until I saw them recognised in her own eyes.

Husband, I thought, my husband, how strange that sounds. And at that moment the odd little bubble we were in burst as a voice cried, 'Michelle! Come on, love, just one more picture.'

I looked over. It was my mother, Tee herself dressed in the oddest combination of flowery dress and felt hat, her legs looking bandy, her handbag looking plastic. She was standing with her hand on Geoffrey Brown's arm. What a couple they made; they looked like the Chairman of the board and the cleaning lady in a bizarre musical comedy. I waved and smiled to show I was on my way, then turned back to Alexandra.

'Are you coming to the reception?' I asked.

'Yes,' she said. 'I'll come.'

'You weren't going to?'

'I hadn't planned to.'

'But you will now.'

'Oh, yes. You can be sure of it.'

We stood there for another few moments, just looking at each other, until she said, 'You'd better go. Look, they're waiting for you.

I turned to join the next photo group, and when I looked back she was gone. Inside me was a tremor, a movement of something woken that had always slept, and I felt as happy as springtime. I took my place between my mother and my father and kissed both of them on their different cheeks. They seemed such a pair of little loves. The camera clicked and our tyrant photographer shrieked that she was done, we were free to go, so I pulled Charlie away from a group of his old friends from way back, married couples that I didn't know, took his arm with great happiness, and whispered;

'Time to move on, handsome.'

'And I know where I'd like to move on to, beautiful.'

'Restrain yourself, you beast.' I kissed him in that tender spot just below the ear where the skin is soft and the blood flows deep that I loved to kiss and he loved to be kissed, and he breathed in deeply then sighed as he led me away, back into the Cathedral proper, followed by our chattering guests.

Then we passed through the same door back out into the world I had entered not that long ago—the whole thing seemed to take minutes—and out into the sunshine and a row of crossed swords held out by the guys from the Regiment in their dress uniforms. As Charlie and I crunched together to run through the swords our guests threw confetti in bucketfuls, and it fell like coloured snow through the sunshine and the flashing blades as our adoring crowd cheered. What more could any girl ever want?

Then we ducked our way into our leather-smelling Rolls-Royce, ready to drive off to the rest of life when I realised I hadn't thrown my bouquet to the hungry crowd.

'Don't go anywhere,' I said to Charlie, and opened the door the chauffeur had just closed, gathered my skirts and hopped out onto the pavement holding the bouquet up high. The unmarried girls shouted and held up their arms, and I made a theatrical show of one, two, three, and then threw the bouquet of subtle cream, violets and pinks and trailing ribbons high into the air. It made an arc, followed by the eyes of the people, high into the blue, blue sky and then down over their heads and straight to the lone figure of Alexandra, who I hadn't noticed till that moment, standing erect in her sharp blackness, off at one side in the shadows, apart from all the others.

She caught it neatly, took it to her nose and smelled the flowers, then smiled broadly and blew me a kiss with her free hand, all in one fluid movement. I watched this happen as if it was all in slow motion. Fate and forces I was only just beginning to detect the existence of once again moved me, unsettled me somehow for a passing moment as the crowd turned and cheered Alexandra, who held up the bouquet with an outstretched arm like the victor in some ancient games.

That was my moment to bob back into the car and fall onto the seat in a flurry of silk. The chauffeur looked back inquiringly and I nodded, and the car began to draw away sedately through more cheers and even more confetti, which piled up on all the horizontal surfaces of the old Rolls Royce.

Moments later we turned the corner, stopped waving, and were alone at last. 'Phew,' I said, and fell back onto Charlie.

'Beautiful woman,' he said, and put his arm round my shoulders. 'Who got the bouquet?'

'My cousin Alexandra. Did you meet her?'

'Can't say I did.'

'She was the one wearing the black trouser suit.'

He shrugged. 'Is she the cousin who you haven't seen for ... how long?'

'Since I was a little kid. Yes, that one. Amazing. She's quite something.'

Then we fell into silence as the car made its way through the very ordinary traffic of Chester on a Friday afternoon. I think we were tired by the whole affair, what with all the excitement, the crowd, the inner tensions, so we just sat there watching the world slowly float by. Charlie, who had the capacity to fall asleep in a moment, even for a few minutes, any time and any place, closed his eyes and left me alone to drift through the suburbs and the open country, lost in my thoughts. It was a gap in the choreographed day, a cast-break where I was no longer the bride and the property of the eyes of many, but just me, alone, and I was actually conscious of relaxing my face now I didn't have to smile.

I looked down at my fingers and now there were two rings, my diamonds and now a wedding band. I was a married woman; how strange. And next to me this chunk of snoozing manhood was my husband; how strange. The car rolled on and the sun lowered in the sky. I had no watch—why would a bride need such a thing?—and no idea of the time, but it must be around four, with the light already leaching from the air and the promise of a chill night in the cloudless sky, where the bright point of Venus was already visible in the dimming light over the Eastern horizon.

The journey gave me time to think, no longer about my fate and the right and wrong of what I was doing, because now it was done. Seeing Alexandra again had unnerved me in a way I could not understand, and as we drove I thought of the times when I knew her years ago, of eating meals in her family kitchen, catching crabs on holiday in Wales; images of past times, long gone and, I thought, long forgotten, swam before my eyes.

Next the reception, the wedding party, the celebration, and I felt so numbed that I would have preferred to cook a simple meal and eat it with Charlie by the side of one of our log fires at home in Saxon Cottage. But duty was duty to be done, my path was set and my future, which had become my present, was not mine anymore to make choices with. Further options had vanished, and the path ahead seemed narrower than ever, but I was resigned; it was the way of the world. Nothing, I thought in my innocence, could get in the way of this future now.

Charlie slept on. I didn't mind at all, in fact I was glad for the time to myself on that day which belonged to so many others. It also gave me a chance to inspect this male creature of mine from close to. I looked at him, slumped there in the gathering shadows with his chin on his chest and those wonderful eyelashes curling out from his dark eyelids. I brushed his hair with my hand, leaned over and smelled that individual man smell of his that I adored. It was as if I was inspecting good blood-stock, and I felt very well with this sleeping stallion of mine.

Then up ahead on the road, brilliant in the twilight of the fast-fading day, was a cluster of cars flashing blue light into the thickening darkness. I shifted forward in my seat, reached out and slid back the glass that separated me from the driver.

'What is it?' I asked.

'Looks like an accident,' he said.

We slowed as we approached the scene. Policemen were directing the traffic around a mess of broken metal and glass that once were two, or maybe three cars. It was awful. Men in uniforms were busying round with grim faces, torches and radios, and as we inched by I brought my face to the window. Charlie slept on. What a thing to happen—in one place people are getting married in hope and beauty and no distance away in time and space other people are screeching into pain and death. What is a time of birth for one is a time of death for another, beginnings and endings all invisibly intertwined, and for us, the actors in the drama, no perspective given by distance to help us make sense of the whole. The scene troubled me deeply without me knowing quite why. It was a feeling that was above and beyond the normal reaction to these things, and I was fascinated by the scene of unforgiving carnage at the same time as I was repelled by my own fascination.

As we crept by I caught sight of a man kneeling on the road amongst a star-litter of broken glass which was flashing all around him in reflection of the staccato blue lights of the police, so he was more of a silhouette against those neurotic points of light than a man.

Next to him was another silhouette, a dark figure on a stretcher, and as I looked the kneeling man sensed my eyes and turned and his eyes met mine. Just for a moment the bride in the passing Rolls looked into the bewildered, shattered eyes of the weeping man and my heart went out to his, and then we were passed and gone and a tear was passing down each of my cheeks, as I felt a tremor of fear for the fragility of my own hopes and loves. And more; beneath that a fear for what had just been made in heaven, and upon which the sleeping heart of Charlie Brown lay.

'Charlie, wake up, for God's sake.' I shook him with both hands, and he woke instantly.

'Are we there?' he asked, and looked around.

'No, we aren't there, we're here. Charlie, there was an accident. We just passed it while you were sleeping. It was awful, police and ambulances and I think people were hurt, maybe killed.' And I burst into tears while he held me and stroked me, not understanding what was stirring in my heart any more than I did at the time, not feeling the intimations of what was to come that were dawning fiercely and as yet without form on my own inner horizons.

In this way we drove the last few miles to Parkgate. He had the goodness not to ask a thing, not to chide me, but just to hold and comfort me, protect me from fears without names that he didn't know or understand, but would, in time.

In the street before the Brown's house I got the chauffeur to stop the car so I could fix my face and compose myself in the wings before we entered the next act in the drama; the reception, the wedding feast, the beginning and the end, the calamity and the wonder, the bitterness and joy of the fire-nest of the Phoenix about to rise.

Chapter 8

As our Rolls crunched up the gravel drive of the Brown pile there was a whoosh of fire as the first rocket of the early dense night—Geoffrey's greeting to us—tore off into the sky and exploded in a cascade of purple light over the house.

I stepped out of the Rolls into the chill darkness, my shoulders covered with a shawl as soft as cream, and was into the house in a few steps. Margaret and Geoffrey were there at the door—they had left the Cathedral well before us—their faces in smiles, welcoming us, escorting us in to sit in the armchairs that were ready for us by the roaring log fire and be delighted with everything.

'It was so beautiful,' said Margaret, hands clasped in an attitude of prayer which showed me the depth of her feeling. This day was to her the culmination of some ancient dream of romance, the longing of her heart revealed in all its strange sadness. 'So beautiful. The Cathedral. That dress. Even your father looked like a prince.'

'I thought it was Charlie who was the prince,' I said, knowing it would please her, and sipped on a glass of hot mulled wine in a crystal goblet, watching for her reaction through my eyelashes as I drank.

'What can I say?' she said, looking at her boy with pride enough to burst, and my heart went out to her. Again, it was the trace of sadness that touched me, the evidence of the vulnerable in poignant contrast with that heartless façade. He was a good-looking man all right; something in that military bearing of his set off the formal wedding gear to perfection and he looked good enough to eat. 'He always was my prince,' she said, her eyes only for him, and an expression on her face that was near to hunger.

With this I felt the odd unease, that chill in the heart I had felt before in that house when mother and son danced a dance from long-gone childhood that should have died a long time ago.

'Oh, honestly, mummy,' said Charlie. 'That's no way to speak of a married man.'

'Maybe my dad could be a Duke, then,' I said, attempting to steer life back to an approximation of the present with a little weak humour. While inside myself feeling a wobble in my foundation-less certainty, yet again, but this time on the far side of the divide; now I was a married woman, and it was too late to change anything, my course was set. Or so I thought.

'A Duke he is, sweetness,' announced Geoffrey. 'And if I'm not mistaken that's the sound of the ducal carriage now. Can you hear it drawing up outside?'

Our peaceful moments were over. He was right, it was my mum and dad, both of them beaming with delight as they were brought into that lush lounge where I stood in my billowing dress from heaven, lit in flickering orange by the great fire.

'You were great,' said Tee,' just great. God, it's gettin' bloody freezin' out there. What're you drinkin''?'

'Mulled wine,' said Geoffrey. 'Shall I get you one, Tee?'

'Gin for me,' she said. 'No ice, just a scrap of lemon. A nice big glass, if you don't mind.'

'And Tetley's for Al,' said the host, lifting his head and smiling at the sound of laughter from the hallway, as the mood of the house changed once more.

The house was filling with guests, and Charlie and I stood there by the fire, smiling and kissing cheeks and being kissed as in they came, just one face after another to me, even my own family, all except for the one face I searched for and didn't find. Maybe she had decided not to come after all—she had a feel of beholden-ness to no-one and no plan that left me uncertain of even her promises to me. And her absence left me feeling as if there was a gaping hole in the fabric of the night.

'Billy,' I called out to my little brother, looking shambly and uncertain of himself in new suit and rich house. 'Have you seen our cousin? Alexandra. Did she get here?'

'Oh, yeh, came with us in our car. Said she was goin' for a walk down by the river and she'd be up later.' He shrugged; she was not contained within his understanding.

Walking by the river in the chill darkness all by herself. Not a one of the other guests would even think of doing such a thing, never mind go ahead and do it. She fascinated me, and I would have loved to slip out of the house myself and find her in the darkness down by the marshy reeds where I had walked myself that very morning, a long time ago. But I had duties to attend to now. I was a married woman, a Brown no less, and since that walk and with my elevation in society my options had become fewer.

As more and more guests arrived and the house filled up to and then past its capacity, they began to naturally spill out into the marquee, the most gorgeous tent I had ever seen outside the dream of a Sheik of Araby. It had walls draped in what looked like silk, thick carpets, crystal chandeliers, flowers in cascades, starched tablecloths, silver cutlery, and heating. It was even joined to the house by a warm tunnel. How lovely money can be.

I excused myself with smiles and made my way upstairs, long skirts gathered in my hands to show my tiny satin slippers, which were actually killing me, conscious of myself looking like something from Gone With The Wind. Then there I was, back in my room, circled back to the beginning of the day but this time alone, no need for my court now that the deed was done. I looked at myself in the same mirror and saw a different person, a married woman, and I curtsied to myself like a child in a loft secretly playing princess with a wedding dress from generations gone by.

Three knocks on the door and I frowned. Who had followed me into my own place? Was there no privacy in this world?

'Who is it?' I called out.

'It's me, Margaret. May I come in?'

My face showed a flash of petulance to itself in the mirror; she was the last person I wanted to see, but what could I do? A wave of desperation passed over me; was my life really no longer my own? For a moment it felt too much to bear.

'Of course,' I called over my shoulder, my own tiny drama having passed, then turned to watch the door open behind me in the mirror and my new mother in law—God help me—march over and stand to one side. For a moment we both looked at me, the dress, the veil flung back now, the once in a lifetime dream come true

'You looked very beautiful,' she said, already putting my present in the past, and I said nothing as I felt one more step taken in possession of myself. I could feel myself already defeated. There was nowhere to go, nothing to do but to continue the submission. Having passed over the divide I was now tasting the flavour of my future, and the old doubt rose and gnawed at my innards for just a short permitted moment in time.

She licked her lips, and I looked at her pink suit with gold buttons, pink shoes with gold buckles, pinkish pearls, pinkish eyes, and had a moment of despair for my sanity in letting myself become indebted in even the tiniest of ways to such a creature, never mind to the extent I had.

'The Lord Lieutenant has arrived,' she said. 'You know he couldn't come to the ceremony. He's downstairs right now.'

She waited, trying to show patience, and I looked at myself once more in the mirror. It was as if I was saying goodbye; I was no longer my own, times had changed. From such a peak as I had reached that day was it now the great downhill?

I smiled brightly. 'I just wanted to check, see if I looked all right. It's been a long time. Let me powder my nose and I'll be with you.'

Still she stood and watched and waited, ignoring my hinted desire for aloneness as I dabbed at my face, ran a lipstick over my lips, poked at my hair, and smiled brightly once more. For the first time I turned and looked away from the mirror and at the real Margaret. For a creepy reason I could not understand, the reversed image in the mirror seemed more true than the person in front of me.

'Come on,' I said with false enthusiasm. 'Don't let's keep him waiting.'

So the two Mrs Browns made their way down the gorgeous sweep of staircase to the crowd of guests milling below. I felt as if I was descending into my place in society with each reluctant step, about to become a real Mrs Brown when I reached the bottom and made false obeisance to the man of position who was waiting somewhere below. Halfway down Anthony Stuart-Guest, our best man and Charlie's closest friend from army days, resplendent in his dress uniform, aristocratic and charming, caught sight of me and smiled with real pleasure. I liked him very much, and smiled back, our eyes meeting for a moment in genuine togetherness and understanding.

'To the bride, to Michelle!' he cried above the hubbub, and raised his glass, so the whole crowd turned and smiled at me too, all raising their glasses obediently and repeating his toast in one chorus. There it was again, the odd sense of the unreal, as if I was in a great opera, about to burst into glorious song.

As it was I stood there and actually blushed. At that moment Charlie, the man himself, slid into sight behind the crowd, visible only to me, and gave me a look of such eye-gleaming animal desire that I blushed again, to the delight of the roaring crowd.

'Come along, Michelle,' Margaret hissed at me. 'The Lord Lieutenant's waiting.' There were far more important things in life to her than wasting time basking in love for the other Mrs Brown.

When we arrived back at the great fire, there was my good ole dad indignantly arguing with this tall, red-faced, gross-bellied character, clearly the great man, who was almost spluttering as he tried to make his point.

Silent alarm bells sounded in both myself and Margaret. It was exactly what we had all been secretly afraid of—the class war erupting there and then—my father, the well-known Trotskyite, never shy of trumpeting his views, matched with one of the privileged and knighted elite, never shy of trumpeting his views, and never the twain shall meet, we hope, especially at my bloody wedding.

'Lewk, Bernie,' Big Al was saying. 'They might've been a good team—norra great team, mind—but solid.' He sank a half-pint of bitter in one easy movement. 'But the truth is—and ya gorra face it—all that went down the drain with Matt Busby.'

His new friend knocked back a quarter of a pint of whisky, fuel for that redder than red knobbly nose, with equally practised ease, and glared back at my dad.

'Manchester United,' he boomed in fruity tones, 'are without doubt the premier football club of this country. Liverpool may have had their day ....'

'Sir Bernard,' Margaret interrupted, cutting through the football war with that voice that could penetrate concrete walls. 'This is my daughter in law, Michelle.' She smiled a sycophant smile.

Sir Bernard turned and looked directly at my shadow of cleavage, then raised his bloodhound eyes and looked into mine. 'Delighted, I must say,' he intoned, his political smile falling into place, and I felt sure he was delighted by my breasts, not by me. 'Damned pretty girl. Henry's a lucky chap.'

'Charles,' said Margaret coldly.

'Charles?' asked the great man blankly.

'My son's name is Charles, not Henry.'

'Of course. Naturally. Charles.' He finished off his whisky. 'I say, would it be possible ....' He looked round expectantly.

'At least, Bernie,' said my dad, 'we have managers actually from Liverpool. We don't have to go on bended knee to catch the scraps that Scotland don't need'

'Hm,' said Sir Bernard, readying himself for the next round. 'Fill your glass too, Al?'

Margaret, who knew that game all too well, caught the eye of one of her cronies and turned us both to fall into conversation with her, as if that was what we intended all the time, and I chatted inanities with this blue-rinsed twit who had not a trace of humour or intelligence in her being, which was, instead, filled with insufferable righteousness. She was Margaret's cousin, a woman I knew had become grossly rich at the death of her husband, one of those injustices of fate which make you wonder about cosmic balance, eternal justice and the wisdom of God.

She didn't have conversations, she just had audiences, so while she told me of the latest outrage to her sensitive life, I detached and let my mind wander. Were these the people I would have to kowtow to for the rest of time? The place in me that had always doubted doubled in power. I couldn't stand it, but once more saw the inevitability of my destiny, and knew that the skill I had to learn was that of making the best of compromise. What a thing it was to have the creeps like that on your wedding day. For God's sake, I thought, you don't have to continue as you begin, but isn't that usually what happens, despite our illusions of choice?

The woman was so lost within herself that she never held eye-contact as she pretended that she too was entranced by herself, so the one advantage of her monologues was that you could keep your eye on everything going on while she spoke. And the more she spoke the more a wave of doubt about the correctness of what I had done, so thick and wide I could have surfed it rose in me and I despaired about any possibility of salvation, who should appear at the door behind her but the black sharp one, Alexandra herself.

She smiled, a broad easy smile that looked alien in that tight English middle-class world, ran one hand through her hair, and then winked at me. It was an outrageous act, pure cheek, a comment on all that was going on, who I was and who she was and the stage drama of it all that I almost dropped my glass. Then she glanced left and right, caught my eye once more, positively twinkled and beckoned me with one finger. I was instantly entranced

'Come,' she mouthed, and that was it. I cut the blue-rinse off in mid-sentence, swam through the crowd, swooshed past my cousin and beckoned her after me. It was time to get to know this person. Annoyingly, two old friends came over to congratulate me in the quiet little nook I found for us under the stairs, and they were very sweet, meant well, so with great impatience I hoped didn't show I spent a few minutes with them before turning at last to Alexandra.

'I'm sorry,' I said as they vanished into the crowd, ' I just had to talk to them.'

'Of course. I thought it was time we got to know each other. Again, I mean. Did you work out how many years it's been since we last met?'

'At least twenty five.'

'My, my, how time flies. I just remember a fat-faced little kid I had no time for, and now look at you.' And look at me she did, in a way no man or woman had ever looked at me before. It was full of an unfamiliar lightness and power that lifted me, made me well, eradicated doubt and gave me a gleam of hope, all in one long look of gleaming eye.

'And look at you,' I said to her, and so I did, and with a shock I saw myself; the same eye, curve of eyebrow, cheekbone, evidence of our shared genes; me and not me all at the same time. It was very unsettling. But she was different in what lay behind the steady eyes, in her there was depth, wisdom, humour, and a voidness that was in the place where most people's defences lay.

'I'm so glad I came,' she said, very easy to be with. I felt something relax within me, and in no time at all it was as if I knew her better than any person on this earth, that we were the oldest of intimate friends, and our apartness had been for no more than a long weekend.

'You had to,' I said. 'You couldn't have stayed away.'

'It's true,' she agreed. 'I guess the time had come.'

We stood there smiling at each other, and beneath those brief words was an unspoken language of destiny, oncoming times, almost straying into the movements of planets and the finger of God. What was this? I never even thought of such things and now in a moment it seemed simple and true, obvious, what all the outer drama was really about; greatness, love and the mystical beauty of who we are.

'Oh, darling, there you are.' Charlie's voice burst the little bubble we were coexisting in, and his large male presence stepped between us. A flash of annoyance passed over me. His arrival felt like a trespass into my own private world.

'We're not far off beginning. The food and everything, the reception proper, you know? Would you mind if I took Michelle away from you?' he asked Alexandra.

'To tell the truth, yes,' she answered, and then smiled and held out her hand. 'I'm Michelle's long-lost cousin. Alexandra is what they call me here.'

Charlie smiled back and took her hand, and just held it rather than shake it. He was a man who had certainty in himself, it was a greater part of his attraction. 'If that's what they call you here, what do they call you where you call home?'

'Depends how good I've been,' she said. 'But as for names, they call me Alessia. It's another given name, and this time not given by a mother but by a lover. Better by far; she named what she knew and loved.'

She. We both heard and neither of us blinked. Ah. She bedazzled me with a certainty that eclipsed even Charlie's.

'Well, good to meet you,' he said, letting go of her hand. 'We should get together later, after the madness has died down.'

'Absolutely.'

Then my new husband led me by the hand through the hallway and into the dining room and out of the French windows and through the tunnel and into the marquee, where our guests were taking seats at places on tables with their names on hand-calligraphed cards, each place as exquisitely calculated in terms of rank and importance as in the court of the Sung Emperors. Margaret had created the seating plan swiftly, without a moment's hesitation; she knew the place of us all to within a millimetre. I wondered briefly on how far I had changed in rank during the afternoon of that day.

The answer was, of course, on that occasion and never again, marked by my central place at the main table, and it was to there that we made our way, breaking our journey time after time to talk to old friends and maybe old lovers, relatives, who knows and who cares? Then there we were, the bride and groom all in their wedding togs, like thousands and millions of others except that this time it was me. I wondered as I sat there waiting for the start of things how many women before me had made a perfect picture, an image from a dream on the outside, whilst inside profound feelings of trepidation such as within myself seethed.

It was a strange business, this wedding feast in the dark of the chill night, but it gave an intimacy, a closeness, and an intensity that would have been lost on some bee-humming June day. Charlie and I took our seats, our respective parents on either side, three out of four of them well-oiled by now, and drinking on with champagne in fluted glasses. Only Margaret was stone-cold sober, her eyes darting round every detail in the conversation filled, guest-crammed, portable room, looking for fault as always, and no doubt finding it, as always. Such is the curse of the perfectionist, to always live life in disappointment.

Charlie and I were left alone for once, and we sat there chatting about the faces on the people sitting before us.

'Which one?' I asked.

'Pretend you're not looking. The one in the weird little Goebbels glasses sitting next to the girl with the hook nose and blonde hair.'

I let my eyes sweep the room. I got him. 'You must be joking. Not him. He kind of looks like a city banker.'

'Some banker. They say the guy made his fortune being the biggest supplier of cocaine to the City. A dealer. Never trust what you think you see, sweetheart.'

'Does that go for you too, Charlie Brown?'

'Absolutely. Who would know looking at me up here in my splendour what I have done in my past that no-one knows or sees?'

We were in one of those worlds of our own amongst all the others, as if there was no-one else there at all and we were alone in a room and a life for only us, and somehow, impossibly and strangely, our talk wandered into the depths of ourselves where we had never before gone.

'So what can't they see, Charlie?' I asked quietly, looking him straight in the eye.

'Time will tell, Michelle, time will tell,' he said, and a wicked flash passed over his eyes. Not for the first time that day, an unnamed fear quivered within me. 'But what about you?' he asked. 'What can't we see about you?'

'I don't think there is anything, Charlie,' I said, in all innocence, believing it, unbelievably. 'What you see is what you get.'

'Well, time will tell,' said Charlie, and you know what, he was right, it did. All that was surprising was the proximity of that time, and when it came, what it told.

Chapter 9

Then that moment passed, as all moments do, as we have that happy capacity for temporary blindness when the thin ends of wedges poke us in the eye during romance and weddings and other times of passing madness, so what might have been foreboding becomes a mere nothing, what might have been brought to the fore is left to wither, and life as it was goes on.

'Who's the woman in the hat, for God's sake?' Charlie asked, pointing with his glass.

I giggled. 'That's Mrs Bee. A kind of auntie without being one really. Looked after me a lot when I was a kid. A total fruitcake, but all heart. She's having a whale of a time. Whose are those repulsive children?'

'The ones in the satin dresses torturing the boy in the shorts?'

'The very ones.'

'They were spawned, hopefully in error, by my cousin Alan, and his ghastly wife Henry.'

'Henry?'

'Henrietta. The big woman smoking the brown cigarettes. Everyone calls her Henry. When they came back from the States she wanted to be called Hank, but we had to draw a line somewhere.'

They did? I wondered why, but said nothing. Were such lines also being drawn around me? In my heart of hearts I knew they were, as well as I knew that with the passing of time they would be drawn tighter, until my surrender was complete and I was no longer who I was. These thoughts came, disturbed me, and vanished, leaving nothing but their unerasable tracks. 'And your army lot?' I asked

'Well, some of them you know. On the whole they're a good bunch. I'm the only one out of that crowd that actually left.'

'Regrets?'

'Small ones, and rarely. But the truth is that it was great when it was and then suddenly it wasn't anymore. I've no idea why'

'Maybe you grew up.' It was one of those times when you wish you could run the movie back and say it again but differently, but it's too late and a part of you which you wanted to keep concealed forever has just emerged into the light of day, forever, no matter what you might pretend.

He looked at me sharply. 'Miracles might happen,' he said, coolly, and looked past me to smile at my dad, who was bellowing and roaring with laughter, slopping beer onto the pristine table cloths, tapping cigarette ash onto the carpet, having one hell of a good time.

I left the scene from my past to Charlie and turned my attention to the gathered guests in front of me. In the same way that when a mother sees a photograph of a whole class of children and has eyes only for one child, her own, so I had eyes only for one person in that crowd, that dark silhouette and flashing eye of my cousin. She intrigued me, entranced me, and I found myself looking over to her through the corner of my eye as people came and went and chatted with me, and she would always know I was looking and looked back and smiled that smile at me and then there was no-one else in the room, no-one else in the world.

What a wonderful thing it was to find such a person in my life. Was she the sister I never had, someone with the ease of intimacy that comes with shared blood, someone with shared roots that was partly what I was, someone who was a mirror to what was the greater part of me? I honestly had no idea; all I knew was how happy it made me feel to have her come back into my life, so unexpectedly and sweetly, after all those years. I had never seen anyone like her, so poised, elegant, natural, easy to be with, disturbingly profound. I was drawn back to her time after time, until I began to be concerned that I was being rude, or at least indifferent to my guests, and to Charlie. What was going on? She was no more than that cousin of mine who shared some genes, some childhood holidays and Christmases, but my attention was taken by her without cease, magnetically; my own will was secondary to the force of her own presence.

Ting ting ting, and Anthony the best man, beautiful, rich, wifeless, girlfriendless, a man I was talking to one day with such undefended ease that I flashed onto the fact that he was probably gay, stood and tapped the side of a glass to call attention to the beginning of formalities. Who better?

'Ladies and Gentlemen.' He paused and looked around the people, waited till he had the attention of them all. It took a short time, he was a man of some presence. 'It is my honour as best man to stand here before you today. I know Charlie Brown well, I've been with him in situations where one's life hangs on a thread and you thank the Lord for the strength and dependability of the man next to you, and such a man is Charlie.'

It was at that point that I began to cry, without rhyme or reason, tears running down my face in front of everyone, and the room watched me while Anthony spoke. He was the sound, I was the vision, and, that being the case, I feel no-one heard him properly and no-one saw me for what I was. Except for one, and I fought to keep her out of my sight, as I knew there was something in her that was the catalyst for the production of my tears.

As I wept in silence—just flowing tears, no sobs—I could see on the blurred with tears faces that they were moved by what was to them an expression of my love, while secretly in my heart of hearts hearing Anthony's clear love for Charlie had touched a vein of sadness, perhaps even grief in me, and it was for that sadness without form or understanding that I cried.

'Michelle I have known a shorter time, but in that time I have come to see that here is a woman to match the man.'

I listened to him closely; could I sense well-hidden tremors of his heart breaking somewhere in the depths of his clear, educated tones, or was it just one more delusion, a mirage, an outer form of what was happening incomprehensibly in my own heart? Oh, what a turmoil of emotions were running through my poor body, as hidden depths, understandings, misunderstandings and loves rose to the surface and began to quietly tear me apart. It was then that the dissolution of my own feebly held delusions of who I was and what I was to be truly began. It was the death of who I used to be, happening in front of a roomful of the guests at my own wedding, and the level of grief was too intense to bear.

'Now I would like you to join me in raising your glasses. To the long and fruitful marriage of Charlie and Michelle Brown.'

The place rose to its feet and repeated his blessing, like a congregation mumbling an unfamiliar prayer, glasses of the best champagne held high, and through the crowd I caught the eye of the cousin of cousins once more and the tears started all over again. What was going on with me? Never in my life had I known such intensity of feeling without knowing what it was. A massive outpouring of raw emotion without name had started haemorrhaging from some part of my being I didn't even know existed, and I was overwhelmed, lost.

Charlie took my hand, and I could see in the way he sniffed and rubbed his eyes that he was being moved himself, but in his case it was the more obvious, the expected motivation—as far as I could tell—and in his dear innocence he thought he was matching the colour of my tears, not contrasting with them. That poor sweetness contrasted deeply with the first hints of betrayal of heart that was beginning to move in my belly, like a child not far from birth, and it only made me weep the more.

Only one face in that room knew what was happening to me, and that was the smooth pale angled face of the one and only, which was looking at me without pause through a narrow crevice in the forest of people, and her expression was of heartfelt compassion, an appalling tenderness. Whatever was going on with me was connected with her, but I had no idea at all of why or wherefore. So I sat at the high table in my wedding dress glory and wept as the person I had always been began to die.

Anthony was done; his message was simple; he sat down. Waiters ran around the tables pouring champagne, frothing over the lips of the glasses in their haste. Conversation buzzed once more, and I was grateful for the chance to pull myself together. Charlie smiled at me and stroked my cheek with great affection, and I smiled back, sniffed, dabbed my eyes with a tissue and hoped my mascara wasn't running down my cheeks. Our best man slid in behind us and crouched.

'Thanks,' said Charlie, in such a heartfelt way that the one word said it all, and I kissed him on the cheek.

'Love you, Anthony,' I said. 'You're the very best of best men.' And from somewhere in the distance came the sound of explosions, a whine and a crackle, a great bang.

'Bonfire night has begun,' said Anthony with a smile.

'I can't wait for ours,' said Charlie. 'Have you seen the size of our bonfire?'

Who hadn't? Geoffrey Brown, who had been held in restraint for a lifetime by mothers, fathers, schoolmasters, colonels, wives and self-doubts had made an awesome pyre, the dream of a schoolboy gone mad looming and towering expectantly into the night sky.

'When will it be lit?' asked Anthony.

'When all this is finished, when we've eaten, which is after other people speak, which is hopefully as economically and well as you.'

As if on cue my father rose to his feet, staggered, searched through his pockets, cursed, leaned down to his wife my mother and stage whispered, 'Where's me fuckin' speech, Tee?'

'In yer fuckin' pocket,' she stage whispered back. 'Where d'ya fuckin' think?'

At this the room burst into laughter, and Dad, who loved an audience, never imagining they were laughing at him rather than with him, pulled a crumpled pile of paper out of his back pocket and waved it at his fans. As one they guffawed and moaned theatrically. The mood of the drama shifted from tragedy to comedy as the great creator of unending tragedies was revealed to be nothing other than a clown. To my right, the lines round Margaret's mouth tightened. This is precisely what she feared, all her beautiful plans just ruined, ruined. That poor woman lived with her knuckles white on the wheel of life, in terror of losing control of what was, in the end, beyond control. As she would soon witness. The minor variations from her excruciatingly planned wedding theatre plans were nothing, mere minute irritations; before the night was out she would rue the day she first heard the name Rafferty.

Dad held up his hands. He was the pure ham on the stage at the holiday camp, all he needed to complete the picture was a bow tie in coloured lights and a pratfall. 'Don't be frightened,' he said in his thickest Liverpool accent. 'I'm not goin' to torture you poor bleeders to death. But this is the weddin' of me one and only daughter.' He picked up his glass and drained it, yet another pint gone, and turned and caught Geoffrey's eye, who nodded, caught the eye of a waiter and pointed.

'Like I was sayin',' said Dad, then stopped and swayed. His audience held their collective breath. 'What was I sayin'?'

'Yer fuckin' speech,' hissed Tee, then turned and smiled at everyone. She looked dotty to the point of lunacy. I began to giggle. Another couple of gigglers snorted, and manic titters began to spread through the tables.

Dad beamed; everything was going well so far. Being the star turn was just great. He squinted at his tatty piece of paper for what seemed like minutes, then made a theatrical expression of surprise and turned it upside down. The audience howled. I was in pain from trying to hold back hysteria by this time, and caught the eye of Alexandra through the crowd. She was bent double, tears rolling down her face, almost falling off her chair, and the instant I connected with her I could hold it back no longer. I laughed till I cried yet again, and all the world laughed with me. In minutes the raw emotions that were leaking from the cage of their ancient suppression mutated from grief to laughter, but it was all expressions of the same force. In time the laughter subsided slightly; Dad raised a hand, time to listen. Everyone bar Margaret couldn't wait for the next act.

'I've worked bloody hard all my life,' he began.

'Must've been when I wasn't lookin'' said Tee loudly, and gave another dotty smile. The people roared again. The mood of elegant Parkgate wedding, all finery and restraint, had been shattered. This time Dad wavered—doubt was entering his befuddled brain. Were they laughing at him, not with him? Danger lurked, and I knew this one, so I stood and took two paces to be next to him. The laughter subsided once more. I smoothed out his speech, all written in Biro on paper torn from a spiral exercise book, and put it in his hand.

'See?' he said. 'See what a good girl she is.' He sniffed and wiped his nose with the back of his hand. We were entering the maudlin stage now, fine by me, one of the predictable staging posts on his alcoholic journey to nowhere with no danger of mad bulls to erupt there. I smiled sweetly, the good girl with her daddy. Then I made the mistake of glancing at Margaret—her face was set in a grim mask, which all of a sudden looked lined, sagged and older, and I knew in my heart of hearts I would never be truly forgiven now, as if her suspicion that bad blood will out was confirmed once and for all. And in a way, from her point of view, she was right. To my surprise the expected feeling of guilt never arose; instead, and for the first time in my life, there was a sense of freedom—to hell with it, what did I have to lose? My own father, who I had secretly blamed for creating repression in me, was, due to what I always hated as the worst in him, opening the door to my own freedom.

'Even when she was a little girl, she was always good to her Dad.' He hugged me tearfully, the lying bastard. I hated his guts when I was a kid, and he hated mine. Or so it seemed—but then I remembered what my mother had said about my beauty in that pub in the Dingle.

'And now,' he continued, 'she's got Charlie.' He grinned wickedly. 'And the best of luck to him.' He raised his newly filled glass and drained a whole pint in one effortless move with a flourish of pride, his own form of punctuation and demonstration of who he was, and took his seat. We never did learn what his speech was about. Phew. Danger veered near and but it swerved and was avoided.

Across the room Alexandra made a show of wiping her brow and I widened my eyes in a show of how close that was. Then we laughed together. You must see that we grew up in the same mould, the same culture, we ran down the same back jiggers, and she knew every nuance, hair and turn of what was going on with Dad and me, my life, who I was and where I had come to and how. No secrets. And more than that, the true compassion of one who had been through the same life, fought the same forces, emerged from the same difficulties. Hell, it was good to have her there. More than good, wonderful. How amazing it was to have such rapport, such easy togetherness with someone I had hardly spoken to, hardly seen, for most of my life.

'So am I going to need that much luck?' asked Charlie, nicely mellowed out himself, tipping back on his chair so I had to turn back to see him. 'Are you going to tell me the worst now it's all too late.'

'Oh, no, love,' I replied. 'That would take all the fun out of it. You'll find it out in time, when it really is too late.'

He mock pouted. 'Not even a clue?'

I put my chin on my fist and leaned my elbow on the table, frowned in the attitude of the thinker, knowing it would create an attractive picture for his male eyes, a not so subtle way of diverting his attention from yet another form of danger. 'Well, all right. But just a teensy little clue, OK?'

He nodded; such humility. This odd game we were playing, full of tongue in cheek self-mockery, was skating on the surface of very deep water, and I felt on edge with the thin line I was walking.

'I hope you're ready for this.' I took a deep breath. A further act in the drama, a way of averting deeper truth by giving a taste of a lesser truth. 'I'm a cross between my mother and my father.'

Panic and horror crossed his face. 'Omigod,' he said. 'Why did I never think of that? And now it's too late.' He buried his face in his hands and heaved in pretend sobs. This was a game played on many levels, which, if we had cared to, could have revealed all that lay in our depths, and may normally have emerged only with the passing of married years.

'Charles.' His mother's voice. He looked up, still in apparent anguish. 'Are you quite well?'

'No,' he said, for the first time in front of me playing any other role than the dear little golden boy. 'I think I've made a terrible mistake.'

'Oh, is that all? We all think that, darling. Part and parcel.' It was the first time I heard her make an attempt at humour, and dry as a bone it was, it gave me a glimmer of hope. But what a virtuoso I would have to be to dance this dance and still hold my head high.

To my joy the formal and proper tone of the proceedings had broken down with my Dad doing his act, and there was now a buzz of conversation filling the air, laughter sounding in different parts of the room, and children were running round between the tables.

'Your new cousin seems to be enjoying herself.' Charlie said, looking over to where she seemed to be acting out a strange pantomime to her table of my Liverpool friends, married girls and their husbands, and assorted Cheshire ladies who were all entranced by her performance, every eye on her, and much laughter rising in the air. It was the table for the odds and sods, latecomers and those nearly forgotten. They seemed to be having a fine time of it, the best in the whole marquee, and I was dying to get over there and join them, see what she was up to now.

'She's quite something,' I said. 'Wise, comic, independent, serious, funny. I find her intriguing, fascinating.'

At that moment, as I was watching her once more, she turned, sensing my gaze, and smiled, hesitated for a moment then stood and threaded her way through the tables, tall and slender and crisp in her black suit, to stand in front of me, then crouch to be at my level.

'It's fun,' she said, looking me straight in the eye. 'I'm glad to be here. You look very beautiful.'

I had to bite my lip to stop the tears. 'You're very beautiful too,' I said, and we just stopped the world for a few immortal moments, looking into each other's separate eyes that were the same but different, right there in the front of the whole affair, and forces, mystical powers and pure magic ran between us. I had never felt anything like it in my life. It was unnerving, intense and thrilling, and for that minute or two I was aware of nothing else in the world.

'Hello there, Alexandra,' said Charlie in his bluff and cheerful way, turning to notice her for the first time. 'Having a good time?'

'Very good, yes.' She stood; the magic was broken, and looked to her left at a movement in the corner of her eye. It was Geoffrey Brown, patrician and elegant in his grey morning coat, standing for attention. Alexandra faded away with a smile, turning and melding into the crowd with such grace, her movements so feline, controlled and plain beautiful that I was entranced.

Geoffrey just stood and waited for everyone to stop talking, with great poise and dignity of his own, and in no time at all he had them in the palm of his hand. Still then he waited in silence before he spoke.

'Friends and family, welcome to our home. What a happy day this is; for me the best this house has known. I am delighted beyond words to welcome Michelle to our family. Charlie, you've done us proud.' He paused. What he was saying had a tone of finality, ending about it, as if things were being wrapped up well, and a tinge of sadness in his resonant words brought the whole place to utter stillness. 'I have lived a good and fortunate life, and now I wish the greatest of good fortune to Charlie and Michelle.' He held up his glass and looked me in the eye, then drank, and for some reason I could not understand it was terribly sad. The wedding guests raised their glasses and drank to us once more, but this time they were subdued, cautious; what a change from the mad comedy of my own father, but both linked by the same dark undercurrent of melancholy.

'And now, food,' Geoffrey announced, and a smattering of applause came from the guests. He smiled, and nodded at the chief waiter. 'Then after the food we have our fireworks and bonfire to cap the evening. Thank you all so much for coming.'

He took his seat once more. This third speech was short to the point of abruptness. It was an odd performance, left us wondering what to expect next; it had all the joy of a wake, and we were all relieved to turn our attention to the arrival of the food, the salmon and foie gras and this and that and the other that I had spent so many awful hours over with Margaret, that I could hardly bear to look at it now it had taken form and was appearing before me.

For form's sake I picked at one or two nuts and a sprig of watercress, and began to look at Charlie's hand where it was laid on the table. He was turned to one side away from me, chatting and laughing, and this hand was just lying there, curled in relaxation, and I could see every last hair and groove and line, the details of his trimmed broad fingernails, the new ring on his thick finger, gleaming through a sprouting of black hairs. What a powerful hand, I thought, so different from my own puny, pointy little things, and I wondered what it must be like to feel at home with such a hand at the end of your arm. I glanced secretly at him, the male of the species, a different animal completely in body, mind and soul, and wondered if I could ever understand such a creature. Or if he could ever truly understand me.

Once again, in this and all other things, time would tell.

Chapter 10

While my guests feasted on the finest, I took the opportunity given by my own disinterest in the food I had spent too much time over already and wandered from table to table, turning and bobbing and gathering my skirts, dancing my own dance alone at the ball of my own wedding. It was my chance to see every guest face to face, to smile into every eye, and, with hindsight, to bid a farewell to everyone from the world I had been part of. I think now that I was, and I am, a creature beholden to destiny, and by that evening was surrendered at some deep level to the power that ruled my fate. The inevitable was nearing, the passage to another world was now inches away, and only one person in that room had an inkling of what was about to emerge from the unseen.

I floated round getting in the waiters' way, blocking aisles in my fantasia of silk, the dress which was just coming to the end of its short and gorgeous life, and loved by me not just for itself but also for the poignancy of its lightly-held mayfly existence, as a Japanese aesthete loves the beauty and sadness in the passing of a spring blossom.

Yes, it was true, there was something of an end in my dance, an unconscious sorrow beneath my bubbles and smiles, but that fated day had already seen such incomprehensible swings in moods and passions that a little more enigma was now a mere nothing to me. As I worked my way through the entire marquee, the silken-draped, crystal-lit fantasy, a bright star in the dark of the November night, with other people's fireworks beginning to crash and whoosh all around under a clear black sky filled with real stars and the sharp crescent of a waxing moon, I felt that not only was the Cinderella dress approaching the end of its time, but so was the bride in it. Was my own midnight coming? How strange it was to be living one great role, the dazzling bride, while inside and all the time there was the oddest sensation of something else going on, like a movie in another room which is more attractive than the one you are watching, but as yet invisible.

Not by chance, it is clear with hindsight, all the people I cared about in my world were there; my mother and father, brother, uncles and aunts, friends from childhood, from my working days, and I talked to them all of the same thing, the wedding, the cathedral, the dress, the house, the marquee, the food, the how well it was all going, and the oncoming fireworks.

As the meal was coming to its end I reached the final table, where I had saved the best wine for last, consciously avoiding even looking at her while I was just dying to. She looked up as I arrived, smiled her smile, and her eyes shone.

'The food was good?' I asked her.

'The food was good,' she replied, and the others at the table joined in with the usual praise and proclamations of happiness and enchantment. While I tried hard not to ignore them all while they nattered away. While my cousin, beautiful, enigmatic, stroked me without warning down the forearm, ever so lightly and naturally, and it felt like a form of electric shock that made light chat an absurdity. All this before the eyes of the world and unseen.

'Next we have the fireworks. And the bonfire,' I said. 'Time to get changed.'

'Oh, no,' cried the women, who never wanted the fantasy to end, never wanted the mundane to begin.

'Oh, yes,' I said. 'If I wear this I'll turn into a bonfire myself. Don't forget to get your coats, right? It's cold out there.'

I stood to go, and Alexandra, very casually, looked me in the eye and asked, 'Would you like some help?'

I looked back at her and knew somewhere in my common sense heart that at that point I should have very casually said in return, no thanks, I'm fine, and chosen the path to the more obvious destiny that I was already treading. But it was impossible, something stronger than sense was leading me to my appointed fate, and as I said, I had already surrendered.

So I smiled, something inside me exulting, and said, 'Oh, yes, that would be great.' So she stood to join me. How innocent it all must have looked; my cousin coming to help me change. But dear me, how much we must learn not to trust the easily visible, learn to distinguish between appearance and reality. I caught Charlie's eye across the room and mimed changing. He nodded once; understood, it was part of the agreed schedule for the evening, everything was going to plan. Or so outer appearance indicated.

Through the dining room and into the corridor, past the busying waiters, following the same route I had taken with Charlie at the start of things, but this time with Alexandra in tow, and as we climbed the stairs where I had been cheered and feted in what seemed like another life, we rose into the silence and darkness where we were alone for the first time.

I stood in front of the big mirror once more, looking at my bridal self for the last time, both the observer and the observed, and at my shoulder this time was my cousin, very sharp in her black against my cream froth.

'Do you like me in this?' I asked her reflection.

'I've never seen you any other way,' she said, and I was amazed at this simple truth. 'To me, this is how you are. And I like you very much indeed, this or any other way.'

There we were, talking to each other's image in the mirror, and all the time between the reality of the bodies in proximity was a flow of ... what? Energy, heat, power, I don't know, as I looked at her mirror eyes it flowed from her body to mine and from mine to hers. I had never felt anything like it in my life, and loved it, was hungry for it, wanted more no matter what the cost, and at that time I now feel that the glorious madness first entered my soul.

'Now goodbye to the princess,' I said.

'Never say goodbye,' she responded. 'The princess never came with the dress, the dress came to the princess.'

I turned and looked at her face to face. She was so close I could feel the heat of her presence, the softness of her rising and falling breath, and it took my breath away.

'Unzip me, will you,' I said, and watched in the mirror as this slim figure who could have been a Takarazuka prince, the woman in the role of man, reached for the hook and eye, and I started as her cool, soft hands touched the bare flesh of my back.

'Are my hands cold?' How calm and cool her voice was, how clear and strong.

'No.' I wanted her to touch me again, but instead she unzipped me in one movement, and I stepped out of my silken mirage, the pea from the pod, and my sweet illusion crumpled onto the floor, a nothing at all, a balloon without air. She was right; there was no princess without me, and for the first time this life I had the intimation of who I really was, of what lay within me, unrecognised, unknown, unhinted at, until now

'Have they lit the bonfire yet?' I asked. I was hanging the dress from the picture rail, shedding white stockings, pulling the headband from my hair, finished with that role that I loved for its time and now eager to move on.

Alexandra moved to the window and looked down. 'Not yet,' she said. 'But men are busying round with torches. I can see flames being carried round in the darkness. It might not be far away.'

She turned as I was dressing in my chosen outfit for after the ball, a trouser suit in the purest of red, the most expensive item of clothing I had ever owned, the costume of a Brown. It was the creation of the perfect eye of an Italian master, cut in a line as simple and taut as a drawn bow, in a wool so fine it might have been silk. How different we feel and are in different clothes; what a different person I was in that suit than the girl in the Cinderella dress. And how fitting it all was for what was to come, as if I was preparing for my future well before I consciously knew what it was.

She looked at me frankly for a full minute then smiled that easy smile and applauded, the sound of her clapping sounding dully in the Edwardian bedroom. 'Perfection,' she said. 'Come and look.'

So I crossed the room to the mirror and stood next to her. When I looked I was shocked; in one move I had changed who I was, and in that change had become more like her than anyone else could possibly be.

'Snap,' she said. 'One black, one red. The colours of anarchy.'

'Are we anarchists, then?'

'Time will tell.' It was the phrase of the time, from the lips of us all, the single undeniable constancy in a world of manic change.

We stood and gazed at ourselves, our almost twin selves, in that mirror that had shown me many reflections of what lived inside me, but nothing, not even the princess, so astounding or fascinating as this.

'Do you have a warm coat?' I asked, look; an expression of concern.

'Yes,' she answered. 'And you?' The voiced concern returned, and instantly we were closer.

'Oh, yes.'

At that moment the wall behind the mirror lit up with flickering orange light.

'Quick!' she cried. 'They've lit the bonfire.'

We grabbed our boots and coats and ran down the stairs giggling like a pair of schoolgirls. When I stumbled she took my hand and we dashed out into the garden holding hands, not like schoolgirls at all. It was the first time I had touched her.

We slowed to a walk, still holding hands, and joined a group of people silhouetted by the growing fire. The flames were licking up one side of the gigantic pile, but having trouble, it seemed, spreading to the rest. When I saw who it was we had joined my heart sank; of all people it was Margaret and her ghastly friends, the sharpest tongues and the bluest rinses in the west.

'Ah, Michelle, it's you,' she said. 'You've changed.'

'Have you met my cousin Alexandra, Margaret?'

'Only in passing.' She gave a cursory smile and turned back to people of greater importance. 'What is Geoffrey doing?' she asked impatiently, and her pals clucked their tongues and despaired of men and husbands, a Greek chorus of impatience, with men who never did what you hoped, never, no matter how much you complained or waited.

'Is Charlie at the fire too?' I asked. It was impossible to recognise anyone from the dark figures flitting in and out of the firelight, shining torches and lighting matches and talking to each other in words that blurred on their way across the black lawn.

'Yes, of course, dear,' said Margaret tetchily. 'Can't you see him?'

'If I could see him I wouldn't ask, would I?' I said in a tone of voice to match, and Margaret looked at me with the astonishment due for such impertinence, but for the first time ever, Madam, frankly I couldn't give a damn. Balances were shifting invisibly before our eyes.

'Come on, cousin,' I said. 'I need coffee.'

I linked my arm in hers to lead her away. 'I feel as if I've known you for a thousand years,' I said. She smiled that smile, and something moved within me. 'But I don't know you at all.'

'This is an amazing world,' she said. 'Full of mystery and

wonder. I long since stopped trying to understand, it just seems to dull the shine of the miracles.'

I was curious; she seemed to swim in waters deeper than those I had known, and knew things I never knew. 'Did you know that we had this specialness before the wedding, cousin?'

She shook her head. 'Nothing in all the experiences of my wild life prepared me for this, cousin,' she answered. 'I just knew as deeply as I have ever known anything that I should go to your wedding, nothing more. Anything else is as much a surprise to me as it is to you.'

We were inside the marquee once again. Now the door was open to the night it was cold and the waiter serving coffee and mulled wine was wrapped in an overcoat, shifting from foot to foot and rubbing his hands. Ahead of us was my friend Tracy of the perfect house and car and child and life.

'Michelle!' she squealed. 'Oh, no, you've changed. Oh, well, all good things and all that. I've still got my wedding dress in a box in the loft, actually.' She glanced at Alexandra. 'I don't think we've met.'

'My cousin Alexandra,' I said.

She looked from my face to hers. 'I should have guessed you were something like that,' she said. 'One look and you can see you have shared blood.'

Alexandra and I turned, looked each other with those eyes that were reflections of each other with a look that said: so that is what we have. At least part of the puzzle fell into place; some essence of our blood itself was shared.

'Nice to meet you,' said Tracy, smiling to excuse herself. 'Got to get this wine to Tim.'

Behind us there was a cheer from the garden and we both turned as a column of flame roared into the night sky. Geoffrey's bonfire had caught. We moved as one, without thought, towards the heat and light, and all of a sudden we were part of what could have been some ancient pagan rite, a celebration and homage to primitive Gods we no longer knew, a sacrifice of blood to earth and fire to the heavens.

At least that is how it seemed to me, because something inside me had shifted and opened and what had seemed like just the world had now become a dazzling chaos of wonder. I felt like a child watching her own secret dawn, trembling on the brink of a new life.

From the direction of the fire a figure came clumping towards us, and as it neared I knew it was Charlie. My husband, my God, could this be true?

'Michelle,' he called cheerfully. 'What a fire, eh?'

'What a fire,' I agreed.

'You two seem to be getting along famously,' he said. 'Nothing like shared blood, I suppose.' There it was again. He rubbed his nose, eyes on the fire, leaving a smudge of black across his face, which was lit in orange flame. I looked at him with distant interest, with warmth, with affection, but without passion. The day that had turned into night was changing me so fast that I had no idea who I would wake up being the next morning, and for reasons unknown I now had no fear of whatever was to come. The force which was taking me was now the master of my fate, and I would accept whatever future it would bring. Deep within me a wild abandon was hatching from the eggshell of my lifetime's fear.

'It was the wind that did it,' said Charlie.

'Did what?'

'Got the fire going. The wind came up and started the fire into life.'

As he spoke I noticed for the first time the keen wind against the skin of my face, and before me the fire grew apace.

'Christ,' said Charlie, watching the flame spread. 'Thank the Lord the wind's blowing the right way.'

He was right; the flame from the mother of all bonfires was stretching out an unlikely distance, and an old apple tree that should have been far enough away to be safe was now smouldering into fire. Geoffrey had made an error; the fire was too big and too near the house for comfort.

'Oh, well,' said Charlie. 'Time for fireworks. Don't go anywhere.'

Off he clumped across the lawn. Alexandra shifted and our shoulders touched; even through the thickness of our coats I could feel that heart-moving heat of the presence of her being, and although my eyes were on the fire, the whole of my attention was on her. What was going on? I had nothing in my life to that time which would explain or clarify the lunacy which had seized my life by the heart; all I knew was how much I loved just standing there.

Above us the sky was clear, and I looked up as sparks from the fire swirled up and away to vanish and join the stars, and I took her arm and hugged it with great happiness.

'I'm so glad you came back,' I said. 'You know I never forgot about you during all those years. When the postcards came from all those far-off places I kept every one and stuck them on the side of my wardrobe.'

'Did you really?'

'Really. And do you remember bringing me back a present from Venice, years and years ago, a little chain with dangly pictures of scenes of Venezia?'

'Vaguely. Yes, maybe I do.'

'Well I've still got it. At home in my jewellery box. Is the wind shifting?'

It was. Whereas before the freshening wind was coming from our right and directing the growing flame towards the orchard, it was now turning a touch our way. The heat was searing. The face of my cousin and all the others, every one of them staring into the fire, were all lit starkly in the light which was becoming more yellow than orange as the fire grew. It seemed to be finding new reserves of fuel in its heart, and instead of flaring and peaking the flames were growing as the great fire ate into its own centre and redoubled its power.

Anthony, our best man, approached us from the side, a concerned look on his face. 'What on earth did Geoffrey put in his pile?' he asked. 'It seems to me that there is more than just wood. Can you smell something?'

We both sniffed the night air and the smoke that was eddying around us. Yes, he was right, there was something other tingeing the wood-smoke, something I couldn't quite put my finger on, something familiar but distant, what was it?

'Some kind of tar or oil.' said Alexandra. 'Is that what it is?'

'I hope you're wrong and fear you're right,' said Anthony. 'I should find Charlie. I'm a yachtsman and that wind worries me.'

At that moment there was the first explosion in the sky above and the fireworks began. As in the bonfire Geoffrey had no longer compromised his boyhood dreams, and the sky was filled with the colours of his wildest fantasies. What a sight it was, what a wedding, that massive fire roaring and behind and around it all the colours and explosions of Geoffrey's Chinese fireworks.

'You don't have to look far to find Charlie,' I said, almost shouting over the roar of the fire and the crash and boom of the fireworks. 'He's setting them off.' And then quietly to my cousin, 'He's just a big kid at heart.'

'They are,' said my cousin. 'And just like with children we love them then despair of them, want them to grow up then grieve when they do.'

'You haven't had children?'

She held up a gloved hand and turned my way. 'I've known other people's. Enough for me.'

'You never got married?'

She shook her head. 'I'm not the marrying kind.'

'Never even tempted?'

'Many years ago maybe, when I was just a kid, but it came to nothing.'

'Regrets?'

'No regrets, no regrets for anything in my life. It's an indulgence I don't permit myself.'

If we weren't so close the noise of the fireworks would have made our talk inaudible, but as it was we stood there, bathed in many coloured flickering and flashing light and talked softly, melding closer and closer, as if our shared blood yearned to flow together. It was the most sensual time I had yet lived, right there in the centre of a symphony of exploding colour in the dark of the star spangled night, worming my way into the heart vulnerabilities of the enigma that had re-appeared from my beginnings to entrance me with all of her mysteries.

'But you must have had lovers and dreams.'

She glanced at me, and I was so close I could see tiny curved reflections of the fire in her eyes. 'Of course. What do you think I am?'

I felt myself move even closer to her, as if that was possible, and said. 'I don't know, I don't know you at all, not really. Does anyone?'

'Oh, yes.' She smiled. 'There are some to whom I am one of the lesser mysteries.'

The whole of this conversation took place in a world apart from the world that was burning all around us, as if we were in some separate universe, watching our own remotely through a window in time.

I noticed some hairs on her head a touch awry, brought my hand towards them to smooth them down, hesitated, then did it anyway. Her hair was very soft. She accepted my gesture, my caress, as simply as would a cat, and I pressed on.

'So those who find you an open book, are they, or were they, your lovers?'

'It depends on what you call a lover.'

I was playing a game with her, cat and mouse, chasing the fleeing core of what she really felt, where she was coming from, what was going on in her heart. I smiled, amused, delighted by her, relishing having her ever so tinily on the run, feeling her in the palm of my hand, at least for a while.

'You don't like to be questioned much, do you?' I asked.

'I have my reasons,' she replied, and in her tone I caught a warning, some hint of danger that beckoned me on rather than stopped me.

For the first time I felt that she was on some sort of uncertain ground so, intrigued, I snuggled in close to her in the way we girls do with dear cousins and sisters and friends, our heads back as we watched and gasped at the fireworks which could have come from the pyromaniac dreams of the fire-master of the Emperor of China, and pressed a little farther.

'But your reasons couldn't have always stopped your feelings.'

She shot me a look of warning, the flames of the still growing bonfire reflecting in the whites of her eyes as she turned. 'Dangerous ground, cousin,' she said, as giant plumes of purple and red fire span, the bonfire grew hotter and the purest feeling of unfettered joy ran through my shared blood.

'Look,' she said, 'I have my reasons, I have my feelings, and the two don't always mix.'

'What do you mean?' I asked, tauntingly, watching the light of the fire on her skin, her hair, her eyes. 'Do you always have reasons which hold you down?'

'Not always.'

'Now?'

'Look,' she said, bringing her hands together in an attitude of prayer. 'Don't make me do this. I beg you.'

'Do what?' We both looked up at a cascade of silver light which crackled as it fell through the night, and she turned to me. There were tears in her eyes, and something in me was appalled by what I had done

'It's too late,' she said. 'The deed is done, there's no turning back.'

'Tell me,' I said, confusion raging inside me, tears pricking my eyes too. ' Tell me, you must tell me, what is it, what's going on?'

She then took my hands in hers and looked straight at me, straight into me. 'Cousin,' she said, 'it's very simple and very terrible.' She hesitated, as if to gather the strength needed, all manner of fire and light shining in her eyes and then said. 'I've fallen deeply in love with you.'

Chapter 11

I stopped dead, the world stopped dead, the fire raged, the fireworks exploded, and in the centre of all that chaos, heat, and noise a great silence opened up within me that overwhelmed it all, and within that silence a piece gently fell into place in the heart of me; what was never quite clear before was clear now, the incomplete was complete and life would never be the same again.

'Yes,' I said. 'I see. It's a bit of a surprise, to say the least. And I feel the same, I do, I love you to death.'

We embraced, hugged each other hard, right there in the sight of everyone, and they smiled to see the two cousins being so affectionate there on my wedding day, how sweet, how touching, while inside me more fireworks were exploding than there were in the sky above, and the searing passion of an opened heart had cancelled all reason, sense and fear of consequence. Thus the last barrier to the fulfilling of my destiny crumbled.

'How long have you known this?' I asked her.

'It was love at first sight in the Cathedral, but I thought at the time it was just a passing madness, it was so unlikely. Then I sat there watching you get married before my eyes within minutes of feeling my heart open in a way I had never known before, thinking, hoping, it was all some strange delusion that would soon pass.'

'What,' I asked with a smile, 'your passion or my wedding?'

'Either one, but the passion seemed the more likely to change or fade. I should have known better and left there and then and never looked back, but I couldn't. Or didn't.'

'Thank God.' I laughed. 'What a pair we are. It never crossed my mind that I could love a woman like this, so when all these feelings for you rose in me I thought they were to do with cousins re-found, the reconnection of the blood, hell, I don't know what. This particular reality was way beyond my understanding.'

It was right then that Anthony came up to us, lost in our own world as the fireworks came to a crescendo, almost unnoticed by us, they were just background to our own form of inner pyromania.

'Ladies,' he said, terribly polite as always. 'You're going to have to move, I'm awfully sorry. Look at the fire.'

We looked and he was right. The wind had changed and stiffened. Anthony's yachtsman's instincts were true, his fears were grounded and Geoffrey's great fire had turned from entertainment into danger, not the only thing that evening that had swung from the safe and unexpected into the wild and unpredictable. The truth was that we cousins had been so wrapped up in ourselves and our amazing revelations that we had noticed nothing else, not even the heat of the flames that were now close enough to almost sear our flesh, and were reaching ever nearer to the marquee and the house. The whole mood of the day had swerved from its well-trodden path, from the predictable and sweet, conservative and safe, into the fearful unknown where danger and destruction threatened from both within and without. In the space of a few short hours the solid foundations were being torn from my world.

'Did you find out what Geoffrey put on the fire?' I asked, as we moved towards the rest of the wedding guests, who were standing in one safely placed clump, talking with animation, pointing at the flames, which were now reaching extraordinary lengths, roaring and veering with the fickle wind. Waiters were now busily removing all things of value from the marquee under the command of Major Charlie Brown, a man born for such things. I had never seen him at work like that, the man in charge of men, and I stood and watched him with interest, oddly remote in myself, as he shouted and pointed and hefted things around in the manliest of ways. It seemed absurd to think I had actually married this person that very afternoon. What amazing timing. Why hadn't she appeared before, years before, even a month before, even hours before, and saved me from this inner anguish? I knew even then that the why's would have to stop, that easy understanding was no longer a part of my world, that I was moving into the land of another truth and no reason at all.

As I watched him I found a finger going to my mouth and I began to chew on a fingernail. What had I done? Oh, Charlie. Could this really be my wedding day? I looked at him with great affection, love even, but it was a slower kind of love, like the love of nature or art, something deep-flowing and calm. Not like the breath-stopping passion that had been ignited in me for my exotic cousin. When I turned my gaze to her my whole being burned and I wanted desperately to hold her so near and tight to me that I pulled her cells into mine and we merged into one. So intense was my feeling that I almost wanted to cause pain, to bite her, scratch her and scream.

I couldn't believe I was thinking and feeling such things. All the rules and expectations of my life were thrown out of the window in one move. You must believe that not once in my life had I ever thought of embracing a woman with love, with passion. The thought had never entered my mind, it seemed ludicrous as I thought of it. Perhaps I was in some strange dream and soon I would wake and the world would be righted, black would be black and white, white, and no longer would I feel overwhelming, hot passion for a woman. And not just any woman, but my cousin, the girl from my childhood, Ada's girl who went away.

It was all too much for my mind to grasp, the suddenness, power and unexpected fire of it all. I took off my glove and pushed my hand down into hers, and she turned and flashed a smile at me which made my heart miss a beat, then she reached over and kissed me on the cheek. It felt like the touch of an angel, the sweetest touch my body had ever known, and with it came the simplest deep happiness possible. For the first time in my life, I was truly in love.

All around us were the guests at my wedding, for God's sake, almost laying their bets on the survival of the marquee. And not just the marquee, but the house itself was being talked of as being under threat, and not without reason. The heat was tremendous, and the wind, the food of the fire, seemed to be rising. I had never seen a fire like this one, so hot in its visible core that it was almost white, darkening along its horizontal flame to the orange that was caressing with all its destructive power the sacred house of the Browns.

'The marquee's going to burn,' said my cousin, the source of the even greater fire burning in me. 'Look.'

She was right; on one corner I could see charring and melting, and now everyone was out of the great tent and out of danger, standing in a still group just watching, no longer attempting to interfere with a power that was greater than they.

Then a thought popped into my mind, and with it, desperation. 'Cousin, what's going to happen to us?' I asked. 'You can't just leave when all this is done. Can you?'

'My love,' she said, looking at me with such passion I could die. Oh, why did she go and call me that? I could have wept. 'You're a married woman. The moving finger has written. I've been trying to avert my mind from this particular reality, but it seems that our time is short.'

I found myself holding back tears, and dug my fingernails into her wrist inside the warmth of her own glove; this I could not bear. Flames began to appear from the fabric of the marquee, and now I could see Charlie in command once more, this time pulling down the canvas tunnel to the house. The danger was spreading, panic was in the air. Where had the simple wedding gone?

'So where are you going when this is over? Back to Liverpool?'

'Good grief, no. My small business there is done. I'm going back to Italy.'

'Italy.' I repeated bleakly. It seemed like the farthest reaches of the universe; a long way from me. Then I remembered; the next day I was going to St Lucia with Charlie, off on my happy honeymoon, body on the plane, heart elsewhere.

'I can't stand it,' I said. 'I only just found you, it's too early to lose you.'

'We'll be together in spirit,' she said, emptily and without conviction. I could see her biting her lip.

'Don't give me that,' I told her. 'We'll have to meet up later. Maybe I can go to Italy, or you could come here, hell, I don't know, something must happen.'

'Yeah,' she said dully; she knew as I did that in truth our time was almost done, our race was run, and it felt like a cruel, cruel world, I'll tell you.

'Michelle,' said an all-too-familiar voice to my side. Margaret. I turned from my own small troubles, once more breaking out of our world made for two. 'Have you seen Geoffrey?'

I'd never seen her like this before; she looked worn and tired, vulnerable and worried. 'No, not for ages. Why?'

'We're worried, to be truthful. Haven't seen sight nor sound of him for far too long. Not like him to be hiding, out of the action on a night like this.'

We shrugged as one—what to do? What was going on here tonight? From what seemed like the most regular of Parkgate weddings, except for the season, there was an over-current arising of something unexpected, something unknown and uncontrolled, not the usual thing at all for Parkgate, believe me. What should have been a wedding in the hand had turned into a conflagration, and the thought actually went through my head that this extraordinary business with the cousin of cousins herself was the psychic catalyst that was the secret cause of the entire eruption.

'How can I love a woman?' I asked her, holding her arm close. 'It doesn't make sense.'

'If only the world made sense, sweetheart, and heroes were true and so was magic, that all things were simple and as you see.'

'What have you been doing out there in your wilder world while I got myself nowhere?'

She smiled ever so easily, a smile without shame, constraint or comment. 'Look,' she said. 'There goes the marquee.'

I could see Charlie Brown, my husband, no less, commanding his troops carrying buckets and hoses. We could see his plan, to at least keep the flames away from the house itself, hose it down, throw water on it, shout a lot, and it all seemed like a distant drama played out on someone else's stage. I no longer felt as if I belonged on that stage, that my part in that drama, which I thought would be long-running, had in fact just run out of time.

I just loved holding that arm of Alexandra, just loved being with her, just loved her. So different from the love I had for men, well, for Charlie; so balanced, so sweet, so tender. It all seemed as natural as the day, easy, effortless, obvious, but at the same time so powerful it nearly made me explode.

The trouble with passion—one of the troubles with passion—is that you enter some kind of magic kingdom where everything looks different and terribly real even though most of what you see is delusion, so excuses are easy and you are morally free to do anything you damn well like because you know how beautiful and true it all is, no matter how it is, no matter what the cost,

So when the wind veered and roared and the long pennant of orange fire licked and chewed at the corner of the house itself, we stepped back out of the feral heat into a fold of building where the shadow was dark and cool, and, as easy as pie, with all the naturalness in the world, we weren't making a point, we were fulfilling a destiny, deep and long, we kissed.

Ah, what a thing it was to kiss that long-denied love for the first time. I had never known such a thing. I was accustomed to the hard and bristly lips and faces of men, that tough masculine that had always been the measure of what made me gasp; the overpowering, the phallic force, the hard chest—hell, you know what I mean. Now this, for God's sake, the softness of a woman, the body, the lips, the skin, all just like my own, and I loved it. I was in a state of ecstasy from which I simply did not want to emerge and all my past, both distant and very near, was of no interest to me if I had such a present as this to live. All this, I remind myself, was going on at my very own wedding.

We parted and looked at each other from inches away, once again the wonder of those eyes of my own on someone else reflecting to me a deeper part of my heart and soul than I had yet known. In some way, uncomprehended by my faintly struggling mind, she was not separate from me, not a different entity, and I had entered a world of reflections, mirage and love that had recast my whole view of the world without my knowing what it was.

'Well,' she said, with a tiny smile.

'You feel the same as me? Never have I known such a feeling as this. What are you doing to me?'

'I have no idea. And yes, I feel the same.'

We were oblivious to the roar of the fire and the shouts of the people, lost in our own world made for two. My mind was reeling, my body quivering, my heart open and raw.

'I would like to kiss you again,' I said, understating a wild desire that I would have torn the heavens apart for, and she immediately leaned forward, her eyes closing as she approached, and I watched her tender lips meeting mine, that touch being like the meeting of two halves of one ecstasy. As we kissed, so long and so sweet, I drank in that which I had always sought but never known, that missing piece that gave me the answer to all my curious doubts and hesitations with other loves. How wonderful she felt, how natural it all was, how right ....

'What the fuck are you two up to?'

Oh, Christ, it was Charlie standing over us, hair wild, eyes wilder, glowering in red-fired rage. We fell apart. What could I say? There were cousin kisses, girly caresses, and then there was this, a wanton display of disregard for any feeling he might ever have had. In truth I had simply forgotten all about him, the ultimate insult. I felt terrible. How long had he been watching us? The bottom fell out of my world and I stepped out of our magic circle of wonder and love where everything was as perfect and pure as fresh snow, and realised what I'd been doing. My freshly created world of perfection crumbled.

'Well?' He was furious, hands on hips, chin thrust forward. 'The house almost in flames, the marquee gone, my father missing and you two are snogging in the corner. For God's sake, Michelle, it's our bloody wedding day.'

'I'm sorry, Charlie,' I said weakly. 'It's not exactly what I had in mind.'

He sneered, faced Alexandra. 'I think you'd better go,' he said. 'I've known trash like you before, and you aren't welcome in my house.'

'Very well,' she said quietly, calmly, with no trace of defence or regret, and turned to go.

'Not yet!' I cried. 'Don't just go!' And in that moment, in the anguish of my cry, was betrayed the depths of my feelings, exposed my burning passion, which closed a door forever.

He turned to me, his breath coming in short bursts. 'I don't know you,' he said. 'I don't know you. What's going on?' He looked as if his head was reeling, as if some line had been passed, and the emergence of a savagery I had touched on from a distance, enlivened by the great fire, was imminent.

I reached out for him, to touch him, to tell him that at some level beyond what he could see and understand from a more limited past that all was well, just changed, and we must have faith, when he struck my oncoming hand with his, and, in the same movement, the side of my face.

As my hand rose to touch my cheek, a breathless shock coursing through my body, Charlie looked at me without a shadow of compassion, coldly, another person, and one who chilled me to the heart. Oh, no, who is this man? I was feeling dizzy, as my safe and good little world burned to pieces before me in the twin fires of the giant funeral pyre of the life that was lighting up Charlie's fury and eruptions of the fires of my fate were cremating my past within.

With a fierce stare, he turned on his heel and vanished.

'Your cheek,' she said, touching it with a hand as cool and warm as Moon and Sun, my whole life feeling healed at her touch. 'Did he hurt you?'

'More shocked than hurt.'

She took my head in her hands, with a gesture of such love that

I felt I had come home at last, then reached forward and kissed me on the place the moving fist had bruised on my cheek. At that moment I knew that the die was cast—I no longer was the person that started that day, so the rules and the promises of that time seemed remote, far away and no longer for me. That blow, the look on the twisted face that followed, these things were enough for me, enough to turn the balance, dismiss regret and step into the void.

Then the first movement in that void, the first coagulation of form in the chaos, the only signpost in the road to nowhere yet, was a keening wail cutting through the roar of the giant fire.

'Geoffrey!' I said, just knowing in my heart of hearts that something had happened to him. 'Please God, no.' What else could this day do to me? We crossed the lawn to a spot by the entrance to the rose garden, and there in the darkness a crowd of people gathered round a figure lying on the ground and lit by torches.

Geoffrey indeed. I kept to myself on the outer fringes of the small crowd, no longer feeling it was my place to join Charlie and Margaret at his side. From someone near me I heard the words gone, finished, all over, and a piece fell out of my heart. Surely he couldn't have just up and died. Was the whole of my life as transient and fragile as this? I realised just how much I loved him, and in that utterly bleak moment when I realised he had gone I understood that he was the last of the reasons to stay, so now I was free to go.

I took her to one side. 'Did you hear?'

'I heard.'

'There's nothing left for me here. Can I come with you?'

'All the way with me? To Italy?'

I nodded.

'Of course. You realise what you're doing?'

'I do. The decision is mine.'

She smiled that smile, that open, without the slightest hint of regret or fear smile that I would have followed to the far side of the universe, never mind Italy.

'Very good,' she said, eyes shining. 'Let's live. We need a car.'

'No problem. We can take ours, I mean Charlie's.'

'He won't mind?'

'In for a penny, in for a pound. Where are we going?'

'Italy. I have to be at the Opera tomorrow night, in Milano.' She paused and put her head to one side 'Maybe you can come too. Why not? I know who counts in Milano. Where's the phone?'

Upstairs I went in that deserted house, leaving the cousin from heaven calling Italy on the phone while I picked up my bags for a holiday in the Caribbean, kissed goodbye to my wedding dress forever, and descended the sweep of stairs for a final time that day of days, no-one there to toast and applaud me now.

She was sitting on the arm of a chair in the lounge in the half-light, calmly talking rapid Italian down the phone. She looked like the most beautiful human being I had ever seen, and now I had a life with her, time with her, and I could feel myself changing with the moments that passed, as in some way I could never describe even to myself I gave my whole spirit to her, and the result was the purest of joys.

She looked up as she replaced the phone. 'Bene,' she said. 'OK, one more impossible seat at the opera, the miracle of connections in Italy.'

We grinned at each other, and moved into another phase of almost naughty, heart-light togetherness.

'The time has come,' she said. 'You got the keys?'

I held them up, the keys to Charlie's prize; his smooth fast Jaguar, one of those older ones in curves and elegance with a fire-breathing engine and a walnut dashboard, the car off on a journey that would give it space to breathe and fly.

'This is the maddest thing I have ever done in my life, by far,' I said, relishing the fact, feeling electric excitement and not a trace of fear.

'If you had any ground to catch up with me, then you just did it,' said Alexandra. 'Even for me this is wild in the far extreme.'

'I only hope we don't regret it.'

She touched my lips with an outstretched finger. 'Not even a hint of doubt ever again, darling,' she said, and for the first time in my life that word sounded like a word of love. 'If there's a price to be paid, let it be. But somewhere deep inside I feel that I've already paid for this, and I must be doing something the gods love for me to be flying into the night with you, love of my life. Let's go.'

Chapter 12

Minutes later I was at the wheel and accelerating out of the drive in that soft and curved sweet car of Charlie's with gravel flying, and turned out onto the road as fire engines in a blaze of blue and white light came thundering past us and into the gateway we had just left.

'Not a minute too soon,' said my new cousin love, turning her attention from the vanishing lights behind to the darkness of the road ahead.

'Which way?' I asked. 'Where are we going?'

'South,' she said. 'Take the road south and drive like the wind.'

It was there and then that the drive of a life began, the lunatic flight from the fire in the night and the merciless death of the past to nothing at all yet known. The Jaguar, built for speed, just the thing for the escape to the future, at last came unto its own, like a racing dog let off its leash.

'Thank God for a real car,' said my divine cousin as I accelerated without effort to a speed that would once have taken my breath away and now felt normal, comfortable, as if we were being pulled by forces as yet not visible at a speed of their choice to a destination only time would reveal.

We drove in silence, and were strangely as one in a way I had never before known with any other person, with a lifetime to talk about and nothing to say, but with space for my mind to work its old tricks and lead me into familiar chasms of doubt, to abandon the rush that came with the release of the heart and follow those old tracks marked guilt, hesitation, self-denial. I was just a good English girl, you see, trained not for freedom and ecstasy, but simply to be good.

'I have no money,' I said. 'Not a penny, no cards, no nothing. Brides don't need such things.'

'Don't be concerned. I have cards with credit enough to buy an empire. You have underwear in that bag?'

I shook my head.

'One of the advantages of a female lover,' she said. 'We can travel lighter, share the knickers.'

'Well,' I said brightly. 'Can't think why I didn't think of it before. So practical.'

Then we caught each other's almost same eyes and burst out laughing. And laughed and laughed so hard that I had to slow down our time machine because, for the second time that evening but for different reasons, I could hardly see through my tears.

'I can't see to drive,' I told her, and she undid her seat belt, took tissues from her bag and leaned across to dab my tears dry, then kissed my cheeks, ran her hand through my hair—while I was still driving and powerless to resist, even if I had wanted to—saying, 'Don't worry, sweetheart. From now I will show you the meaning of tenderness.'

So the tears started all over again, and now she was kneeling on her seat holding me while I wept for the passing of an old life and the joy at the coming of the new, the actual moment of my rebirth taking place at a steering wheel but in control of nothing, driving at almost no speed at all now down the inside lane in our stolen car on the way to our stolen life.

Then suddenly I was finished and an old skin was shed and the tears were done, at least for now, and I pulled in on the hard shoulder to kiss her again, on the lips and with passion, and I felt as free, burden-less and clean as a gull sweeping over the sunlit sea.

We drove on, this time even faster as the different driver that was the different me took the car to her natural speed. By my side all the world in human form riffled through Charlie's music tapes, as we sped along through a night young enough for there to be fireworks still shooting off into the night sky. They took my mind back to the house in Parkgate, the bonfire, the fireworks, and Charlie. He hit me, he bloody well hit me, I thought to myself, knuckles whitening on the wheel, how could he bloody well hit me? In that moment was the full drama that would have normally been played out with time, slowly over our married years, was revealed and known and played out before the day of our wedding was done. Life had accelerated into an arena of breathless speed in all things to match the speed of the car, which felt happy at last under my hands, finally, like me, set free from normal restraint.

Too late and not too late for me to see something of what was hidden there inside dear Charlie Brown, the savage at the heart of the man, perhaps. Was it the greatest of good fortune that I should have had this revealed to me, I wondered, so at least I could flee into chaos and truth rather than remain as I would have been, in order to others, and falsehood to myself.

We hardly spoke, the car fled on, and my new cousin-lover slid a tape into the deck. 'Listen,' she said. 'Do you know Callas, Maria Callas?'

'No. Just the name. I know nothing of opera.'

'Ah, you will. I have a world to show you. Amazing that Charlie should have this tape in his car. Charlie of all people. Callas, Madame Butterfly at La Scala, listen ....'

The mood of mad abandon had been set, the direction set, the place, a road from the past to the future under a starlit sky exploding with fireworks, and now the music that would set the mood in heart-sound forever. For the first time this life I was living in the full sensual waters of the life of the living moment, and there was something way down deep in the core of Maria Callas that she had the nerve to not only find but become and then sing from, that resonated with some same place deep inside me. The danger I was living on the outside was a mere shadow of the danger I was living within myself as I hurtled into me, with an inner scenery of feelings of such power that never in my life had I dared go there, till now. My guides on the way were the cousin I loved and that opera which was the sound of my life, sung by one who knew, two forms of La Divina taking me to yet another form in me.

I play it now, far too loud in the middle of the night as I write this, and it is the music of that time, the sound of my passion for Alessia, my passion for me, my passion for life. To read this best, have Callas sing Madame Butterfly to you as you read, and have La Divina tear out her heart with sound as I tear out mine in words to share with you.

We fled past Birmingham, the car cruising with apparent ease at a regular hundred and twenty miles an hour, the natural, effortless speed for our flight, somehow in magic safety beyond the awareness of earthbound police and other such possible nuisance. As the music played on while my head span and we seemed to be on a rocket-ship to the stars, streaking past factories, night-driving salesmen on their way to the next lead, lads in sports cars, the whole of the world not moving as fast as we.

'My goodness, you're so lovely,' she said from her seat at my left. It felt like a caress, not a seduction, and I warmed a degree more to this new life of mine, this life without home or friends or family where such delights were part of life. In one stroke I had cut myself off from my world and even though I looked hard within me I could find not even a trace of regret.

Freedom, freedom and love, how sweet. We stopped for coffee and fuel at one of those bleak motorway places in the middle of the night, and sat at a plastic table looking at each other, so obviously pleased with what we had.

'Who would have believed it?' she said. 'My cousin, little fat-faced Michelle who used to bug me on those ghastly holidays by the freezing sea in Wales, oh so many years ago.'

'It was the kiss that did it.' I said. 'One kiss like that and life can never be the same again.'

She looked at me and shook her head slowly. 'What are you doing to me?' she asked, and I shrugged; how could I know? Could it be anything like what she was doing to me? I was excited, flattered that such a marvellous and profound creature as this should be so moved by me.

'So we're going where? Milan?'

'Right. La Scala tomorrow night.' She looked at her watch. 'Past that I have no idea of any future.'

'We can get there on time? It's an awful long way ....' and I hesitated. 'What do I call you now? Not Alexandra, it's too long and not you at all.'

'Alessia, call me Alessia, that's who I am. Alexandra died some years ago and now the name feels like someone else's from another life. It's short for Alessandra; what they sometimes call Alessandra's in Italy. And yes, we can, and we will get there on time, but we'll have to drive very hard. OK with you? One sleeps while the other drives?'

'Alessia, Alessia, I like it, very beautiful, like you. Have you been with many girls, women, Alessia'

She saved her answer until we were hurtling south at unvarying speed once more, keeping the needle at 120 and steering and let the miles just vanish. Why had I never moved like this before? And the only answer was that never before did I have anything so gripping to flee from and fly to. On the tape deck, Maria Callas, coming near the end of a first performance of an unending round of Madame Butterfly.

'Yes, I've loved women.' And she glanced at me as Maria hit a note that almost made me shout out loud. 'But this doesn't mean I can't love men; I have done, but not for some time. Everything changed when I became myself.'

She was so unaffected, so pure. A form of advanced simplicity that we might aspire to after we have lived all the complications life can bring. I looked at her in wonder. To her it was obvious, clear and uncomplicated. For me it was so far outside the life I had just left that my mind groped, found no meaning, so it gave up, and I settled down to the exotic liberation of my personal springtime.

'You're quite something, Alessia, Alessia. You are doing things to me that no human has yet done. Will we go to bed together too? Is that in the master plan?'

'This is my clear intention.' She grinned like a naughty teenager. 'I know the bed too, it's where we're driving to in such haste; a very beautiful bed in a very beautiful apartment that belongs to a very beautiful man who lives not far from La Scala.'

'The show after the show.'

She grinned once more, her eyes and teeth shining in the half-light as we sped ever farther southward, serenaded endlessly by Puccini.

'The show after the show, exactly.'

I loved watching her drive; so balanced, so attentive, so decisive, so bloody fast, fearing nothing. This was a breed apart from the women of the world that was fading into memory, the women of whom I used to be one. In Alessia not a trace of hesitancy or self-doubt, no false bravado, but a curious and delightful mix of the power of certainty and the sweetness of the flower; humour, incisiveness, fearlessness; she intrigued me totally, mesmerised me, and I sat watching her drive, drinking in all of what she was. Mmm, how much I wanted to kiss her again.

'D'you think Charlie'll call the police? About the car.' It was my single doubt.

She shrugged. 'Time will tell. For myself, I don't think so; this trip was the creation of the minds of the Gods, no human could have dreamed this up, and if they want us to arrive, arrive we will.'

Ah, what a lovely idea, our dear selves somehow in the lap of the Gods, this whole drama that we were living a great work of magic in which we were spirited away from one universe to another, mere mortals given no choices they could understand, just directions to follow. Simply relax and lie back and let this messenger from the Gods, or Goddesses more like—the only way of seeing my Alessia that made any sense—drive me at breathtaking speed on the journey from a freshly shattered fresh marriage, like an egg from which I emerged fully formed and flighted so I could wing off to an opera house in Italy.

'I don't even know what I'm going to see,' I said happily. 'I hope it's good.'

'It's better than good and more than worth it,' she said. 'Trust me. We must drive through the night and we can be at Enzo's apartment with time to spare—eat, sleep, and off to the Opera.'

'But I haven't got a thing to wear.'

She brushed away my concerns with a sweep of the hand. 'We wear what we have,' she said. 'Relax.'

So I did, half-lay there in the comfortable silence with Alessia—I kept repeating her name under my breath like a magic incantation—and let my mind float back to the scene I left behind; the burning house, the dying father, the outraged son, every one of Margaret Brown's dreams crushed casually underfoot by me. One thought of the effect of our disappearance on that world and I hastily averted my mind from that snarling scene. For one moment I hoped that no-one would realise what Alessia and I were, that we were actual lovers, but then I remembered that Charlie knew all, and I had the relief of knowing that nothing was hidden, that concealment and shame had no place in my love.

'Do you live in Italy, then?' I asked her. 'I know nothing about you.'

'I've spent years in Italy,' she answered. 'It's as much home as anywhere else, maybe more so.'

'What do you do?'

'This and that,' she said vaguely. 'One thing I do is to paint, and I want to paint a portrait of you.'

'Me?'

'You, carissima.'

'Carissima. What does that mean?'

'Dearest of dear ones. You're so beautiful, I love you, so I want to paint pictures of you.'

'It would be kind of like painting pictures of yourself.'

'Not quite but almost,' she said. 'It's all very wonderful. You've opened up a new world for me.'

I'd opened up a new world for her? It was all too much to take in, so I didn't try. Let the future bring what the future brings is what I thought, and settled down to the present as the car hurtled on, Alessia at the wheel and, despite the opera still playing, I found myself drowsing off. I fell swiftly into a half-sleep full of images from dreams and operas, of passions and blood, agonies and caresses, sweet warmth, horses running wild through the night, gremlins taunting, fires burning, revenges falling; pictures from childhood, from my wedding, from lonely times and happy times, and always returning to a glint of fire on knife that in the end shocked me awake. I had been deeply asleep in a maelstrom of dreams; it was a shock to be back in that car, in that life, and I was cold.

Alessia reached over and touched my face. 'You've been sleeping,' she said, 'twitching and whimpering, curled up in the seat like a child. My heart went out to you, but what could I do? I thought it best to leave you to lose your own demons. Look, we're at the Channel, we'll be in France in no time.'

'Time for you to hold me a little?' I felt as fragile as a small child woken in a strange place.

The great lights of the Tunnel complex glinted on wet rimming her eyes. 'My God,' she said, as she looked at me in a way no human ever had until that time. 'I thought I had loved before. What are you doing to me?'

Then in the Tunnel, on the train, we sat and held each other and the gremlins of the dark past faded. It seemed too much that this wonderful creature, this cousin of mine, this blood of my blood, not only was there to be loved by me, but also loved me in return. Exhausted from driving, she fell back against me and I cradled her in my arms, indifferent to the eyes of lesser mortals, and kissed her brow, stroked her temples, and realised that she had already fulfilled her single promise; I had already tasted fresh depths of tenderness, and just not hers, but my own.

It was in the first hours of the morning that I drove the Jaguar out onto the road south. Our route was set, and without a moment's hesitation I tore off into the French darkness. In some way, crossing the Channel had made the tone of the journey different; now it was a journey to something, not a fleeing from anything anymore, and because of that, far freer. To me there was the sense of my butterfly wings spreading now, and with them not only beauty but also the freedom to fly.

As Alessia fell asleep, I slipped the tape of Madame Butterfly into the deck again, and yet one more time that astonishing night the heat of the operatic passion filled every pore of me, accentuated somehow by being temporarily alone. I had woken up from the night-sleep of a half-life, and now I was becoming alive, every cell electric, my heart burning with love. My new life had begun.

Once more I headed south and drove like the wind, with total disregard for legal limits, driving a car that was by rights stolen, the reflection of a greater me and yet not me sleeping by my side. As I drove I was alone, just that eternal tape rolling on, and I had time to think, muse on my life; the past, necessarily, as I had not the faintest idea of a future. Isn't it strange the way sometimes hardly anything at all changes for what seems like years, life plods on, and then all of a sudden one small thing happens and then another and the world turns on a dime, performs a somersault and lands in a different place?

Now the nights are long in November, but even considering the darkness of that time of the autumn equinox, more had happened that night and more had changed than any day or night or week or even month of my life. The sun had not yet come up on the morning after the night before, and I thought back to the wedding, unbelievably just hours, not days before, and it seemed like a distant event in the life of someone else. Never before had I felt as I felt as I drove that car faster than any car I had driven in my life down the foreign roads of France. Because I was no longer part of a social world, I'd blown it all, I no longer had a part in a play that once was mine, I was like an actor in a cast break, just being myself. Which was very simple and very moving, very real and very alive. I turned the rear-view mirror so I could see myself, looked into my own eyes for once in the half-light from passing cars and saw who I was for the first time.

You know what it was that changed everything? It was that kiss. Until that moment it was all just potential, rain in a cloud, then with that kiss I knew that life was not what it had always seemed, that there was a city of gold beyond my own inner horizons. Once I had tasted her, melded into her, felt her caress, there was no going back, there was only going on.

So go on I did, relentlessly forging the way into my future, the clock at 120, the tape of Callas still playing, the immortal Gods still holding us in the palms of their hands as I drove ever onwards and southwards, like an arrow loosed from a tensed bow. Tiredness came and went as I slipped into a state of empowered animation that was on the other side of sleep.

I drove and drove like I had never done before, stopping rarely, only to check maps and pay tolls, and Alessia slept on, silently and without moving a muscle. One time I actually came up close to her to see if she still breathing, in the way that new mothers do when they live on the edge of the fear of their new wonder being taken almost as soon as it was given. She was still alive, all was well.

The tape ran out and the radio came on automatically. The BBC, Radio Four, a trace of Charlie in the form of his taste in radio coming in clear. How unreal people and things are when they are not before our eyes, and exist only in the mental forms that we fabricate from doubtful memory and flavour with our own hopes and fears. Even though I had left Charlie just hours before and sat now in his seat in his car and listened to his radio as I sped south through autumnal France, he seemed at that time to be long gone, reduced to someone I once knew.

It surprised me to hear the BBC still working in France, as if there was a barrier to the passing of radio waves that came with a changed language and a stretch of sea. I listened with fascination to the measured tones of cultured Britain, a professor of something or other telling me about secrets in the bones of dinosaurs, new discoveries in the Rift Valley, and somehow it reminded me of all that I had left behind, all that polished opulence, everything in its place but me in the Brown's little big world that I had seemed heir to and now had lost forever, thank the Lord. Just think what I would have become what with babies, expectations, and my own little weaknesses. Oh, Charlie, I thought, I'm so sorry, I had no choice. I never was a Radio Four girl.

Still the unending night rolled on; French roads with few cars travelling. Now and again yellow headlights swept by on the far side of the road, but nothing passed me on mine at that speed that I had set as my own. If they did, I thought with a smile to myself, they could look after themselves.

The long night stretched on as if it would never end. Alessia slept and slept, and I restrained the urge to wake her on some feeble excuse so that I could break out of the growing sense of being totally alone in a black world with no other people, just me at the wheel of that car that felt as if it could eat up roads for eternity. Instead, I sat there with my own feelings for company, listened again to that opera that had within it some secret I couldn't yet grasp, and let my mind wander over the past and into the present, where it stopped. My future was now unimaginable. But, I thought, if it had anything of the power of the day I had just lived I was looking to times to be remembered in even further futures, when the present me was no more than the memory of yesterday's bride was to me now.

And on we sped.

Chapter 13

I seemed to drive forever down featureless highways through the darkness of my own first night, the windscreen spotting with rain, following the numbers of roads and the names of cities that meant nothing to me but a direction south and a life I had never yet known. Through this all Alessia, the woman who had turned my head at the altar, slept on like a child next to me. This stretch of time when the flight was in my hands alone, when I was dependent on no other will but my own, was the time when I came to know that my destiny was my own too, and such was its inevitable power that, like me, Alessia was its inevitable servant, and we were doing no more than fulfil that which must inevitably be fulfilled. Ultimately, it was now clear, there were no choices, either that or the choices had been made a long time ago.

Petrol and coffee, maybe even food, I thought, and maybe a little of the best of company as I pulled in, feeling very weary, to what came to me as an island of lights in the oncoming sea of darkness and turned into restaurants, filling stations and a hotel. Such was my degree of aloneness—but certainly not loneliness—as I drove through the centre of that night that stretched from one life to another that I was surprised to see other people living and working in the same world. Alessia woke as I drew to a halt.

'Where are we?' she asked, looking around. She made the transition from sleep to wakefulness with the same easy grace she applied to every move she made. Never did she waver from poise, and never did that poise seem anything but a natural expression of her own inner being. I found even her waking up in a car in a bleak French night-time motor stop entrancing.

'I don't have a clue. France, a lot farther south than when you last looked.'

She looked at her watch. 'Michelle,' she said, 'you've been driving for hours. Have I been asleep all that time? I don't believe myself. You should have woken me.'

'Buy me breakfast, beautiful, and all is forgiven. My goodness, I feel tacky. And so much for my beautiful new suit, look at it, all crumpled to death.'

'We'll get it pressed in Milan. Look, there's a hotel here, why don't we get a shower and have breakfast in comfort?'

She thought differently from me; money was a servant for her, to be used as a tool without embarrassment or any other unnatural colour. So we took a room, showered, changed our convenient underwear, all very chaste and businesslike, ate croissants with cafe au lait and looked at the map.

'We're doing well,' she said. 'Very well. You've driven long and fast but there's still no time to lose. Let's hit the road.'

Within no time at all there we were again, Alessia at the wheel, pounding down that concrete strip, the car oiled and watered and fed like us, doing what it did best, taking us on to our unknown future at a speed its creators made it for. That car by now had become our home, our travelling house on wheels in which we had lived almost all of our short hours together, and, ironically, it was the property of Charlie Brown, so all the while we lived under the vague shadow of the man I had left behind.

'Why Italy?' I asked as we sped on once more, Maria Callas serenading us yet again, around and around, and we never tired of that singing that became imprinted on our minds forever, the sound of a flowering of a new life. I felt that brief rest had given me all I needed to carry on forever. Did I no longer need to sleep? Was that another consequence of my reincarnation within one lifespan? 'What took you there in the first place?'

'Simple; I met an Italian, Enzo Corelli, the rich and beautiful, who courted me with glamour and glittering dreams when I was just a kid, and I heard what I wanted to hear and bought it all. We're staying at his place in Milan tonight, the spoiled, lying bastard. You'll like him; he's a bit like Charlie.'

A bit like Charlie; at the name a small tremor passed through me. 'So no hard feelings, then? I mean with you and Enzo. Are you all kissed and made up and good old friends now?' I was seeking solace, looking for a little hope that in the end all would be well with Charlie, hoping against hope that the odd ache that lay beneath my joy could one day be assuaged.

Outside the car the first grey specks of a grey dawn were filtering into the sky, and with it the first sign of the shape of land I had seen since the drive from Chester Cathedral in that old Rolls. Could that really have been just yesterday? It seemed like something I read in a story I read a thousand years ago in a book that I then lost.

'Look over there,' she said. 'The beginning of the mountains. No, no hard feelings with Enzo. It was a long time ago before we knew what and who we were, and now we're the best of friends. Enzo. He'll be there today, a face and a man out of my past, one of the people who made me. But more importantly tell me about you—you say you know nothing of me, but I feel the same, all I know is the child and the bride.'

Once more the focus was deflected from her, with an ease that suggested long practice. She was an odd creature, and all the more fascinating to me because she was impossible to grasp—powerfully present and at the same time hardly there at all, and I could imagine men being driven mad by this will of the wisp, chasing her with hungered intent and in the end getting nowhere.

'You're a funny one, cousin; a woman without a past, but with a past. For me there is a yawning space between the kid on the beach and the first woman who kissed me, and I'm intrigued about what filled it, what made you what you are.'

She shrugged. 'I just led my life like anyone else.'

'Really? Just like anyone?'

'Well, I just lived it, no matter what it was, like anyone.'

Those tracks to nowhere in her I left to her—I didn't need to know, understand and grasp and own her—and focused on the track I could see, the eternal road ahead.

'Where from here?' I asked.

'Cut across Switzerland, through the Alps, the Mont Blanc Tunnel and into Italy. Home and dry.'

And we drove and drove, relentlessly onward, with such intent that I could imagine this journey having a life of its own that we were subject to, with a relentless driving power that kept us forever on the highway without ever letting us arrive anywhere. I was entering the world of Alessia.

'So am I just like your other girls, Alessia?' I taunted, all the while watching her slim wrists at the wheel, thinking how beautiful she was in all ways when I noticed my own wrist, lying on my thigh, held it up to compare and found it the same as hers. Was I finding my own beauty undeniable by finding it in her?

She just smiled. No need to answer, and it was true, I knew there was no-one like me.

'Have you noticed just how similar we are, physically I mean, in so many little ways?' I asked. 'It's almost creepy. I was just looking at our wrists and hands. We could be sisters.'

'Unidentical twins even. It's fascinating. But what I like best is the eyes—I look at you and I see me, I pull back and it's not me, but at some level I am never sure. Where do you begin and I end?'

'But have you loved someone the same? That's what I mean.'

She turned her eyes, my eyes, from the road to briefly hold mine. 'No. There is only one of you. I've felt many things in my time, but nothing so deep as this.' She smiled. 'It's all way beyond my control or understanding; fine by me. Life on the edge, the only place to live.'

It was morning now, full-lit, and another day, my first as another person, and we were entering the mountains somewhere past Geneva, practising our old Liverpool accents like a couple of tarts out for a bevvy down the Dingle and howling with laughter at our own great humour. Just talkin' like that made me laugh, and y'know, that's where we both came from, like, so we could do it great, ya know worrImeanlike? And to tell the truth, it sorta stuck, like, and that's how we gorralong for a while, in like our own secret dead funny language, but it was no code in which we could speak our language of the heart.

'So tell me, cousin, have you always been sweet on other girls.' This whole business of love for woman was a new one for me, you see, and I had some catching up to do.

She said nothing, filled her time overtaking a giant truck which was labouring up the slope as we were flying. I paused, reached over and stroked her hair. It was so wonderful to be so free.

'You don't like to talk about yourself?' I asked.

She shrugged.

'Even with me?'

She reached over and pulled me to her, so my head was buried in her neck—while we were driving over one of the highest bridges I had ever seen, with rivers and valleys and trees way below, plunging deeper into the high mountains, travelling just a little slower than our accustomed space rocket speed, but not much—so I could smell her lovely skin, feel her body warmth. I ran a finger down the line of her jaw, down her neck, over her collar bone, and then down to the curve of her breast, curiously touching that softness of another woman for the first time.

She reached down and kissed me quickly on the forehead.

'If this is some sort of test,' she said. 'I'm failing. Maybe it's safer if I tell you of the kiss that led to the kiss that brought us here today.

It's true that I keep myself to myself, but you are different, you are so inherently close that to tell you about myself does not violate my own inner trust.'

Strangely, it all made sense. I was not at all tired, and the shifting moods and the delight of our dance together, along with the sun breaking through a gap in the clouds to light up the great mountains all around, made me feel alive, awake, and full of the joy of life. I was entering an area of privilege and secret trust, and my heart warmed. I moved back to my own seat and said:

'Tell me.'

We were now over the long bridge in the air and were tearing through tunnels cut into the side of the mountain, flashing in and out, darkness and sunshine, darkness and sunshine, and she was driving outrageously fast, playing with the colours and the light and me.

'It was some years ago,' she began. 'I am no longer interested in times and dates and ages, it's all part of me and exists not in the past but now, my memories being my present. I'd been living with Enzo, the already famous Enzo, the Charlie in a way of my early years who taught me so much and grew me up so fast.'

'What did he teach you?'

'Oh, about dreams and realities, about what goes on in the hearts of men, and women, and me. He dangled a lifestyle in front of me, girl from the Dingle who knew nothing of these things—elegance and beauty, refinement and courtliness, perfidy and sin. I learned well, fell into the trap, lapped up the thin flattery of this rich Italian aristocrat and believed, hoped he would marry me and make me his Contessa, and that all his delightful friends thought I was just wonderful. Now, of course I know the sort of thing that they must have said behind my back. Makes me blush to think of it.'

'Then came the inevitable day when the truth was revealed in all its glory in the form of another girl, so much more beautiful than me—there's always someone more beautiful than you—and I was out on my own again, ranting with tears and recriminations, not so much for the man I'd lost but for the shame I'd found and the lifestyle I'd lost. That time and that man left me with a taste for elegance and beauty that I thought could never be satisfied in the damp North of England, till I set eyes on you.'

'So what did I do when unforeseen realities made me homeless? I did what I do best, I hit the road. I'm a wanderer, as you can see, a traveller at heart, and when times get hard I move. I left all the fine clothes and bits and pieces in storage with a friend and bought a ticket east, a single to Bangkok, not just inspired I think by old romantic memories of movies of the King of Siam, but rather by some ancient longing deep in my bones. I'd always yearned to go to the Orient and I now I wanted to be as far as I could from bloody Enzo. I had money, from bloody Enzo, no-one else to cling to, nowhere else I would rather be, so off I went.'

It was odd, the way she was telling her tale, as if she'd never done it before and was a touch uncertain about how it was done, no matter how well she spoke, and she kept on driving and driving the way she did, flashing her lights at those in her way and indifferent to the squeals of men in lesser cars who were overtaken by a woman. Her eyes were mostly, and necessarily, on the road ahead, the snow-covered mountains all around, snow by the side of the road itself now.

She kept shooting glances at me, and I knew that she was letting me in closer and sooner than any human being yet. It was one more move into the heart of my Alessia, one more move into the heart of myself.

'I wandered round South-East Asia, finding my place the moment I stepped off the plane in Bangkok and smelled the East. Do you think we have lived before as other people in other lives? I do. I know that in some way I was coming home to a place I knew. But it was only when, after wandering over half of South-East Asia, I arrived in what we call The Island—it has a name, but not for now—that I felt I had arrived where I belonged, that I'd come home at last. The people there took me in as one of their own, made me feel I was right and this was my place and my immediate past faded as I moved into this slow, sensual lifestyle full of dance and music and art, babies and good humour.

'I met men, as I always used to so easily in the days when I was still long-haired, fresh-skinned and happy to please, moved in with a circle of artists and writers who lived in and around the forest, and felt this was the life of lives. I then began to feel that the rich Milanese life I thought was the ultimate was a thin yet elegant veneer over no depth at all, but now I had arrived. And no, I had not even the tiniest of ideas that ever once would I have any sort of intimate relations with women. The idea never passed through my mind.

'Then I met Luisa. She was an interesting woman, half Javanese, half Brazilian, and all artist. She had a wonderful house, one of those combinations of the best of the East with the best of the West, all polished wood and Javanese batik, light and shade, hibiscus and bubbling fountains, and I began to hang out around her place and watch her paint. She was in her mid-thirties, I suppose, and one of the most striking looking women I had ever seen; dark, fast, intense, short-haired, long-limbed. She seemed to speak all languages equally, had travelled to all parts of the world, knew about myths and ancient religions and educated me in ways that gods and goddesses, heroes and villains and demons lived within all of us. She played music to me on a lute and showed me the basics of the rhythms of drums. She could dance too, had danced the traditional dances when she was a child but said she was too old for them now, although she looked wonderful to me when she showed me what she claimed she couldn't do.

'Believe me, in all honestly, as I was drawn in, entranced, mesmerised by this fascinating and beautiful creature I was still entirely innocent. I thought my own fascination was just natural fascination; after all she was, and still is, a remarkable person, a very special soul, and I learned all I know about the rich textures of life and art and religion and myself sitting round her house, cooking Nasi Goreng and living in sarongs. She opened up new worlds for me, opened this world for me, opened up the rich depths of myself to me.

'The Island is like that. I think maybe it's somehow half in the land of the spirits, a place where the gods are still free to roam, where magic happens easily and we can see into the world behind the world, the world of strange forces, loves, demons, ghosts, art, enchantment.

'Luisa talked to me, hour after hour, took me to see the men who carved the best statues of the Gods, showed me girls learning to dance, had dinners with men and women who painted and carved and wrote and talked themselves far into the night about the things of mystery and beauty that are so natural when you surrender to the spirit. All of this was new to the me I had lived, but easy to take on, as if it was a reminder of what I'd always known somewhere in my depths but had lost track of, so it was familiar, my own, and loved.

'Then she took me to different places on the Island, to secret temples, caves, great ceremonies where lines of people gathered to witness the dawn, and music was played, dances danced. We swam at dawn in mountain lakes; saw things Westerners saw, saw things they never saw in a companionship that filled my waking hours with magic and my sleep with coloured dreams.

'It was the most wonderful of times of my life, and it was from there that I sent postcards to you, a little girl I'd never quite forgotten on the other side of the world, trudging off to school in a dark English winter.'

'I'm glad you did,' I said.

'Me too.'

We were climbing now, zig-zagging up to the mid reaches of Mont Blanc, approaching the tunnel which would take us through to Italy, and this exotic cousin of mine, my lover, seemed lost as she drove, part of her in memories and dreams from another time, way on the other side of our world, which stirred something in my heart too. The surprising thought passed through my mind; had I once been part of her life at that time as well? Had we once had lives in that place that suddenly seemed like a home I had never been to, and in some bewildering way was returning to now? As she spoke odd currents of feeling and thought strayed through me, as if memories were trying to emerge from a past beyond the past I knew, and I too was lost in another time and another place, one I had not been to this life, but was returning to now.

'Then one time she took me to the other side of the island to meet an ancient Mexican lady who had lived on the Island for sixty years, a poet and cook who had a ramshackle house full of mangy dogs on a black sand beach up which turtles crawled at night to lay their eggs. The magic and mysteries of that time and place seemed never ending and I thought by then I had tasted them all, but the best was yet to come.

'That night we stayed in a little guest-house in a place perched on the lip of the crater of a long-extinct volcano. This crater is huge, maybe fifteen, twenty miles around, and when we arrived as the sun was going down we could look into the crater and see lakes, people working and living their lives in what was once a pool of fire, a life going on down there, and in the centre a new volcano, a much smaller affair altogether, sticking craggily up into the air. All well and good. We ate, talked, and went to bed early.

'Then, in the middle of the night I was woken by the sound of my name.

"Alessia, Alessia," Luisa was whispering. "Wake up. I want to show you something."

I was with her in a moment, swung off my bed and was led by the hand outside. The first thing I saw was the silhouette of the statue of an ancient God, stark black against a bright full moon, bulging eyes, fangs, full of life and power. The suddenness of this sight shocked me for a half-asleep moment, in time to gather myself to be fully awake to see the vision of another world which opened up before me.

'The sky was cloudless and full of a million stars, the moon, as I said, was full and silver bright. The great wide crater had filled to the brim with fleecy clouds, feathery and pale in the moonlight, and in the centre of the clouds the new volcano stuck up starkly through their softness, and it was erupting, cracking and banging and sending up smoking chunks of glowing lava in arcs through the clear sky, leaving trails of smoke where they passed, and the whole scene; the carved god, the crater, the clouds, the moon, the stars, the volcano, the orange fire, all made a scene that was out of another world.

'Luisa stood next to me as we wordlessly gazed at this transcendental vision, put her hand round my waist, and naturally I moved in closer to her, so as to share the body warmth of this great woman. She pulled me in gently a little closer, and I melded into her body, the way we do with the ones we love. We stood watching for a while, drinking in this scene that we knew would never be repeated this life, then, in the most simple way you could imagine she turned, caught my eye with a smile of a quality I had never known before, slipped her hand under my hair to take my neck in her gentle grasp, drew my face softly towards hers and kissed me deeply, on the lips and with great sensuous joy.

'For a moment I was shocked—never in my life did I think that I would ever kiss a woman like that—but the feeling was so wonderful that I instantly relaxed and took what was mine, and we stood under the waxing moon with a volcano erupting in celebration, and I understood that I was in love.

'It was the kiss that started everything, and it felt like no ordinary kiss, to me it was full of magic power, blessed by the ancient gods, and it touched me to the depths of my soul. From that moment, life could never be the same again.'

'Just like with me,' I said. 'It was the same kiss.'

'Yes,' said Alessia. 'The magic of that kiss, you understand completely, in the only way one can. Luisa knew too; she knew all about such mystical things, maybe it was her blood, a mixture of geomancer, shaman and Portuguese artist, who knows, but I do know that night we went back to our room and made love and I reached levels of pure happiness I never knew could be found on this earth. Then later we talked, and she told me of how she knew I was coming before I arrived, how the signs had been revealed to her in the stars and the voice of the sea, that we had been lovers before, as other persons breathing other breaths that she had glimpsed through windows in time, and this was the fulfilment of what was left undone in lives gone by.

'I am convinced she was right; we had a naturalness together which could only have come with more time than we had had. I moved in with her, shared her house and her life, and in that magic time she passed on to me as much as she could of what she knew, about the messages of stars and the language of animals, about art, passion and love. She opened my eyes to the spirits and the forces of nature in the world around me, in trees and wind and the call of birds, about how nothing is chance, how every move we make, every person we meet is a small ripple in a greater destiny.

'Then one night when we were walking down a road in the darkness of one of those hot tropical nights when in the paddy fields all around were a million frogs singing, in the air above were countless million fireflies dancing, and in the moonless sky above them were a blaze of eternity of stars, she told me that one day I would meet the other half of my soul, and I would know who this was because at that time we would greet each other with the same kiss, and that the fruit of that kiss would be fire, love and freedom.'

Chapter 14

We were now in the pale rock, water-dripping tunnel under Mont Blanc, Monte Bianco, the White Mountain, the channel between France and Italy, the past and the future. We drove slowly and in silence.

'So you think we're two halves of one soul?' I asked, my mind racing, my body filled with the oddest sensation of manic joy on a foundation of quiet completion. Time had passed enough from the telling of her tale for me to digest, ruminate, then hold up the crux of the whole matter in the cold, pinkish light of that channel we were passing through, to try to make sense of an idea that held all sense and no sense at all.

'How can we ever know?' Alessia said. 'Just to think of it fills me with the strangest of feelings, a deep fulfilment mixed with a kind of mad ecstasy. I've never felt anything like this before and am not struggling to understand the incomprehensible. What does this all mean? Is it true or is it just one more delusion? All I know now is to go with the voice of the heart and know that you are more than the rest of the world together.'

We drove on through that oppressive tunnel, countless millions of tons of rock over us, and it felt to me as if I was being squeezed, compressed, while I tried to grasp this idea of being just the one inner entity, that Alessia and I were, in fact, not separate. Funny thing was, in some way I couldn't fathom it made perfect sense. While in most ways I'd ever known it didn't make any sense at all. But you see, a whole new deep old magic had entered my being, flooding into me, and with it had come the power to see and know what had previously been unseen and unknown, and my faith in the new, that deeper part of me that had been touched on by the gods, opened and made my own, was becoming more me than the past with every mile passed, every breath breathed. If I hadn't been my Alessia before, then soon I would be.

The gloomy tunnel seemed to stretch on forever. I felt I could hardly breathe, my chest tight, my breathing short. For once we had no choice but to creep along at the pace of the rest of the world, for once our lightning flight restrained, constricted, and it seemed never ending. Alessia reached over and took my hand in hers. I knew without her saying that she could feel every last tiny spark and ache of what I was feeling, and felt truly un-alone at the deepest level of what I was for the first time this life, and in consequence truly comforted.

'Not long now,' she said. 'Not too long and we'll be through the tunnel and into the light.'

'Whatever happened to Luisa? How long did you live with her?' I asked, my mind still alive with the colours of her life in the distant East.

'Almost three years. It seemed like a lifetime and was gone in a flash. I left her a different person. The end was very simple; she had to go to New York for an exhibition of her paintings, I needed a new visa for Indonesia, and we both knew our time had run out—we were aware this was going to happen and had talked about it openly, and so we went our separate ways. We had fulfilled what had to be fulfilled, we were complete, and we had separate paths to our different futures. It hurt but it was true, so I could never feel regret, just sadness.'

'You really loved her, didn't you?'

'I love her to this day.'

Ahead of us was a pinhole of brightness; at last, the light at the end of the tunnel.

'How can we know? Are we really the one person?' It's all I could think of. 'Is this just mad romance, or is it the sort of simple fact of life I had never before known?' For some reason the whole of existence seemed to weigh down on me for one tight moment in time, then all of a sudden the light grew and in a flash there we were in expanded relief, out in the open air on the Italian side of the mountain. The sun was shining softly through high clouds, and as we accelerated away and down the slope that would lead us to the sea the dark oppression that came with that tunnel fell away, and I was filled immediately with hope, freshness, and a heart full of joyful expectation.

'Let me drive now,' I said. 'Let's stop for one of those Italian coffees that you love, then it's my turn. I don't feel tired at all.'

We stopped at a phoney log cabin Alpine restaurant for coffee and sandwiches, Alessandra stretching and rubbing her eyes as she left the car. 'We've been travelling forever,' she said. 'I can hardly remember living any other way.'

'You could remember that island.'

She took me by the arm, shivering slightly in the chill morning air, and grinned. 'Sweetheart, that was living this way.'

'Was it the same kiss, then?'

We pushed open the door of the restaurant and entered an empty room. 'Never the same kiss,' she said. 'And I love the touch of jealousy. More like the same gods were behind the magic touch; it was like a gift from her to me and then to you.'

'Thanks, Luisa.'

'Yeah, thanks Luisa.' She paused in herself and her eyes went vague and I watched her go back in time to the flavour of an earlier love. We took a seat with a view over a car park and a dull stretch of valley wall and Alessia suddenly shouted a torrent of Italian, which was answered in kind from some invisible source.

'So why Charlie?' She had to ask sometime.

'It was more like why not. And I really had—still have—a real love for the guy. Tell the truth I'm a touch confused; I don't know what I think.'

'Regrets?'

'About running off with you? No.' I looked around—the invisible waiter was still invisible, so I leaned over the table and kissed her, not with great passion, it was an early in the morning kiss, brimming with sweet affection. She really liked it—and so did I.

'While you were living this amazing life with the woman of the goddesses, there I was slaving away in offices, going home on the bus in the rain, fighting off men I had no interest in and wondering what the point of it all was.'

'Simple; to bring you to here, the same as me, and who knows what the future might hold. Not long now, this is the final run, get down to the Autostrada and we're home and dry in no time.'

Once more we were on the eternal road. The scene changed, the language changed, the weather changed, but the car stayed the same and we stayed the same in it. We could have been in a movie, watching the changing sets, all of it unreal, one scene following another, on and on eternally, and in one sense maybe we were.

'I'd like to have my hair cut like yours,' I said suddenly. 'I'd like to look even more like you.'

'If you want,' she answered, simple and unquestioning. 'Make it even more like making love to myself.'

She unlocked her seat belt and moved over towards me—and remember we're driving at 120 again, not a speed to play round at, although after the first few hours it feels like nothing at all—and began to stroke my hair. Then she kissed the skin along the line of my silk top—my jacket was on the seat behind—running the tip of her tongue from my shoulder and up my neck. The car swerved wildly—the feelings she brought up in me were too much to bear, never mind drive sanely with—and another car blared its horn as its driver shook his fist and cursed.

'Ah, Italia,' she said, and proceeded to kiss me gently, with exquisite attention, on the soft and delicate spot below my ear where the blood runs deep. It felt electric; my instincts were to close my eyes and surrender to love. 'Men,' she said, 'certainly have their place in this world. But there is nothing like the skin of a woman.'

I'd slowed right down to a crawl, barely able to steer in a straight line. 'More,' I said, my body coursing with ecstasy.

She rolled her eyes and kissed me briefly on the lips, then sat up in her own seat once more. The show was over for now. I changed down and accelerated back up to cruising speed, slower now in the denser traffic of the working day.

'Do you know what we're going to see tonight?' she asked. 'Did I ever actually tell you what we're tearing across Europe to witness?'

'Not a word.'

'Wagner,' she said. 'You know Wagner?'

I shook my head. 'No'

'Good. Nevertheless, you need to know the story. Die Valkyrie is its name, played by the best orchestra, sung by the best singers, with the best conductor, the best everything in the world just for this one occasion. Not to be missed. I know it's for us, I just know for some reason I have not yet grasped that we have to be there, that it too was pre-ordained and part of the essential pattern of things.'

'For us? Which way at this junction?'

'To the right. Just follow the signs for Milano. Now listen, and don't take fright as you hear the story, have faith that our tale is our own and the only good outcome of our love is more love. Such is the fruit of being true to the urgings of our heart.'

Again, movements of forces within me that once I had no idea were mine, began to stir, and I was grateful for the need to focus on the road ahead—and even the road behind, as these Italian men did not take kindly to women who were faster than they.

'The story of Die Valkyrie could have come from an Indonesian myth,' she said. 'In fact, at the deepest of levels the two become one, in the way all the myths of the world become one, and where they become one is in the heart of our hearts.'

She paused, and I could feel her gathering herself, while in me, as we were approaching the end of our journey that at some level in myself I wanted never to end, I felt a growing trepidation, an uncertainty; not about the past, and the outrages I had perpetrated, but about the shape of the oncoming future. My God, what seeds had I sown?

'This is all part of a greater story, a story for another time.'

'Which?' I asked. 'Die Valkyrie or our own?'

She smiled, that smile for which I would give the cities of Tashkent and Samarkand. 'Both,' she said. 'Siegmund is the boy, the man, and he finds himself in flight through a dark forest, comes to a lonely homestead, steps inside and falls asleep, to wake up to Sieglinde, the girl, and, of course, they fall in love. But the path of true love is never easy, right? Also there is the husband, the great warrior Hunding, who is less than keen on what he rightly senses is going on. But those who fall deeply and quickly in love are more than a little mad, right?'

'Right.' I laughed nervously.

'So Sieglinde drops a sleeping draft in her husband's evening drink, Siegmund seizes the magic sword and off they go.'

'The magic sword?'

'The magic sword. To cut a long story short, this sword was left embedded in a tree, impossible to pluck out for all but an unknown brave hero, guess who. So Siegmund grabs the sword, grabs the girl, and just before they flee off into the night, he realises that she's his one and only long-lost twin sister.'

'This sounds vaguely familiar.' The odd undercurrents of trepidation I had been avoiding so neatly up to that point in time began to rise in me.

'Then the lovers flee into the night. When the husband wakes up, naturally enough, being a warrior, off he goes after them.'

'Did you know that Charlie is, or was, a soldier?'

'No,' said Alessia. 'I didn't. It's just a story, a drama with music, relax.'

'So is ours. Which reminds me, put the tape on again, my love. I miss Callas, it's too quiet in this car without her. And I'm not taking fright, I just want to hear that passion again. Do all operas end in death?'

'Not all, but many. A twist in the tale of Die Valkyrie is that the father of the lovers, the twins, is the great God Wotan, and he is forced to send his Valkyrie, his war-maiden Brünnhilde, to aid the cause of the wronged husband.'

'Why? Surely love is love?'

'Ah,' said Alessia. 'But the romantic love of brother and sister is unholy love, and cannot be countenanced. Therefore the father of the twins, Wotan himself, has to punish them.'

'Sounds rotten to me. Which way do we go now?'

'Follow Milano Centro. This is wonderful timing, I wonder if anyone has ever driven here so quickly. And yes, Siegmund has to die. But enough of this for now. There is beauty and passion without death, our world, our living myth, is a different place, and our gods are more forgiving.'

'So our love is not unholy?' Despite myself, despite the certainty which had made leaving all of my life in a moment without thought of a look behind, a touch of desperation had entered my heart. Why did we have to face such demons? Surely to God we were well in what we were doing? Was it never possible for there to be a simple and unalloyed life, where love was love and in its naive openness there was nothing left but springtime?

'No,' said Alessia fiercely. 'Our love is pure; the uncertainties are merely fuel for the fire in which we can further purify our gold. I love you with all my heart.'

Once more, as so often happened at that time when we were riding the needle-point of fate and synchronicity with all that was around was the norm, Callas hit a heart-thrust of pure passion coloured with sadness and grief and I began to cry yet again, just tears rolling down my cheeks without sobs. It was as if there was an ancient and unspoken grief for some heart-felt loss that I never knew was mine, never knew existed, and now it had risen from my darkest depths to fill me with some exquisite sadness which was now being expunged by love. The form my love for myself had taken, Alessia who shared my blood, once more dabbed away my tears with that tenderness that she was teaching me to accept as my own.

'Pull in at the next place, my love,' she said. 'I'll drive the last stretch, it's my home ground. No more driving for you.'

More coffee for the travellers at a filling station on the Autostrada, this time with comments and eyes from moustachioed truck drivers and other travelling men at the bar, fun for us both; if only they knew.

'Is this where you live? Milano? Surely even you have home somewhere?'

She laughed. 'No, I don't live here. And yes, I do have a home, a sort of studio, a secret place just for me. Soon for you too. In Venice, Venezia. We'll go there soon, it's our true destination. I think you'll like it, it's full of my things, art from Bali, from Luisa, and a million other beautiful things I picked up in other parts of my life.'

'When can we go? How soon?' All of a sudden I was desperate for a destination, a safe place, a feathered nest, a warm home in which to be with my new and ancient love.

In front of the leering men she kissed me sweetly on the lips; there was not a trace of shame in her. 'Tomorrow,' she said. 'We'll go tomorrow.' Then we smiled at those men who muttered and gaped as we stalked out, back to the dear swift car, dirty and travel-worn now from the long road it had eaten, and started its tireless engine one last time this time.

Moments later we were on the road once again, slow now as we entered the smaller arteries of Milan on the last of the long ride from Parkgate, the high speed chase over now in the traffic of the big city.

The tape of Madame Butterfly ran out once more; its time over for now as well, at least for now, and I watched the dull suburbs of the city of Milan pass by the window, reminding me of watching the suburbs of Chester pass by the window of the bridal Rolls. Yesterday? Could that have been just yesterday? It was unbelievable, incredible that any of that life should have existed at all. Incredible too that it all should have seemed real, a firm life that was my all. What had happened? I wondered. Is life truly as fragile as all that? Is the whole thing no more than a thin dance on a moving screen, with its certainties eradicable at the snap of a finger? In that case, was it the same folly that led me to believe in my present joy? The whole of life felt baseless, no more than a dance of coloured light creating illusions for me to call myself, but in that rootlessness was the clearest happiness I had ever known. Alessia, or the time which created Alessia, had changed all of how I saw life to be. It was like being in one movie, blinking, and then finding myself in another, which made neither, or both, unreal.

As we threaded our way through the hooting traffic, I wondered about Charlie, found myself fingering the rings on my finger, watching my diamonds flash and feeling odd tugs on the heart, confusions of pain and freedom, anger at his blow, gratitude because it was the gift of freedom, guilt for my selfish madness, certainty because of my certain love and the wonder of the new world that had opened for me. All of a sudden I was tired, so tired, after all the hours of high-strung energy my reserves were depleted and I was exhausted to the depths of my being.

'Can we sleep soon?' I asked.

'Of course, love,' she answered. 'Minutes away now.'

She was right. This was a place she knew. She forced her way through mad traffic by use of the horn and sheer courage to take a parking place from a furious man, and even lowered her window to trade insults with him before he accepted defeat and raced off snarling. Then she turned off the engine and turned to me.

'Made it,' she said. 'In time for lunch. And a nap.'

The apartment of her old lover Enzo was in an old building in a narrow street that looked like nothing from the outside, but from the inside was a gleaming palace of marble, simple furniture that reeked of simple money, pictures from heaven and a charming hunk of man, much older than I imagined, grey at the temples, elegant to the fingertips, and, as Alessia said, very beautiful. He spoke delightful English, straight out of a thirties movie.

'Enchanted, enchanted, so beautiful, like another Alessia.'

He regretted having to leave, an assignation he could not possibly break and so on, could he leave us with the houseboy? Please to take the two rooms at the end.

'We'll just need the one,' said Alessia. 'My old room, OK?'

Not even a raise of eyebrow from Enzo to justify my faint embarrassment but rather a courtly gesture of invitation to whatever we wanted. Then he left, smiling and expressing unending regret and we were alone in the quiet, for once no vibration, for once nowhere to go. We'd arrived. I felt very strange, for once the stranger in another world, but it was clearly Alessia's world, and in no time her ease of being in it became my own. It was all very beautiful.

'This is all very beautiful,' I said, looking round. Its artistic simplicity, the perfection of every nuance of colour and texture made the Browns and their heavy, polished oaken life look like country cousins. 'Is this how you've been living? Bit of a change from where we came from.'

'It was always natural for me,' she said. 'I like style. Come here.'

Then we kissed once more, for the first time not stolen, hurried, or dangerous, and we could afford to linger. What was it about her strong, soft body that made me feel that way? A kiss alone from Alessia was enough to make me want to faint, swoon from pleasure. What she said was true; there was some quality in our togetherness which was beyond separateness, and the physical closeness which approached a kind of melding of the sameness of our flesh, was no more than an approach to some greater oneness.

'Maybe we are the one being,' I said to her. 'There was a moment back there when I felt I had lost myself completely, that I had almost merged back into you. Do you feel like this?'

'Oh, yes,' she replied. 'We've come very close to abandonment.'

'Your loves before? Were they like this?'

'No. They were fine, wonderful, but not with this quality of mystical savage splendour, made truly wonderful by the possibility of losing myself in you completely.'

'You are so wonderful,' I said, 'oh cousin of mine. What have I done to deserve you?'

'It isn't a question of what you've done or not done,' she said, smoothing my hair back from my face. 'It's a question of who you are, what you are.'

'Will you show me more of your wonderful world?'

She laughed, open and free. 'Nothing more wonderful than to show you to yourself,' she said. 'How about a shower? I'll wash you.'

Then we stopped speaking and went into this shower fit for an Emperor, where we washed off the journey and the remains of our pasts, each one washing the other, with that exquisite, electric tenderness which was the mark of our love, dried each other with scented towels, then she led me to the great bed, fresh and white and cool, and we slipped between the sheets together, wrapped in each other's arms, our matching bodies touching from head to toe, and fell asleep cocooned in the sweetest of innocence, like little children.

Chapter 15

Now remember that the last time I'd slept was the night before the last when I'd woken up after a nightful of fevered dreams in the Brown's house on the icy morning of my wedding day. So when I came to in this strange bed in a strange room after the deepest short sleep of my life, I was more than confused, I almost had no idea who I was. No wonder; I wasn't who I used to be. Next to me, inches away, sleeping so sweet I could have died, was the single most loveable human being, or perhaps divine being, I had ever encountered in all my life.

I lay there in the warmth as my mind slowly reassembled the unfamiliar facts so I knew where I was, who I was, what I was doing, while I looked closely at Alessia in detail, in a way I only could because she was asleep. I found her entirely fascinating, beautiful in a fashion I had never known—not just classical of feature, but entrancing in poise, depth, wisdom, humour, sensuality, style .... I caught myself, carrying on like a besotted lover, and smiled to myself. Well, it's what I was. A woman lover of a woman. A cousin lover of a cousin. That very cousin of mine that I hadn't seen for years and was so hoping would make it to the wedding. Unbelievable. Life would never feel safe and predictable again.

She was lying with one arm draped over me, both of us naked as the day we were born. I made an attempt to wriggle free, then realised I didn't want to and sank back into her warmth. I thought of Tracy, my friend with the perfect house and car and husband and life, and wondered what she would make of it all, what she would make of me, and started to giggle to myself. So much for a life of bitching about all the perfection of life over cream cakes in the conservatory. Trying to restrain myself made the giggling even worse. To tell the truth, thinking of my narrow escape from what every girl wants into the mad freedom of what this girl wanted after all turned my giggles into laughter. After a while Alessia, who used to be my cousin Alexandra in a life gone by, opened her eyes inches from mine, the eyes that were unnervingly like my very own, and once more I was lost, entranced, as her vivid life force seized me anew.

It took her a much shorter time to arrive at our current reality than I did, and I watched with interest and pleasure as she focused in on me; the moment of questioning, the moment of recognition, followed by that easy wide smile I would cross the earth for, coming to be just inches from my own. It was like watching the dawning of the most beautiful of days.

'Nowhere to drive to, beautiful,' I said.

She kissed me lightly on the nose—she is a great kisser, that one—then closed her eyes and snuggled in deeper to me. I couldn't believe how lovely her sweet body felt to me. How come I'd missed this whole section of human possibility all these years? It simply never crossed my mind, that's why, never once did I think of it, but believe me, I had now.

'How about this opera business,' I said. 'Don't we have a short time, things to fix, places to go ....'

'Oh, sod it,' she said without opening her eyes. 'I'd rather stay in bed with you.'

But in time we sat up, examined each other, looked at the time, decided we were ravenous, went to the bathroom, dressed.

'Eat in or out?' she asked. 'We can do either.'

'To tell the truth, cousin, I don't know. This is your world, you decide.'

'Out.' She was brushing her hair at a mirror set in gold, and caught my eye in the reflection, smiled and said, 'I want to show you off.'

I felt shy at the force of her current of love, and pleased of course, but hesitant of my unschooled self in her sophisticated world. It was all very well for her, she was oddly besotted by me, and I knew that the power of the love that she had for me coloured her vision, in the way that love does. At the same time I had such trust, such deep faith in her—more than any other person in my life, after so short a time that seemed forever—that I knew all would be well.

Once more we stood together at a mirror, the black and the red once more, but you know what we'd done? We'd changed; now I was in the black and she was in the red. The clothes fitted perfectly either way; the boundaries between us, never firm and strong, were melting, and with the melting an unbelievably even greater happiness swelled to contain us both.

'Remember the mirror in the Brown's?' I asked.

'You in that wedding dress, how could I forget?'

A pause. 'I wonder how Charlie's doing.'

Her eyes narrowed and she looked at me intensely. 'I'm sure we'll find out, sooner or later, probably sooner. Remember to have faith. Look at me and Enzo; ten years ago we were homicidal, now the best of trusted friends.'

'Homicidal, now there's a word. I wonder if that's how Charlie feels. It reminds me of how much I don't want to see his mother.' The passing thought of the power of her wrath clouded my bright world with darkness. I took in a great breath and sighed it out. 'There was no choice'.

'There was no choice,' she agreed. 'It was beyond the two of us.'

'Or beyond the one of us.'

She looked at me in a way that made my heart turn—such passion, such love, tenderness, compassion; all of the great qualities of the heart joined in a single look.

'You know, if I had my hair cut like yours I could almost be you. Dressed like this.'

'We can try. It is Saturday, not easy.'

'Maybe we are magic.'

'Not maybe; for sure; the only question is what kind of magic, and what miracle it will create next.'

With that the magic twins entered the world of Milano on that drear Saturday the sixth of November, the shops and restaurants shining bright in the low light, and we walked arm in arm, getting so close now in heart that it felt wrong, strange, unbecoming, to be any more separate than need be even in body even for a moment.

The sleep—and it was no more than two hours—had made me feel I had entered a new day. The whole of my normal reality had shifted; days were longer and shorter, I was no longer who I used to be, I loved a woman, I was in Italy, the past belonged to someone who had died on her wedding day, the future belonged to ecstatic gods of love that I had never known till the kiss by the fire that was the end of a world. All of this seemed more natural to me than all the life I had lived before, because now, despite the blazing wreckage of all I was lying behind me, along with inevitable consequences looming round some oncoming corner, I had not the faintest of doubts of the truth and correctness of the life I was living.

We ate in a busy restaurant where Alessia was known, greeted like a lost love. My own tinge of self-doubt in her world fled as I was taken in immediately with the same affection, my coat removed with infinite care, seats pulled out, and waiters who seemed like moustachioed uncles opened napkins for us, fussed as if we were the only and most dear of customers in the world, threw their hands in the air and made cries of Italian joy and wonder at me the cousin of Alessia, took orders for God knows what, brought drinks, and left us to ourselves.

'To us,' said Alessia, raising her glass. 'Welcome to my world.'

We drank to our single self, and I looked around at this new planet she had brought me to; busy, lively, noisy, passionate, and I thought of Charlie with a pang. He loved that kind of place.

'It's not that I don't love him,' I said, and she knew who I was talking about. 'It's just a different kind of love.'

'Ah,' said the divine one. 'It's one of the lessons I learned from Luisa, who understood all such things. I remember sitting with her in the warmth of a tropical night that seemed beyond time and listening to her talk, on and on, about the different kinds and flavours of love.'

'How come I've never thought about or talked about such things before? What have I been thinking of all my life? I can think of my love for you, for Charlie, both quite distinct; does it go on?'

'In infinite colours, it seems; father for son, son for mother, man for man, woman for woman, man for life, girl for woman—like me and Luisa—on it goes; some short in life, some long, some turbulent, some smooth, some passionate, some cool ....'

'Which is the greatest? The one you're living now?'

'That, and love for yourself.'

Along with, for me the love for her, the passion for her, the love for her wisdom, kindness, strength, the love of her love. Never before that kiss had I known or even thought of such things. I was in the same world but a different world. The world had changed because I had changed, in essential vibration, opening of heart, becoming true to me. It was like putting on new glasses which brought a once hazy but accustomed world into focus. Now I looked around and all I could see is what was always there but somehow concealed by my own hesitations and fears; love in different forms and moods, textures and colours. So this was being in love, I thought, it's a literal thing like being in Milan, it's where I was and all I could see.

'If you could live a thousand thousand years, what would you choose to do, who would you be?' I asked, sipping on a glass of golden wine and nibbling piquant little pieces of I have no idea what.

'I've already chosen. And what I am and what I have is so sweet and true there is no room for even a single regret.'

'You seem to have no doubts, no fear of what might come, no

fear of the consequences of our maybe unholy love, no fear of Charlie and what he might do, no fear of unknown futures.' I was fascinated by her; she was a creature from another universe and I was probing into her being, looking for the source of her qualities so that maybe I could make them mine.

Alessia, she had become Alessia to me now completely, any idea of a past identity vanished along with a vanished name, swirled her wine in her glass, took a sip, looked at me even and long, and said, 'I've had the good fortune to have faced most of my fears, and once our inner demons have been faced, eyeball to eyeball, they disappear. What seemed real instantly becomes unreal and we realise our chains were of our own making. It's not easy, but it seems to be the only way through. It's the path you are on yourself, travelling with me at the speed we do. Now I can be here with you and our destiny—which could be anything, anything at all, I honestly have no more of an idea of the future than you. Through all manner of events, all of them the astonishing consequences of my ruthless commitment to knowing myself, I have given myself to the hidden force that rules my destiny.'

'I understand completely. In a flash I have joined you, it's what follows faith and trust. We might have minutes or we might have a lifetime.'

'Precisely. So let's eat.'

Then we ate and we ate as if food was going out of style, and we ate well, believe me. And we chatted of trivia, small things, girl things; face creams, favourite perfumes, the price of clothes in Milan, and then we were done. More expressions of long-lost love and impassioned thanks from our avuncular waiters and we were on the street, the next scene in the changing drama, a dull Milanese street on a dull afternoon turning to evening with the fading of the light. Along with, for me, some confusion; we had hared across Europe for the performance of an opera—or so it seemed—and now we were here it was as if we had all the time in the world.

'Do you think there's any time to try for a haircut, cousin?' I asked. 'I don't want to miss our Wagner.'

'All the time in the world,' she said. 'Actually, it's already begun, we're missing it as we speak.'

'Missing it?' My mind looped. 'Still we have time for a haircut?'

'These Wagner pieces go on forever,' she said. 'Hours and hours. The last act is the best for me, and long enough. Let's try my old friend Mario, my first great hairdresser. His place is near here. It's a shot in the dark, but he's a sweetheart and he's the best. Nothing less for you.' She kissed me on the cheek, and I vanished for a moment into the tiny coolness that lingered on my flesh for a passing infinite moment.

Milan seemed to me to be a dreary city, not at all a place of romance, with glimpses of wealth and style here and there as we walked, but mostly a business town with all the allure of Manchester.

'So this isn't your city?'

'Oh, no, not Milano. My place is Venice—Venezia we should call it now we are in Italy. Like I said, we'll go there tomorrow.'

'Why Venice, Venezia?'

'It's a question I have myself, Michelle. Something of the sadness and beauty of the place, the style and the ancient art—a city built on water that has no right to exist, and does exist due to the benevolence of the Gods alone. I like it best in winter; that's when I live there.

Wagner himself died there, you know.'

'I know nothing of these things.'

'Soon you will—look, you're learning already.'

We turned into a hairdresser's, a very elegant place indeed, reminding me of Enzo's apartment in the simplicity of its wooden floors, minimal use of beautiful furniture, maximum use of money. Once more there was the kiss on the cheek for Alessia, effusive greetings, rapid Italian, then faces pulled, shrugs, looks of impossibility, more fast language, that smile from the cousin, a glance at a watch, a hurried conference, smiles, and she turned to me with a gleam in the eye of triumph. 'Just for you,' she said. 'They'll squeeze you in somehow. As you're my cousin and all that. There's always room on planes and in hairdressers if you know in your bones it's yours.'

It was like taking part in a strange ceremony of a religion from another time and place; the Cutting of the Hair. My hairdresser could speak no English and I could speak no Italian, so for the first time ever in a hairdressing salon, the whole thing was done in silence, adding to the odd sanctity of the occasion.

Only if you're like me and you've had hair past your shoulders all your life and it's come to be a major part of who you are to the world and yourself, will you understand what I was doing. It was a further removal from the Michelle I used to be, a great leap into an unfamiliar void, a great move towards not just looking more like Alessia, but, in some way I was being compelled towards, actually becoming her. I could feel myself melting, dissolving into something larger and greater than that which I had always considered me.

Part of me was scared, but a greater part of me was exultant, and as the prized hanks of hair fell from my head I felt as if chains were being cut from my life. From inside the screen of my hair, out came me.

Alessia appeared in the mirror behind me, spoke a few words to the young guy who was the doer of the deed, and smiled encouragingly. 'Well,' she said. 'You do look different.'

I said nothing, and she faded out of sight once more. I picked up a long waved tress of my dark brown hair, the hair that Charlie loved. Oh no, yet another irretrievable outrage, a further step away from the comfortable illusion that even yesterday was to be part of the making of a life.

That hair had taken years of my life, hundreds, thousands of pounds, millions of brush-strokes, gallons of shampoos, conditioners, endless concern, the eyes and touch of a series of men, and it was being cut off and tossed aside like the remains of yesterday's dinner. It felt more significant than getting married had—was that really just the day before?—in some way I couldn't figure. Then I saw it—the hair was for men, for my image of myself to the man in me, and it was beautiful, alluring, took the attention off me myself in there, and it was time for me to step out from behind the curtain and take my bow onto my very own stage.

He was done, and yes, it was just the same as the cousin's; short, swept back at the sides over my ears, and the shape of my face was changed forever.

'Mm, I like it,' she said. 'You've got good taste; my own. Time for a little Wagner, time to meet the Valkyrie?'

'What's a Valkyrie again?' She was paying once more for me, I always seemed to be a receiver, Alessia the giver; it was like being a girl to a man once more, only altogether different in tone, in expectation, in the distribution of power.

'A war maiden. Always very beautiful, warlike, masculine and feminine all wrapped up in one.'

'Like you?'

She smiled, her eyes glinting. 'That's right,' she said.

'So where does that leave me?'

'Beautiful, warlike, masculine and feminine all wrapped up in one?'

I blinked at her. This didn't sound like me at all. Then I caught sight of myself in a mirror; the nearest thing to Alessandra the great on this planet; her face, her hair, her black suit from the distant memory of someone's wedding a thousand years ago. A wave of nervousness passed through me. Was this all moving far too fast? Had I lost control completely, and was that OK?

'Let's go to La Scala,' I said. 'Before we get into even deeper water.' Not knowing that La Scala was precisely where the waters ran deepest of all, at least on that particular day, and all the preparations I had made were for entering those waters at their fastest and darkest.

For once it was easy to choose what to wear, all we had was what we stood up in, but at least it was class, and once pressed by the smiling Filipino houseboy back at Enzo's flat, my face made up more like hers with that Kohl around the eyes, we thought we looked just great. At least we did for each other, and that's all that counted.

'Is this the right thing for La Scala?' I asked.

'Relax, you can never have the right thing for that place. Maybe we should have skirts, hell, I don't know—just don't feel intimidated by the fashionable crowd, there's no way we could or would ever even want to compete with that bunch.'

'Is it time to go?'

'It's time. Will you go in on my arm?'

Of course I would, and of course I did, and I must say I was dazzled; the beautiful men and the beautiful women and their beautiful clothes, the opulence of the Opera House of La Scala, all made magic by my lover myself. I can't say that I remember details of that place, all I have is an overriding vision of shine, light, polished stone, bright metal, gleaming wood, and then stepping out into this tiny box that was our very own and looking out over this scene of sumptuous beauty, the lit boxes like our own all around, the buzz of interact conversation from the oiled and bejewelled ones below, the orchestra tuning up, the whole thing like a princess dream, and for that night it seemed all ours.

'Oh, it's lovely,' I said, no doubt my eyes shining.

'Worth the drive already?'

I kissed her in reply, chastely, a peck on the cheek. 'So where are we in the story now?' I asked.

'Our own? Or the tale of the Valkyrie?'

'I thought they were the same.'

'Don't say that,' she said. 'I know the end.'

Another cool current of doubt ran across my childlike heated pleasure at being in this magic place with this magic person. Was this an unwelcome touch of dark prescience, the first chill and deepening shadow as twilight fell on a perfect summer's day? Or was it no more than the last of the tracks of doom my mind was accustomed to running down, applied even to this heaven?

'Remember the story?' she asked. 'The twins re-united fleeing into the forest, Hunding the warrior chasing them, their father they don't know, the Father God Wotan and his grim duty to punish the unholy love?'

'More or less,' I said. 'But where does the Valkyrie come in?'

'She takes tender pity on the two lovers, defends our Siegmund against the enraged warrior husband, until Wotan arrives on the scene—look, the curtain's going up.'

For me it was a scene from the magic play that was in the opera that was my life; unreal as the orchestra began to play, music I had never known, chords of deep unearthly beauty that resonated at the heart of the innermost core of me, took me away from that seemingly eternal Madame Butterfly and into something beyond myself and yet myself. It was my story, I knew it, unfolding before my very eyes, but in truth I could make little sense of all of the mythic depths of Wagner and me that I was witnessing within and without. I was moving too fast for comfort, my understanding trailing behind the rapid unfolding of my folded life. Without Alessia beside me in all her certainties of who she was it would all have been too much. In the narrow space of just twenty four hours I had been taken from a small innocence and hurtled into a world of mystic depth, passion and the reach of strange gods. It was thrilling and I was without a hint of regret, but I felt at my limit of what I could take, what I could live, what I could handle.

Then I saw him.

Chapter 16

I was casting my eye over the wonderful scene below me, not just the stage, the singers, their divine voices and the austere setting, but also the sumptuous auditorium filled with the beautiful people of Milan all dressed to kill each other, making complete the drama laid out before me. I was entranced. In a similar way to how Alessia and I found it hard to define where one of us began and the other ended, so I found it hard to define where the opera had its boundaries, in its story that was my own and not mine at all, and the audience, without whom there was no opera, no story, and then the me watching everything, without whom there was nothing at all. The show was us all. Something was happening to me without my willing it that was making me into a removed observer of my own self, moving from being lost on the stage of my own drama to being the audience of myself.

I was part listening to the music, part watching the singers, part watching the audience, part watching Alessia, basking lazily in the richness that was filling my senses, when my eye caught eyes watching mine, and my blood froze. It was Charlie. Charlie Brown the one and only, the man I had married and then spurned all in the same day. It couldn't be, no, surely I was mistaken, it was impossible, inconceivable. I felt like rubbing my eyes, having someone pinch me to wake me from this particular living nightmare. My heart was thumping, a great Wagnerian baritone was filling every part of that gorgeous place, and I was staring, chewing a fingernail as Hunding the warrior was hunting those who had betrayed and shamed him on the stage, while my husband, abandoned inches from the altar was in the audience hunting me. No life I had lived so far came anywhere near the fast and unlikely intensity of this new way of living. It seemed that now life was being boiled down to some essence where events that might normally take years could happen during a single afternoon, and the pace was quickening.

'Alessia,' I whispered, panicked, the bottom falling out of my new and wonderful world. 'Alessia. It's unbelievable. Charlie's here. In the audience.'

Without taking her eyes from the stage she said, very quietly, 'I'm not surprised.'

Once again my head was reeling. She wasn't surprised? I was astounded, shocked to the core, torn in pieces, quivering, and music and singing that my mind did not understand but my inner core felt and grasped every note of set my teeth on edge. It seemed to her this calamity, this appalling reality, was expected, as she calmly watched on. Once again events had accelerated out of and beyond my understanding. This new world of mine took some getting used to.

It was him, it was, there was no mistaking Charlie Brown. It was unbelievable, irrational, that the man I fled from and left in the blazing ruins of his life appearing like magic at the end of the long fast journey, like an unavoidable curse. He caught my eye that once alone and then just turned and watched the unfolding of The Valkyrie before him. I wonder if he knew the story well enough to think that, in a way, I was Sieglinde, Alessia was Siegmund, then he was Hunding and our fate was in the hands of the dark All-Father God of infinite retribution. Scary is not the word.

The acoustics in La Scala are such that it was no place to talk, but I simply had to know why she was so cool, unsurprised, apparently indifferent to what may have been the beginning of the closing scene in the opera of our love.

'How come you're not so shocked?' I asked as she turned to look at me, the stage and it's singers moving around out of focus behind the silhouette of her face.

'Remember when I phoned here to fix our seats? From the house in Parkgate while the fire was burning?'

I nodded. Of course. Could I ever forget? For God's sake it was only hours ago, less than a day in mortal time, as clear as day but in another galaxy, millennia from where I was. The sound of the orchestra surged behind her, the ongoing operatic background to our shared life.

'Well I realised later that I had left my notes on the pad by the phone; the telephone number of La Scala, and even a note of the time of the performance. I realised later that it was in the hands of the gods whether or not the note was seen, and then whether or not it was acted upon. There are no chance events, no mistakes, the whole thing works in one great intricate correctness, no matter how it might seem. Clearly, Charlie moves swiftly and well. Look, listen, here comes Hunding now.'

With that she turned back to the stage, relaxed and unsurprised, to the scene that chilled me to the bone as the ghastly warrior arrived in a storm, thunder and lightning crashing all around and Siegmund dashed forward to meet him, sword in hand. Such was the time, when all my most ancient of fears came to manifest before me, but rather than be alone I was safely in an aura of love in which these things can be borne.

'Oh, no, please, no,' I whispered to myself, and Alessia's hand reached out for mine as the music reached a crescendo. What did she say, how did the Valkyrie end? Death? Just like Madame Butterfly. Were these two operas intimations, portents of what my own was to become? Again, please, no, surely this sweetness, this purity, this simplicity, is forever?

How could this be happening to me? So swift, so final, and the fear at the bottom of the fears—that our love was forbidden, what was the word? Unholy? And that unholy love is punished by the Gods as a matter of course. Oh hell, what have I done, what destiny am I living, that the greatest of love should be given to me, only to become uncertain in a flash and thereby accentuate my long-slept longings which were now fully awake? With the music, my music, how lovely those chords, those voices, exactly the sound of the torn agonies and loving passions in me.

'You must tell me this will be all right,' I whispered.

'Faith, love, faith in the goodness of it all, in the goodness of what we are and where we are all going. There is no other way in this world.'

On the stage, such voices, out of heaven in their beauty; where did they get those voices from? Had people lived what I was living before? They must have done to write and sing like this. Where had I been all my life? This new world of mine where people lived with passion and gods, beauty and death and woman's love for woman, was almost too much for me, except that I loved it so more than I was afraid of it, and would pay any price for such an alive and vibrant life. For sure for me there was no going back, so there was only going on, and, as always, maybe trembling but courageous as I had to be, walking knowingly into the unknown.

'But I am so afraid,' I whispered.

'Of course you are,' she whispered back. 'It's how you know you're on the path to freedom.'

Then she kept her hand on mine as worlds crashed within me, and love, fear, joy, anger, bewilderment, strength and every colour of feeling coursed through me. Over the stage there is a clock, and one of the things I was watching was the creeping hand of that measure of how time was passing, and with it, I suspected, feared, dreaded, the new world of love for my woman cousin. Why did she bring me to this terrible drama of our own life? All I wanted was to avert my mind from the possible retribution that was the fruit of my betrayal, and within hours her mistaken messages to him, directions to our end, had brought Charlie to witness our own doom on the stage of La Scala.

Not for a moment could I deny the sublime music that kept drawing my mind away from my own chaos of thought into the drama unfolding before me, more than half of which was lost to me in detail but ever so complete in feeling.

'Who is that with the spear?' I whispered.

'Wotan, the All-Father God,' she answered, light in her eyes, and I had no idea of why, at such a time that darkness seemed to be gathering in my heart. It was due to him that Siegmund, his own son, died at the hands of the warrior husband, who was himself then killed by Wotan. It all seemed a terrible mixed up waste to me, as the best were killed for reasons dubious, and guilt and shame took the place of love, fulfilment and happiness. Was this my destiny too?

As I watched and listened, my heart went out more and more to the Valkyrie herself, Brünnhilde, the only one, it seemed to me, to have compassion and good heart, caring for the distressed Sieglinde, who has just lost her new and all-embracing lover-twin at the hands of bloody men.

I looked down at Charlie and my heart went out to him. How rotten that I should be the instrument of fate that must have torn him apart. The singing went on, Brünnhilde and Wotan and their own torture of love and duty at odds, and I watched Charlie, unmoving, watching it all, and at one moment he must have felt my eyes because he turned his head and looked at me once more. Our gaze met with a tremor, cutting through the music and the single direction of the eyes of the audience. It just took a moment, but in that flash was everything beyond the drama of the time, a touch of the heart that lay at the depth of what we were and I panged within for the fragility of his heart.

'We have to meet Charlie,' I said to Alessia, feeling a new strength, a new certainty, a new kind of higher duty growing in my bones.

'Of course,' she answered. Why was I still surprised by her? 'We must welcome the inevitable.'

'But not here, not in Milan,' I said. 'Not this business city. We need a place where there is magic in the air.'

'Venezia,' she said. 'Your home from home. Wait here.'

Once more she surprised me yet again by slipping from our box like a wraith, leaving me to the music, the singing, the beauty, the theatre of dreams and the man that I loved and betrayed because I loved a woman more.

Above the stage the clock moved on, on the stage the drama moved on, poor old Brünnhilde, the Valkyrie herself, demoted from divinity to mortality for her compassion in helping the brother-sister lovers, being cast into spellbound, flame-encircled sleep to await her fearless hero lover ....

Then all of a sudden something snapped in me. I too was waiting for judgement, the harsh hand of retribution, punishment, tears and death for my unholy love, when I saw as clear as day that my fate was only in the hands of heavy Teutonic male gods if I sat back and let them; if I surrendered weakly to some assumption that had been secretly set in my heart as if it was truth and inevitability, but in reality was my own learned script for a life of denial and anguish. Within me was the dawning of the knowledge of my own power which came with the flowering of my love, and with which I could perhaps mould endings of compassion and love, acceptance and beauty, rather than those of doom and endless tears.

As Alessia slipped back in, near the end of drama now, and truly beautiful to me, a form of Goddess in the wild opera of my own life, I wondered with the spark of hope I had ignited within myself whether she was the truest of portents of the future, greater than, and overriding all else. 'OK?'

She glanced at me and whispered. 'Fixed.'

'Then let's go now. Right now. We don't have to wait for the end, and this is not the place to meet Charlie.'

She nodded, not a question, not a hesitation, scooped up her coat, and we slipped out, not before I gave one last glance to the head of the man of my life, blew him an imaginary kiss, and left him to his Valkyrie and All-father God.

We hurried down empty corridors in the Opera House, the sound of our footsteps drumming louder and more urgent than the now faint thundering scenes of Wagnerian myth behind us.

'What a place,' I said to her. 'Funny how familiar it seems.'

'You know that recording we've been listening to, Callas and Madame Butterfly, she sang it all here, in this place. Maybe that's why.'

I smiled. Circles and circles, somehow proving to me that we were in the hands of destiny and that Alessia was right, we should put our trust in goodness and faith, and walk a fine line over a chasm of fire. Outside in the street a chill rain was falling in the darkness. Yet another world.

'Can we go to your place in Venice right now? Is it too far to drive?' I asked, feeling cold and tired, my exhaustion rising. 'I want to be in your own bed with you.'

She kissed me and held me close for a moment in reply, and within twenty minutes we had picked up our few things from the apartment of Enzo the once-lover and were driving for one final time in that car that seemed now like an old friend, picking our way through the rain-shining streets of Milan, on the road again.

'What's the name of the lover who is to come to Brünnhilde? The guy who wakes her up and brings us all to love in the end?'

'Siegfried the Fearless, the greatest hero in the world.'

'Ah,' I said, and told her, as she drove in her usual fearless, heroic way, cutting through the traffic, driving far too fast for normal mortals, of how I had touched on this gentler form of divinity that seemed to live in the depths of my own self, one that could and would make new worlds.

'Ah,' she said, her eyes shining, as we reached the Autostrada and the car leapt forward, its engine serenading us with its sweet song, and once again we were cousins, lovers, now Goddesses, cutting through the night in a chariot of fire.

'And Charlie?' I asked.

'I arranged to have a note given to him.'

'Saying?'

'Tomorrow, 3pm, Saint Mark's, Venice.'

I slid the familiar tape into the deck, and as the first bars began in our portable Scala, side two, Va Via! I found myself moving into some new form of the unknown me, richer of depth, sweeter, stronger. Who I was even the night before seemed far in memory, callow, a place I had once visited when I was young.

As we tore past Breschia I asked, 'How come you came from where we came from and came to be what you became.'

She laughed, laughter like music to me, the Puccini of laughter, and zoomed by a clot of cars in the outside lane by passing on the inside. My God, how much I loved her.

'I won't feign humility by pretending I don't know what you

mean,' she said. 'I've always at least suspected who I am, and when I was a tiny child I would go by myself to the playground in the Dingle and spin round and round and round till I was dizzy, then fall to the ground and look up at the sky and see myself as a magic princess.' She glanced at me. 'When I did, I knew that it wasn't just the silly dream of a silly girl, but me making futures, casting my will off into the blue.'

'Were you surprised at what you came to be?'

'Yes, I was. It was better than I imagined; you see I just made a track, not a final destination, that was left in the hands of something else.'

'Is what we are living now? Tearing down this road to Venezia, the true end of the road in the hands of that same something else?'

She reached over to me and stroked my cheek. 'You move so fast,' she said. 'There is no doubt your time has come. I sense that soon you will be leading me, returning the gift.'

On we fled, and I put my head on her shoulder, drowsy, and watched the place names whiz by; Verona, Vicenza, Padova, all in a rainy Italian dream.

'Not long now, cousin,' she said. 'Soon we'll be home.'

Home, a place I'd never been; if home is where the heart is, does this mean I'd never been to where the heart lies? Ah, questions and questions, and in the end who cares? Just drive on, the immortal music playing, sitting there up against my love, her arm round my shoulders as we watched the lights of the Italian night flash by, this time approaching the certain end of our journey of journeys as we came to Venezia and the sea, over which no roads ran.

It was as dark and cold as a North of England night when we

finally arrived in Venezia. Alessia parked that fine car in a place she knew, and left it with thanks and a kiss, then from somewhere found a boat for hire. It was some sort of taxi on water, and the last stage of our flight was slow and quiet, chugging our way with an unspeaking pilot across dark water, lights reflecting, dark shapes of buildings looming. It was for me like casting off from the land that had always held me and heading out into the final darkness of the mythic unknown.

I shivered in the damp chill, and Alessia put her arm round me. 'Ten minutes, sweetheart,' she said, 'not much more, I promise.' With that I surrendered one step deeper, and felt myself relaxing into her, like a child into a mother, grateful for her warmth and protection in this world which was long hers and only newly mine.

Slowly we traversed the open stretch of black water in unspeaking silence, then passed into one of the invisible cracks in the faint looming silhouette of buildings and the mood changed; open to enclosed, and the underlying feeling was of closing to the end of the longest trail of my life. I felt exhausted, tired to the core, finished, every reserve gone.

Then, very quietly, our boatman began to sing, sweet and low, a pure tenor that was his own—and ours, that night. I lay back and way up above the clouds were breaking over a bright sliver of moon; the rain had stopped now. As the boatman had stopped singing as we turned from one canal into another. Alessia looked at him and spoke in a soft Italian that sounded like a form of music to my ears that loved the very sound of her voice.

The boatman laughed softly. Then to my amazement and warm

joy he began to sing one of the arias I had come to know so well on the long track back to where I'd never been, one of those songs from Madame Butterfly that would haunt me for the rest of my life, that I have playing now as I write, and without which none of this could have come to be.

'Did you ask him to sing that?' I asked.

'Of course,' she said. 'How could we travel without?'

I kissed her, my perfect lover, and as we kissed, the boat bumped gently against land, or what passed for land in this city of islands on an ancient sea . The song ended, the journey ended, and by torchlight we stepped from the bobbing boat onto worn stone steps.

'Grazie,' I called to the boatman, and there was just enough light to catch a flash of white teeth.

'Prego,' he responded, and the lights of his boat started to draw away down the canal. We were alone, car-less, in a place I had never been but I knew was the home of my heart.

'Come on,' said the dearest of voices. 'Just a few steps.'

We were standing at a doorway under a light; it could have been any one of thousands of old buildings; no signs, no numbers, no names, just stonework lit by a single bulb, a wooden door and no people. 'So this is where you live?'

'It's where I'm living. Like I said, I have a studio here. It's a good place to work.' She smiled. 'And a good place to be alone.'

With that I knew that she was taking me to her place, her centre, the private secret lair of a most private of persons, not a place she took others, but I was not others. She turned a key in the lock and swung open the door. Click and a light came on; ahead of us a set of worn stone steps between stone walls. Up we climbed and there was another door, another key, Alessia slipping inside, click, another light, and I stepped into the most beautiful room I had ever seen.

Chapter 17

The place was small; I imagined something grand, sleek and stylish like that apartment we visited in Milan, not this intimate fairyland. A long rectangle in warm yellow stone leading away from us, down one side a row of pillars supporting arches which contained windows, and over every other surface, hanging from the walls, from the ceiling, draped over tables, were bolts and stacks and piles and swathes of cloth, in every colour and texture, every stripe, spot, swirl known to woman. Dazzling pinks clashing with peach, tufted reds in a cascade turning to orange, the palest violets, pinks and yellows in cobweb silks; rugs on the floor, one over another, Turkey and China overlapping. There were cushions of every style and size and type; big fat beige and turquoise, twinkling, mirrored Indian ones in a heap, dark as midnight velvet ones, on and on. It was a cornucopia of colour. As I stepped into that Aladdin's cave the whole place seemed to look back at me. It felt alive, friendly alive, and I had the feeling that all these living cloths and colours had scurried back into place as we arrived, in the same way that toys do in magic stories for children.

'This is you, this is Alessia,' I said. 'So now I know the whole story.'

'Well, at least you know more of the story.' She looked shy, exposed, revealed, endearing.

'It's wonderful, like nothing I've seen on earth. But why, what's it all for?'

'It's something I do,' she said. 'I work with textiles. It's a passion of mine.'

Gratitude surged in me, and I reached out to touch her, this emissary from the land of passion. Without whom I may have spent my days in correct, passionless safety, living a life in form without content, like a fruit without juice.

I walked the length of the room with an immediate sense of belonging, picking up, examining, touching and feeling all manner of designs, colours and forms. 'How did you start doing this?' I asked in wonderment. Again, it was a long way from her beginnings, a million light years from the small world she grew up in, and in a direction I would never imagined. I had thought that I was doing well with my education, changed accent, elegant clothes, but in truth, in comparison, I had only just scraped the surface. Alessia was a constant source of amazement to me; she was so concealed, so private that anything revealed would have been fascinating, but whenever I did get to see something from her depths it always surprised me for reasons richer and deeper and different from anything or anyone I had previously known. More and more and more I was being pulled into a world that was unknown, but once there I found it more home than any other. Somewhere within me passed the memory of the odd longings I had lived with all my life, especially as a child, when I had felt that somehow a terrible mistake had been made and I had been left, bereft, with the wrong parents and the wrong life, like a princess foundling in an ancient myth. It was as if I looked around at times, throughout my life, wondering when they would come and take me back home to where I belonged, but they never did. Until now.

'It started in the East,' she said. 'Remember Luisa? Come and sit with me while the place warms up, it won't be long, and I'll introduce you to my first loves.'

She talked about her textiles in the same way others talk about their dogs, as if they had souls, lives, understandings, and as she showed me lengths of hand-printed batik sarongs from Java, she stroked them as if they were cats. 'Look,' she said. 'Look at the indigo, faded ever so beautifully into that kind of grey sheen, the way that brown meets it, the way the pattern falls, a work of art, this.'

'What's this one?'

'Ah, Japan; here, look at these kimonos, did you ever see such perfection? These are my special loves, the obi, the sashes that go with the kimono.' She tore herself away and smiled. 'But you must be frozen to the bone, carissima.'

'Ah, carissima, call me that again.'

'Carissima, carissima, carissima. Would you like tea, coffee, wine, food or just bed, carissima.'

'Feed me, Alessia, I want to eat your food, something made by your hand.'

'Then pasta it is. I love fine pasta with olive oil from Lucca and a little fresh parmesan. A glass of red wine. Feel free to explore, it won't take long.'

It didn't. There was the one main room, a kind of gallery for textiles that you lived and ate in, a bedroom, all pale wood and stone, a peach-coloured carpet, a mirror the size of a wall to look at my new haircut in, a four-poster bed all in cream, a modern bathroom in dark blue, then a kitchen which meant business, where a pot of pasta was bubbling away.

'Come quick,' she said. 'Let's get changed.'

We strode down to the bedroom, took off those suits which had been us for far too long, and she draped me in a robe of the finest silk in a range of colour from the palest lilac to the royal-est purple. It was so beautiful, so soft, so delicate, so powerfully coloured that I hesitated. Was this me?

'I thought so,' she said, standing back, hand to the chin in contemplation. 'Good colours for you. Do you like it?'

'I love it. I just never wore anything like it before.'

' High time, then. It's yours.'

I looked at myself in the mirror—short hair and purple silk—and liked what I saw, even though I hardly knew the person who was looking. Behind me my cousin lover was slipping into her own silken robe, all in a particular shade of blue, shot through with a single flowing line of scarlet, also very beautiful.

'Gosh,' I said. 'How pretty. You look very beautiful.'

Once again this life she looked into my eyes in the mirror and said, 'Snap.' But this time we were both the feminine same, some great balance had been shifted from the time of the wedding dress and the sharp black suit in the mirror on the day of the sacrificial feast, hours ago when I still knew nothing.

We both smiled at the same moment, that moment for the flash of cameras, and I still have that picture, not in a silver frame on top of the piano but in my deepest hidden place, to take out and remember the wonder of that love when I am old and such moments are long past.

The first time the cousins had been a matching pair in the mirror of the Brown's house in Parkgate, a hundred thousand thousand years ago, they had not touched, not yet become lovers—in spirit maybe, but not in flesh—but now, in Venice, things were different. We turned to each other, silk against silk, silken flesh against silken flesh, and kissed once more, and I swear that there was a moment then when Michelle was almost gone, melted in a single ecstasy of love.

When, after an eternity when the world stopped turning and the full meaning of life on earth was revealed and then almost lost again, we separated by inches, looking into our same-blood eyes with such love that I almost cried out in pain.

'The pasta,' she said. 'We have all night for love.'

A kiss of butterfly tenderness on the nose, and the pasta was rescued. Then we sat in the light of candles fat and thin, red and long, white and squat, in candlesticks of brass and silver, wood and glass, on Persian rugs in our Italian silk, and ate out of bowls hand-painted with animals from myths in jungles full of flowers.

'Tomorrow,' said Alessia, casually, between mouthfuls, 'tomorrow we have Charlie.'

Ah, yes, Charlie, never forgotten, the force that brought us together and lurked unresolved behind all of what we were. I nodded.

'Are you afraid?'

I put my head to one side to think. What was it? 'Hmm,' I said. 'There is fear in me, but other things press upon me stronger.'

'Do you dwell on the end of the Valkyrie, the punishment of the gods for unholy love like ours may be?'

I reached over and touched her lips to silence her cares with one finger. 'You're concerned,' I said, touched by the vulnerable soul she so rarely revealed. 'What is it? Fear of Wotan and his fire and brimstone, hell and judgement?'

'Hardly Wotan,' she said through a mouthful of pasta, sitting there cross-legged on the Persian rug in candlelight, looking lovely in her silk and shadow of uncertainty. 'You said Charlie is a soldier?'

'Was.'

'Then yes, I have fear of Charlie, fear of the wrath of the wronged male and the power of his revenge.' She lay back with the grace of a cat. 'Does he have a capacity for violence?'

'Did you bring the Callas tape with you?'

'You want it on?'

'Our journey isn't quite finished.' More's the shame, I thought to myself, the road seems to lead on without end, in one form or another, when all I want to do is to stop where I am forever. Moments later the familiar passion softly filled the room that was something out of a dream of sheikhs of Araby, as the strange creature that was my love incarnate took her place once more.

'Charlie Brown,' I said, my attention straying for a moment as that aria which contained all the beauty and pain of my opened heart called 'Un bel di vedremo', the beautiful day is coming, when Butterfly in her impassioned delusion dreams of the arrival of the lover who has betrayed her, began yet again, with that heartbreaking catch of underlying sadness which gave such colour to its beauty. Once more, art and life mixed in incomprehensible quantities, a key to understanding of my life with no code to unlock its secrets.

'Charlie Brown is a soldier, a warrior, he has killed men; he has blood on his hands,' I told her. What could we do? The truth was the truth and the ghosts of the past were with us, not to be resisted, turned from or ignored, but taken into our world without fear.

For a moment we listened to the aria, then Alessia smiled and said, 'So our Hunding has come; we have welcomed the avenging warrior into our midst. Maybe we should have fled to that Island of dreams and hidden out there for the rest of our days.' And she laughed at the futile impossibility of such dreams. 'Coffee? Or do you want to sleep?'

'Coffee, yes.' I followed her to the kitchen, bare feet on cool stone. Once more tiredness had vanished, now I was in warmth and safety, now I had arrived home.

'We should be ready for the worst,' she said over her shoulder. She was so brave, so strong; even the worst of nightmares were tamed by her forthright acceptance of all the colours life had to give.

'The worst?'

'Yes. What has he killed with?'

I shrugged. 'Different things. Guns, knives, I really don't know.'

'So we must be ready for the possibility of death, later this very day?'

'It's the worst of my unspoken fears. He has a dark side I never got to know—except when once we talked about the times when he killed as a soldier. And again when I saw his face the night we fled. But he slept easy with the death on his hands; he felt it was duty; he has a clear sense of correctness in all things.'

'Which makes my unease greater. We have mortally offended that correctness.'

What a place my passions and my destiny had brought me to, with such speed and certainty. I still felt as if I was moving swiftly down a track to heaven knows where, wild forces within me opening, coursing madly through me. My mind, my way of thinking, perceiving and being were altering at the speed of our drive across Europe, and sometimes I felt one part of my understanding was lagging behind, so now and again I would have to pause and wait, as parents do for their little children.

Once more we took our places in the candlelit cave of the million colours of Alessia, thoughtful now as we sipped coffee and the Venetian night moved slow steps towards the unknown quantity of the oncoming day.

'Faith, love, and more faith, your words, cousin,' I said. 'I know we have no idea of what our destiny will bring, but I now believe less in the dark power of the avenging gods, and more in goodness, happiness, love. I can't say I am wholly certain and without fear—not yet—but some inner tide has turned from fear to hope, and it's flowing fast.'

'I knew you would start to return the gifts soon,' she said. 'I just had no idea of how soon and how well. Maybe what we believe in comes to exist; if it exists then it's because of our belief, of what lies imprinted in our hearts. So great power lies in a simple change of heart, and ours are changing by the moment. Now we have a time to see what we can do, to see who we are, create our own destiny.'

Once more the world began to change, fears transmuting into new forms of faith and hope as we looked them in the eye, and in the cocoon of her magic house with the catalyst of our very ancient love working miracles, it felt as if the greatest of lives were dawning within our own.

'If by chance death is coming this afternoon of this day that has not long begun,' I said, 'then we have little time, cousin lover, and should treasure every moment we have.'

'Yes,' she said. 'No past, no future.'

Then the two of us in our silk wedding gowns made our way, hand in hand, to the bedroom, where we lay in each other's arms, kissed, stroked, held, laughed and simply existed in an odd electric timelessness in which every moment was all of life.

Never before had I lived right now in all the richness of the immediate present with no reference to the past, therefore no possibility of projections upon an unknown future, treasuring every moment, living without excuses, hesitations, doubts; the shadow of the possibility of death bringing out all of the joy in life.

And I'll tell you something you may find strange; nothing of our physical love was limited to the purely sensual, not really, no matter how it may have looked from the outside. It was more a kind of new unfettered togetherness, in which we relished every morsel of time as it strayed by, and the containers of our souls, our bodies, dense and slow, were almost no barrier to us touching at some hitherto unknown point of divine singularity.

In time we slept, and slept easy, no avenging warriors in our dreams that night, because that was the night of the greatest love and was a gift from some unknown goddess, a peep into the world beyond ours, a taste of the final home. In fact, that night there were no dreams other than the one we were living, and that was enough for any mortal.

Time had become without meaning to us; we slept and woke and rose for the day that had arrived, still taking every living moment as our last, no baggage of the past to clutter the present and foul up the way to the future.

Was I happy? Oh, yes, entirely, and all we talked about were clothes, the weather, and breakfast; we were that free of the oncoming events that would shape the rest of our lives, our life. It was like living a dance in which every step, move and turn had been choreographed for us a long time ago, by the greatest master of the dance that ever was.

'We have no bread,' said my reflected half, no, not my half, myself. 'Breakfast out?'

'Breakfast out.'

The weather had changed overnight. It was warmer now, and although the sky was still massed with clouds there were now great blue patches, through which bands of sunlight shone like rays onto buildings and water. I was delighted to be in Venice, surprised once more by what Alessia had brought to me. Every move she made was, to me, fresh and alive, unrepeated. Nothing she did moved in patterns, one surprising act leading to another, and all of them in balance, pleasing and enlivening.

I was now dressed in her clothes completely—soft wool trousers in lilac, a Kaffe Fassett sweater in a thousand subtle shades—and we walked arm in arm through a faint breeze along the side of canals.

Alessia dressed in all manner of colours, always in clothes of such elegance and style, and it took me some time to become used to the woman outside the severe black suit. As it was the only way I had seen her I imagined that was how she always was, but that suit was something she had chosen for the wedding alone as a contrast to pale froth, the pink wedding suits of the ladies, and, she thought, to provide an appropriate touch of mourning.

'So why Alessia? Did someone else call you that?'

'It's what I called myself; I am self-named, I created myself, so why not?'

I loved it, and told her so, for me it was the most wonderful name in all the world, and I was delighted as she led me into a restaurant where she was greeted by all with—Ciao, Alessia!—like an operatic chorus of her name to confirm it forever, and I was glad that they loved her too. Once more she explained who I was to attentive faces, and they all looked at me and nodded their heads, and made exclamations of wonder as they saw the same flow of the bloodline, then served us with great coffee and pastries fit for the Empresses of the Universe.

'I wonder what's happening in the world?' I said, my eye caught a man deep in his newspaper. I wondered what he was reading about, and this reminded me of the world out there all about its business, which in turn made me conscious of our private dreamland. 'Governments are falling, wars are breaking out, babies are being born ....'

'Men and women are getting married ....' She caught my eye and we both laughed. This was the mood of things, light as a feather on the wind. And you know, something of where we were in ourselves had made the unseen seen, and we were both conscious of some invisible hand fashioned from an enormous compassion, holding us in the palm of her hand, letting us live these hours, this time, imbibe this fragrance of the Garden of Eden.

Still we had hours on hand, enough time to live a whole life, and we walked through the streets and passages, over bridges, through squares. After all, we were lovers in Venice, and Alessia knew every inch of that sad and beautiful city. We called into churches to see frescos of masters, ran our fingers along the lines of great statues, and she pointed out details of buildings, towers, windows, and my sight was opened to the finer points of possibilities of beauty in this man-made world.

'Lunch?' she asked.

'Something small at home. I want to be alone with you.' And something unsaid was; maybe for the last time, who knows? But we said nothing.

I watched her shopping with fascination; the way she picked up fat tomatoes, squoze them, sniffed them; the way she used that merciless smile; the speed of her decisions, the certainty; the way she threw her pale brown shawl back over her shoulder. I was entranced, mesmerised, a creature hungry for love being fed to fat repletion.

What it was to be walking with her, carrying bags of shopping back home for lunch, fully arrived now at a state of being the one in two parts, troubled by nothing but a slight frustration that total merging into oneness was impossible for the now.

Cooking, oh, what it was to cook. Every leaf of lettuce, every tomato sliced, every crust of bread, every crystal glass filled, was an act of grace, full of colours I had never before noticed, shades and textures as varied and delicate as her textiles. I was entering her world, seeing through her eyes, and we moved in a ballet of harmony with our knives and pots and pans, not needing to speak, working as one creation made into two, so we could better love ourselves.

'Is it far to Saint Mark's?' I asked over lunch, the first direct reference to the inevitable afternoon.

'About fifteen minutes,' she said, and glanced up at me. Then smiled, and I was relieved of the oncoming black clouds on my horizon.

We ate, hardly speaking, and as we did the sunlight that was shafting through the arched windows moved slightly in the direction of San Marco, bringing with it some ripples to the placid lake within me.

What did I, we, feel like? Was it something like the feelings of the condemned man, or woman? For sure there was a growing sense of the truth that life would never be the same as this again, whatever came to pass with my warrior from the North. Once more I was cast into the uncertainty of the future of the revolutionary, between structures, between lives, one form gone and the other yet to come. And I felt that place, the home of insecurity, the life of faith without tracks, was where Alessia lived always in a wisdom without form, on a parallel road but not of this earth. Me, I wanted to travel with her. More than that, it felt that not to move with her would be wrong, even sinful, a denial of an appointed destiny.

My question, my doubt, was whether it really was to be my way too, despite our oneness, despite my utter happiness and my heart-desire to stay there forever. Behind a screen within me, I had a vague panic that just as I entered this magic world of hers and all the colours of life lit up, secrets of the heart were revealed and I touched on the divine, another form of fate that I had averted my mind from would force me to leave it and return to the perplexed sense of dissatisfaction that had previously haunted my days.

In this, as in all things, time would tell.

Chapter 18

I guess everything has its time in this world, when movements of planets and ancient destinies meet to produce those momentous moments in a life, all of them forms of the beginnings and endings, births and deaths that put shape and form and meaning in our passage from one eternity to another. Not always, not usually, do we have notice of what is coming our way, and when we do have notice, despite the dark pictures of our own fears, we never know what we have lost and what we have gained until the dust has settled. I suppose Alessia and I knew that what we had, love in the form we had it, would not survive that day intact, but would be replaced by something new. The problem was that what we had was the sweetest fruit we had yet known, and secretly we feared that from here everything would simply be less, as dark duty replaced freedom, distance replaced togetherness, and, who knows, death itself replaced life.

So we lay together, gently passing time, not needing to do anything; the joy was simply in being with each other, existing keenly in the same shared, electric fraction of moving time. The imminence of change brought no hurrying, but rather a kind of breathlessness, a hush before what was to be done.

'It seems like a thousand years since I first saw you in that Cathedral,' said Alessia. 'And since then we've lived an entire life in what, would you believe it, just two days.'

The first cracks of melting of our singleness of thought of the present were beginning to show. What could we do? My goodness, how well we were doing, holding the shadow of what was to come on our distant horizons, but it was beyond us to not feel the first touch of chill of its imminence.

'Don't, love,' I said. 'Anymore and we'll be dreading the future, taking fear with us to meet Charlie when what we need is the best of our love. Do we need to go soon?'

'Soon. Do you want anything?'

'You mean any last wishes?'

We managed to laugh, a little weakly, granted, but even as we were tearing ourselves out of her magic cave of dreams, with a mixture of feelings mixing away inside, still we could be light, see the humour in ourselves, in life itself. But it was hard to leave, believe me, hard to gamble the best of life on the unpredictable form of the unknown that awaited us. But such was the life of uncompromising directness and Valkyrie courage of my Alessia. What was to be done was to be done; one day stealing a bride from before the eyes of her husband, the next to meet him face to face, and both acts done because they were correct unto the moment they were lived.

By the time we were once again outdoors even the breeze had dropped, and we were back into the magic of our utter togetherness and could walk along the bridges and canal sides, threading our way through the maze of tiny ways of stone and water and sky as if nothing else was happening. Venice never looked more beautiful as it did on that walk. It was a magic place at a magic time, with autumn mists lying low over the still waters and towers, domes, campaniles, palazzos and churches rising out of its vagueness into the clear afternoon sky. I wondered with grim humour if this is how condemned men, or women, felt on their way to the gallows, alert to every breath, every memory, every beat of the heart, every footfall on this temporary earth.

'I hope I don't lose you,' I thought to myself, to her, walking up against me, eyes bright and alive, shining with the light of her own self. That was it; she was simply more alive than any other person I had set eyes on, and that living presence nourished my soul. Without altering my pace, my poise, I opened myself to become even closer to her in spirit, if that was really possible. Immediately my heart rose and my altered world altered once more, it became even brighter, sharper, and Alessia turned to me to flash that smile of smiles at me that tore at my heart more with every fleeting moment. She was astonishingly attuned to every nuance of what I was and what I did. I let my mind think of Charlie again, after not letting it for some time. Nothing had changed. I was still moving forward into a future of utter uncertainty, returning to that which I had rejected, facing that which I feared most in all the world. And, oddly enough, I felt entirely content, given to my fate no matter what it might bring.

Then all of a sudden we popped out on that famous square, the domes, the lions, the flying flags, the pigeons by the café tables, the brilliant water beyond. My heart missed a beat as my eyes scanned the scene for the familiar figure of Charlie Brown in that unfamiliar setting. It seemed impossible that he should be here in this place with us, someone from another world and another time entering our own private universe just made for two.

I looked at my watch—it was two minutes past three, and Charlie was always on time, precisely, I had never known him be late. He was a military man still in his disciplined ways.

'Maybe he didn't come,' I said, my hope weak and futile.

'Maybe,' said Alessia. 'There again, my note said Saint Mark's, not the square.'

'So he may be inside?'

'Who knows? But we should look.' Then just as we reached the entrance she said, 'We should cover our heads. This is a church, and it is Sunday.'

I followed her example and pulled my soft scarf over my head, so we entered into that place changed entirely from the sharp-suited anarchists on the run the day before to looking like a pair of nuns on their way to mass.

Inside it was oddly oriental, like a Russian or Greek church to me. It wasn't a familiar sort of Christianity but something eastern and exotic, like a dream of Persia. There was a service under way, with chanting priests genuflecting in the gloom as they swung censers, filling the place with sweet smoke which billowed in the shafts of light streaming through the windows and onto the sparse congregation. For a moment I was taken back to that other church, the cathedral in Chester with its own other light and people, and for one eerie moment it felt as if I should now walk down that Venetian aisle on the arm of Alessia to another form of marriage from which I would never flee.

I looked around, searching the dim and unknown faces for the one I knew so well, or used to in another life just two days before. 'Can you see him?' I whispered to Alessia, my heart thumping, using every ounce of my strength to stop myself from running back into the light of the day and thereby losing all that I had gained.

'No.'

We tiptoed down the side of the great church, peeping round pillars, checking every face, many of which looked back at us with disapproval. It was a terrible place to meet anyone, and just as I was about to give up, suggest we waited outside, an all too familiar voice behind us said. 'So you came.'

We turned, and it was him. Charlie, Charlie Brown. My heart leapt a somersault. A thousand times I had secretly rehearsed what I would say when this moment came, and at none of those times did anything even half worth remembering arise. As it happened I turned to find him right in front of me, so close I almost gasped, and I said. 'Yes, we came.'

It was no place to talk and at the look in his eye, the cold distant look of the stranger, and not a happy stranger at that, I wanted to get out of that church, which felt constricted, tight, a place for other people's worship in which our drama was some form of heresy. The die was cast, we had met, and now we had to do what we had to do. It was almost a relief for the worst form of the inevitable to have manifest. He stood there for a few moments just looking at me in stony silence, the man who had followed on my heels when I fled from him on the day we married, deserting him in front of his family and friends to run off with a female cousin lover. Dear Lord, what had I done to this man?

My heart went out to him, hesitantly, as I had no idea of the ground on which I stood. What had brought him here? Whatever motivated him to such action was certainly powerful, but what was it? Maybe outrage, maybe loneliness, maybe revenge, maybe anything between, but certainly pain. The emptiness of his eyes told me nothing. We stood there for a full minute, looking into our familiar stranger's faces, with nothing happening at all but a strange churning of unfathomable forces within me, and then I said, softly, 'Maybe we should go outside.'

He nodded. Not once had he looked at, recognised the existence of Alessia, an unreadable guide to his inner world and his feelings towards her which somehow chilled me to the bone. There was something going on in him that I could detect the presence of without knowing what it was, and, as always with uncertainties at times of danger, I projected all my deepest fears onto that nothingness. The time had come, yet another promise of the future made real, one more oncoming frame in the movie of my life on screen, and my initial relief at the arrival of what had to arrive was swiftly turning into alarmed fear.

Charlie turned and walked slowly out of the old church, and I caught Alessia's eye as we followed. We were calm and well, and now the reality had arrived, prepared for anything despite that which raged within me. I wanted comfort, a caress, a word of warmth and hope, but those times were passed for now and this time I had to handle my world alone.

Out in the square and under the sky and there was an odd stillness in the air, that feeling that comes just before the rain. Charlie walked on, the two of us following obediently behind, then stopped right in the centre of that square from a thousand postcards and turned to face us. At that moment I realised his courage, his warrior power, his male intent. What a masculine force had arrived in our feminine world. He was acting out a role I could never handle, doing something I could never do, he was a person I could never be. Or so I thought.

There we stood, calm and erect all three, Charlie this time looking at both Alessia and myself, his eyes flashing from one to the other, for the first time showing us the fire of his rage.

'What can I say to the lover who turned into the greatest of bitches at the drop of a pin, Michelle?' he said. Hunding had arrived, his spear of righteousness flaming, all the power of the father male condemning Gods at his side.

I shrugged slightly. What could I say?

'And you,' he snarled, glancing at Alessia with a look to kill. 'You.' I could see his hands clenching and unclenching, unconsciously expressing his fury. He looked around. 'This place is not for talking,' he said. 'We need somewhere quiet, no other people. You know somewhere, bitch?'

Alessia was unmoved to the eye, rather pale, but standing proud. 'Over to your left,' she said. 'Through the gap between the cafés.'

I suppose anyone looking at us crossing the square then passing between two buildings and out of it would have just seen a trio of two women and one man, creatures of no particular note, no evidence on the outside of the past, the inner chaos, and the unknown immediate future coloured with peril that we were moving into. Just three late tourists seeing Venice before the winter arrived.

We walked without speaking, Charlie outwardly calm, except for the clenching and unclenching of those hands, which I couldn't keep my eyes away from, and which filled me with deep trepidation. I stole glances at his face as we walked, that face which I had taken unto my own, made promises to, sworn vows to before man and God and then abandoned.

Did I feel any love for him? Did I ever? I was so uncertain; the fire of my love for Alessia had overwhelmed all other feelings, and now I walked beside this cold fury on the way to some unknown ending and he was not the man I once knew, but still I could maybe detect a spark at the core of me of the love that was, I thought. Something in me felt like reaching out to him and saying, look, Charlie, this is nothing at all, everything is fine if you only knew, this love of ours is so pure that nothing can come of it but good, but how could I when his world was in flames and the last time I reached out to him ended in such pain?

In time we reached a small square set on three sides with blank buildings and on one side with a passing canal, on the other side of which were further blank buildings. In the centre of the square was a stone bench, and this was the place, the stage set chosen by Alessia for the death of our present and the birth of our futures.

'Love, faith, goodness,' I was repeating to myself, trying to prise my mind away from its first habits of despair and doom, but nothing could stop my heart from pounding as we came to a halt by that single bench. There was no need for complexities in setting other than space, stone, water and sky. As in the setting of Die Valkyrie, austere simplicity made clearer the underlying power of our emotions.

Charlie turned to me, and I knew him well enough to know that he had been storing and fuelling his pain and rage for this very moment, and I had to admit the truth was that I felt I was owed what he had to give. In fact, in the way that sometimes swift response and retribution can be a relief, a cleansing, a return to balance, I actually welcomed it.

At this point in time, when all the forces of betrayal were focused on the next moment, what did he say? As if it was the greatest outrage of them all; 'You've cut your hair.'

How odd it was to witness anger from the place of my love for Alessia. I could see in what he said that my hair, the long feminine tresses of yesterday, were part of what he felt he owned, part of what I brought to him that he felt he lacked in himself, and it was a piece in a game that we both played that had denied us our fuller selves. The faintest of faint hopes dawned in me. Once more the world had shifted on its axis, once more I had moved on, and instead of anger all I saw was pain.

'Yes,' I replied, and touched it with my fingers.

'So now you're even more like the bitch.'

I said nothing; once more what was there to say? I was what he said.

'Do you know what you've done to me? Do you?' At least as he talked he was with me, communicating with me, telling me how much it hurt, and with that came the re-dawning of my affection, the return of caring, the heart of the mother for the wounded child.

'I don't. I can guess, but ....'

'But in truth you can never know the bloody humiliation in

front of everyone, everyone in my life. I can't face even walking down the street in Chester ever again.'

In me, a flicker of hope; he had lost so much, maybe he was near to losing it all. And with that gaining it all.

'I'm sorry for the pain I've caused you, Charlie.'

'Sorry!' he snorted. 'You're sorry. I'm sorry, the bloody world is sorry.'

Alessia stood watching all this in minute silence. She didn't move a single muscle. A wind was springing up now and darker clouds were scudding over the roofs of the cold stone buildings. The mood was changing, shifting; dialogue had begun.

'Is Geoffrey all right?' I asked. Leaving Geoffrey Brown at that time was, for me, the worst of what I had done. How impossible it would be to try to explain that my truth to myself was even more important than comforting Geoffrey, although I felt Geoffrey himself would understand completely. He was a man of the heart.

'No thanks to you,' Charlie said with curled lip. How strange it was to hear anger, and now contempt, and see only a display of unhealed wounds, all with beginnings from before my time. 'He had a heart attack, survived. More than my mother, who has been shamed into the earth.'

Again, nothing to say.

Then, all of a sudden he turned to Alessia, took her by the throat with one of those great flexing hands that I knew so well, knew the strength of so well, and said, 'I blame you entirely for this, you bitch. 'She continued to look him calmly in the eye, made no attempt to move his hand, no attempt to struggle. 'I know in my bones it was you that cast some spell on her, took her heart away from me.'

'You diminish her,' said Alessia. 'She is the mistress of her own heart.' Even at such a moment she would not deny me; how could I not love her entirely?

'Ohhhh,' moaned Charlie, a noise of the final straw breaking the back of his teetering restraint, a sound full of impotence and rage, and he reached inside his coat with his free hand and took out a knife, one of those you touch a switch on and the blade flashes out, and that is what he did.

My body stiffened as he touched the side of her neck just below the ear with the point of this knife. I knew his knives, all of them sharp as razors, and I stood there in my own world of terror on the brink of losing the greater part of what I valued and loved in our passing world.

'You've taken everything from me,' he hissed, his eyes bulging. 'Everything. Now I have nothing to lose, so I've come to rid the world of some poison, to even up the balance, to make things right. I've killed men before, you know, with this knife too, so I know what I can do.'

'You may have killed men,' she said, her voice muffled under the press of his hand. 'But have you ever killed a woman, Charlie?' What daring; she used his name, talked to him about death on the point of death. We were on the finest of fine points, the very fulcrum of our shared destiny, where the faintest of psychic winds can tilt the balance, bring birth or death. Right now, I thought, hoping that Alessia would hear me in her heart, we must tread more carefully than at any moment in our lives.

He sneered, drew the blade lightly down her golden skin, blood welling up along the razor line. 'You aren't a woman,' he said. 'You I can kill.'

'What of Michelle?' she asked, ignoring her wound, the lifeblood running freely down her neck. 'If you kill me, what of her?'

'Ah, now you begin to understand,' he said, his voice tinged with what sounded like evil. So now we were witnessing what had been hidden in the depths of Charlie Brown. No wonder he buried it so deep. 'The plan is that she then understands grief, carries a lifetime of loss, joins the human race.' And ever so casually, he once more drew the blade down the side of her face, as gentle as a mother with a babe, and once more the blood flowed. He was playing with her like a cat with a mouse, relishing his cruelty, and despite my horror all I could see was the pain of a great lost boy, and with that, love rose in me.

The wind was gusting round the square at this time, setting up a whirlwind in one corner which lifted up bits of paper in a spiral as spots of rain began to fall. It brought a slight shift in mood, but it was a darkening, and I felt tears begin to well in the back of my eyes. All of a sudden any last trace of hope had gone, replaced by a bleak certainty of the end of all goodness this life.

'Very well,' Alessia said. 'If this is my time, this is my time.'

Charlie glanced over at me, standing there powerless, all the power in his hands, and he smiled a smile of petty triumph. 'Ready to see your girlfriend go?' he asked.

'No,' I said truthfully. 'Never. But at the same time, we knew this may be our destiny.'

Yes, the warrior messenger of the wrath of the gods was with us. Maybe my worst fears were true and our love was a delusion, a madness which needed to be expunged, removed like an excrescence on a healthy tree. Look, there were the doubts within me, those hesitations that had, as always, brought their own fruit to my life.

We three were in a space of our own in that dismal square. No-one passed by, no boats, no walkers, no-one, and we could have been the only people on the entire stage of this world.

'Don't talk to me of destiny, bitch,' snarled Charlie. 'I'll show you destiny.'

Then there were a few moments when time stood still for me as I watched him tense his arm, ready to plunge the knife into the blood-hot artery that pulsed invisibly beneath that soft place below the ear which I loved to kiss on her.

And on him. All of a sudden I remembered the love we had shared, and with the memory of love came the eruption of the sweetest of sensations I had ever felt. Inside me something opened like a flower, and out of the flower stepped something divine, a goddess which was me.

Up and over to my left, the clouds parted and a beam of sunshine shone through the still-falling rain, to me a proof, if I needed one, that what was in me was true.

Somehow I had been granted the great good fortune to have a spirit implanted within me, and as I thought of this, way down deep inside me I saw the traces of a vision of a volcano, a full moon, a carved God, and a kiss.

The power of the angry gods had gone, Wotan had faded, and with him my fears, guilts, uncertainties. Now I knew who I was. I took one step forward, with one hand took Charlie by the head and kissed him on the lips, with all the tender love in the world.

For a moment he resisted, but in truth it was what his heart was yearning for beneath the woundings and the rage and the lostness and in no time at all he relaxed into my kiss, and with that opening the spirit of the Goddess entered him.

All of this time he had Alessia by the neck, knife up against her bloodied skin, and I was squeezed somehow between them. How easy it is to see when the dark glass is removed. Now I could see that what we needed to do was to expand our world, open our embrace to Charlie so he could join us in some way not yet revealed. Our magic and love was simply not exclusive, its nature was to include, and in that was the key to the changed form of the greater future for Alessia and myself.

I stood back, one hand on his arm, looking him straight in the eye. In those eyes I watched a short battle, a confusion, then a clearing as he looked at me with a tenderness that seemed newly revealed but which really always lay at the core of the love he gave me. Slowly he took his knife from Alessia's neck, removed his hand, looked around himself in an odd, stiff way, shivered slightly.

'I don't know who I am,' he said, like a simple child, and my heart reached out to his exposed, raw soul. Death in Venice yet again, but this time with birth on its bloody heels.

'I admire you,' said Alessia. 'This route is hard for a man.'

'I feel confused, lost, I don't know what's going on anymore,' he said, and then looked down at his knife hand, the blood on the blade, and threw it far, high in the air, and it arced, spinning and flashing in the sunlight, to fall with a distant splash in the dark water.

'Don't be concerned, Charlie,' said Alessia, my cousin, my lover, myself. 'None of us know that, it's how it is from here on in.'

I took him by the arm, so good to touch, to hold that pure and beginning man.

'What do we do now?' he asked.

'God knows.' I answered. 'Round here we make our roads by walking.'

He paused, turned his attention from us to where rays of the lowering sun were shafting between buildings and onto the rippling water of the canal. I don't know how long he stood there, unmoving, while Alessia and I waited, at ease, the blood of death and birth still flowing ignored down her face. We had entered yet another space in time, a void in a life where something unbeknown from even deeper depths than before was coagulating in the inner oceans of Charlie Brown, warrior reborn.

In time, enough time for clouds to shift and light re-angle, he shifted himself as something moved within him. I caught my breath; was this the first sign of the emergence of the track to my unknown destiny? Was this slight movement the evidence of the unknown coming to form and the road to the future forming from his own clearing mists?

Once more he paused, at home, at ease in himself, and let further time gather. Alessia and I waited with him, all danger passed now, and we had time in hand to drink in the form and colour of that ancient city of the sea, living newly given life together that even moments ago we seemed uncertain to live.

'I feel as if all my life I lived in a shell,' he said finally, still looking away from Alessia and me, as if he was talking to himself.

Silence followed, all three of us gazing out over the waterway, the only movement ripples in that water, billowing clouds in sky, and a single white bird that winged slowly across our line of sight.

'Now the shell has cracked, and it was an egg all along,' he said. 'With me inside.' He smiled, and so did we. 'Are you really Michelle?' he asked suddenly, turning to look me directly in the eye.

'I don't know anymore,' I said. 'I'm certainly not the Michelle I used to be.'

'And it seems that I am not the Charlie Brown I used to be.'

He had entered our world, as I had entered Alessia's world and made it my own, and was faintly feeling around for sense, some rules that would give this formless place the tangibility it could never have.

'So we simply aren't Charlie and Michelle at all anymore,' he said. 'All of that is gone?'

I nodded. Alessia had moved silently and unnoticed out of our immediate orbit and was standing off to one side, head raised, watching the shifting sky.

'All well and good,' he said. 'But how do we go from here?'

'Step by step, it seems, Charlie. Things are no longer as they used to be, you just seem to know what is next and that is good enough.'

He frowned slightly, raised his hand to his mouth and squashed his lower lip between his thumb and first finger, turned away and looked out over the canal once more.

'Alessia!' he called to the slender figure silhouetted by sunshine on water. 'Are you all right?'

She turned and smiled that smile. 'I'm fine,' she said.

Charlie paused. 'I must have scared you badly.'

She looked at him evenly. 'Yes, you did. I thought I was past such things, but when it came to it, I too feared for my mortality. And listen, Charlie, don't be too hard on yourself; everything that existed in you existed in Alessia too. To me everything I see and feel is nothing other than a reflection of what is somewhere in the depths of myself, so all of your feelings were mine too.'

Charlie just looked at her in silence, and then said; 'I think what rose in me frightened me more than you.' He paused, looked inside himself. 'In fact, it still does. Will it ever leave me?'

'Perhaps not. But the trick is not to fight it but befriend it, make what was the master through fear into a servant through love, and turn that great male power into something sublime.'

'You don't despise me, then? Look how I have wounded your face.'

'No,' said Alessia. 'I don't despise you, far from it, in fact I have come to respect you greatly. The wounds are skin deep and will heal.'

Charlie turned to me. 'And you, Michelle? Can you now love me?'

'I never didn't, Charlie. As I stand here I love you deeply. Please understand; what I feel for Alessia is simply a different kind of love, something beyond me, something impossible to resist. It's not like love of one person for another, this is the love of coming home to myself.'

I could see him struggling, but faintly, then with a sigh he let go, and finally was with us in the love-filled void in the heart and soul. I looked from him to Alessia, my two loves, as if there was a possibility of choice, but in truth there was no choice at all; for better or for worse my heart at that time of fire was hopelessly lost to Alessia.

'Somehow, in a way I cannot understand, I can see the truth in what you're saying, Michelle,' said Charlie. 'And even odder, what it does is to make me free. For the first time in my life I feel beholden to nothing and nobody.'

'It's how I feel,' I said. 'The world in the palm of my hand with me on its top.'

'I don't want to go home,' he said, drawing himself up and gazing round. 'There's nothing for me anymore; at least for now. I want to go away and be by myself, visit Machu Picchu and Tibet, swim in the South Seas, dance under tropical skies, see a volcano erupting; I keep thinking of volcanoes. Where can I see volcanoes?'

'You might try the ring of fire around the Pacific rim,' I said, 'I have heard they have volcanoes there.'

'You know what,' he said with a big smile. 'I will.'

'Shall I come with you?' I asked, my lip trembling as I teetered once more on the brink of the unforeseeable. Still the tracks to the future were denied me, still I hung in surrendered uncertainty, still I was nothing and no-one, without past or future, before my first breath in the silent womb of the present.

He shook his head. 'Not this time,' he said, a calmness and depth in his eye that was already far away from anyone he had ever been. 'I want to be alone for once in my life. No reflection on you.' He smiled at me with a smile that rivalled that of Alessia as he glanced over at her motionless figure, 'And something tells me that you have business to complete here in Venice.'

Then he reached over, hugged me and kissed me on the cheek, which was now flowing with tears. What was happening to my heart, what was happening to me? Did I ever know what it was to love before that time?

'I'll be in touch,' he said. 'Don't be concerned, I'll find you. The truth is that we haven't even begun.'

He turned to Alessia. 'Look after her, won't you?' he said.

'You can be sure of it,' she replied, statuesque in her poised magnificence.

Charlie smiled, turned and walked away, leaving me in total aloneness while never alone again, standing there watching him as he reached the spot between building and canal where the sun was now shining directly off the Venetian waters, and as I vanished into myself and myself into Alessia, he there vanished into the brilliance of its light.

Lightning Source UK Ltd.
Milton Keynes UK
UKOW07f1858080115

244226UK00019B/475/P